BADLAND PUBLISHING PRESENTS

sOmEThInG 2 DiE 4

VENCEREMOS!!!

A Classic Novel By PLEX

BADLAND PUBLISHING, LLC

sOmEThInG 2 DiE 4 is a work of fiction. Names, characters, places and incidents either are the product of the author's imagination or are used fictitiously. Any resemblance to actual events, locales, business establishments or persons, living or dead, is entirely coincidental.

Copyright 2014 by: PLEX
Written by: PLEX
Cover design by: Cedric "Ckills" Killings & PLEX
Graphics by: Cedric "Ckills" Killings
Book design by: Ivette Santiago & PLEX
Published by: Badland Publishing, LLC
                        P.O. Box 11623
                        Riviera Beach, FL 33419
                        www.badlandpub.com

sOmEThInG 2 DiE 4
ISBN: 978-0-9839123-0-9
First Edition

DEDICATIONS & ACKNOWLEDGEMENTS

I dedicate this book to Dorothy Ann Killins and Troy Cannon, because you are both sOmEThInG 2 DiE 4!!!

God, I have to thank Him. Then there's Tracey Carter, Kimberly Adams, Pam Quigley, Pam Little, Erma M., Ivy Ervin, Roshonda Nesbitt, Tosha Dixon, Elga Wynn, Shavondra Killings, Sherry Tyson, Kwannah Rouland, Dawn Westbrook, Sharon Pless, Laura Bennett-Coleman, Diane Ferranti, Summer Rose, Shanika Brown, Kesha Jones, Mrs. Howard, Ms. Wise, Lucinda Killings, Ivette Santiago, Tikeisha Reid, Altonise Hills, Lisa Banks, Tonetta Chester, Debra Harrell, Fattima Khalil, Mrs. Buffy Uter, Mrs. Shekita Estes, Enna Waters, Marquiesha, Monisha, Artoria, Jai, Arlexus, Jasmine Sellers, Mrs. Daphne Johnson, Tara Johnson, Ms. Jay, Rhonda "Ronni" Sims, Ebony Moore, Susan Gibson, Katrina Taylor, Marvelyn Brown and last but certainly not least, Virginia R. Killings...you all have added *something* to my life and are all sOmEThInG 2 DiE 4.

Homies Call. Robert Thomas, Cedric Killings, Michael Shorts, E4, Bondy, Tarrence Taylor, Jonathan Carter, Boobie Black [Love Ya Boy!], Marlo Moore, Dwayne Gladden, Steven Polk, Ronald Tinsley, Mr. Gerald Estes [Thank You For Being There For My Children], D-Boi, Chris Hayes, Bo Brown, Kwame Teague, Shakim Bio, Al Monday, G-ALI [The 7th Letter], Jeff Jr. [treazyradioshow.com], Terrance McClurge, Johnny "Crusher" Jackson, Bill Ashby Jr., Omar "O" Grant, Dwight Fleming, Jimmie Williams, Junky Jit [Junk Out the Scotts], Gerald Adams, Christopher Ross, Frank Hill, George Ross, Lorenzo Flint, Palmer Bradshaw, Ismael "Flaco" Guzman, Carlos Dubois, Troy Jones [Love Ya Boy!], Jimmy Barkley, Big KD [Big

Homie], Turk [Outta Arkansas], Jimmy Da Saint [Urban Celebrity], Diamond, Marquis, Isaiah, Arthur, Travis, Artraveus, Bernard & Jon-Jon, Malik, Freddie Simmons and E...thank you all for everything!!!

BOOK GANG. Michael Harper, Bernard [Gemo] Moore [I love ya boy!], Seth Ferranti, Benny Redd, Bling, Seven Supreme, Bino, LaMont "Big Fridge" Needum, Nathan "Big Nation" Welch, Jesse Cage, K-1, Abman Glaster, Wood [Skip], and Rodderick Vann...Capo Cat Freeman, Slim & Beam, Chrizac, Mae Dog, Mal...One Love!!!

My Teachers. I owe whatever that's good from this work to Donald McCartney [R.I.P.] You were my first example of a man... Reverend Moss, Bishop Curry, G. Hopkins-Bey, Minister Louis Farrakhan, Malik Zulu Shabazz, Khadid A. Shahid Muhammad, Stacey Culbert, Luther Campbell, J. Prince, and Robert Beck.

To The Readers. I'd be nothing without yall! Thank you so much for your love and support. This is the first novel I ever wrote, yet it's the sixth and last to be published since 2009... it only gets better from here!!!

This is a letter from my homegirl. Real Talk! It's in the spirit of this letter that I sat down in 08-08-04 and began writing sOmEThInG 2 DIE 4. I completed the book in '05 but was afraid to put it out...It's something different, it's something old, yet it's something very new. It's for you! It's sOmEThInG 2 DIE 4. I pray that you enjoy, but first please check out the letter that sparked it all.

8/8/04

Dear Plex:

I want to first say, "I love you more than you will ever know." I'm so grateful for you and what you've contributed to my life. You have really applied yourself in a world that's competitive (capitalistic). That in itself was so much for me to witness. You are "a man of a thousand dreams" and "definite vision." I've silently admired that about you for years. I always make mention of you to male and female counterparts. You're not afraid to dream and put forth the effort to make your dreams become reality.

You probably did not know this, but all during my time in the Navy I got phone calls from people telling me all about you (your business ventures and activities with the people). You were always "holding your own". Outside of Christ, you're my sole inspiration. I'm going to visit you as often as I can. "Man of magic words and indefinite wisdom". This is your prize attribute. You are a visionaire! I picked that up when you said, "My life will not end in mere death but on the contrary, it will just begin." And something to the affects of "affecting the masses". I said to myself, "where did he get this type of thinking from?" I don't know "any" men your age that speak about having their own parks and schools for the people. You are the greatest!

Your presence in my life has been unparalleled to that of anyone. You were only eighteen when I had to come and live with you because my mother and I were having serious issues. You were so hard on me about education and working. You were very strict about a lot of things. But I needed it, and I'll always love you for it. I did not understand it, or you at times, but it all prepared me for now. Thank You!!!

Do not be moved by your present situation. You're maximizing in an intangible state right now. The area (state) which is unseen but will be evidenced by your future.

I'm your biggest supporter (for now) and your loyalist and biggest fan!!!

Love You,
Tasha

THE MOVEMENT
By PLEX

It was said to my people, that our time had arrived,
Still all I see is suffering, the loss of black lives.
To this day, held captive, beaten and punished,
In this cruel white-man's world,
where the black-man means nothing.
Can you explain the situation? The desolation of a race.
With more symbol than substance, white-men with black faces.
Give me the understanding, of this sales pitch that you preach.
For my conscious vision unveils your deceit.
You promulgate patience, while we're steady dying in the streets.
More symbol, no substance, I say we war for the peace!!!
Come to success, let's move toward revolution,
And continue to link opportunity with solutions.
Power will not be legislated, or delivered to us,
We must move as a unit, Black Justice, for just us!
One family, One love, One struggle to be equal,
One God, One movement,
"POWER TO THE PEOPLE!"

sOmEThInG 2 DiE 4

Part 1NE

...for how we live is so far removed from how we ought to live, that he who abandons what is done for what ought to be done, will rather (soon) learn to bring about his own ruin than his preservation. [So] a man who wishes to make a profession of goodness in everything must necessarily come to grief among so many who are not good...

[The Prince]
Niccolo Machiavelli

Prologue

Hello, my name is—for this instance—Bishop Michael. I am the spiritual leader and founder of The Christian Liberation Against Racism and Injustice (CLARI). I embarked upon this mission in August, around 2010 or 11. Up until that time I had been blinded by the illusions of this world's system; and my eyes were very much closed to the true realities of my people—a grotesquely hideous and violent reality brought about through false indoctrination, lack of education, and a criminal economic freeze out.

Being a man of God, I was very much removed from the criminal element of that time. After all, my congregation—the supposed righteous—were not a part of that. They were well off and in no-way connected to such people and practices. So I spent my time preaching and catering to my congregation, thinking that I was very much doing the Lord's will. As I would later learn, I, like many of my fellow clergymen, was guilty of "preaching to the choir," and leaving "the blind to lead the blind."

I know that you're probably asking yourselves, "What brought about this revolution?" Indeed, it was an absolute revolution of my mind and I received it from the bowels of hell. You see, in 1999, a young hustler from BADLAND, Miami was indicted, arrested, and convicted of conspiracy. As his mother told him and the world would later learn, "he was not arrested, he was rescued." The man I speak of is Arthur Cruz. He was betrayed by the system, and almost everyone he had ever loved. Through their betrayal Cruz was delivered over to his enemies and spent all of nine years in the Belly of The Beast – hell or prison – being re-educated, and in my eyes, divinely prepared for a far greater mission and purpose than he could have ever imagined.

It was here in my church that I met Arthur Cruz. Prior to our meeting that late-night in 2010, Cruz had been released all of two years from prison and he was in a drunken and very confused state. It was on this night that I learned his life story, the story of his people, and the dedication and love of a man for his people. A man that had been truly resurrected from a "hell-of-a-condition," that he might shine a new light on humanity's plight as a whole. It was on that night that I began to re-evaluate my teachings, my outlook on life, and on Black people. Oh, did I mention that I was white?

It had been a very long day for me, what with three services which began at 8:00 a.m. and the last ending at 10:00 p.m. After all of this there had been a lengthy meeting of the deacons' board which concluded around 11:45 p.m. After which everyone except myself left for home. I spent the next hour or so praying and cleaning my office. It was at this point that I heard some rumbling about in the next room and went forth to find the cause of the disturbance. As I drew closer to the door of the room I began to smell the vile stench of alcohol and human waste. There sitting in the dark I saw the outline of a man. Nervous, but very sternly I asked, "Who is that in there?"

He replied in a drunken slur, "I am that I am. The cause of it all! Beelzebub, The Dragon, Devil." Taken aback by this outrageous reply, I preceded forward in an attempt to get a better look at this nut that had broken into my church. Flicking on the lights, I saw as he raised his arms to cover his eyes, that he was wearing what was once an expensive suit and Bally hard-bottoms. A handsome and solidly built man that appeared to be in his mid or late thirties, though at this demarcation he was very dirty and unshaven. But most of all, I noticed that there was a half drunken gallon of Remy Martin V.S.O.P. in front of him and on his right hand was tattooed "M.O.B." I observed this while staring at the rather large gun in which the hand clutched. Further observation proved this gun to be nothing at all! Because on his lap sat some sort of machine gun. As I think back, it was just like the one that B.A. carried on The A Team.

"Kill the switch, Bishop!" he yelled. "I'm afraid of the light. I've been in darkness so long, I'm scared of what I might see, or what you may see of me."

"What do you want?" I asked him, now more nervous than before. "And how and why did you break into my church?"

"I'm here because I'm confused and very mad with God. I'm here because I'm losing everything I've ever loved, including my mind! Look Bishop, I'm here for some answers."

Still quite nervous I sat down across from him. He gestured towards the bottle. Me being a man of God, I'd never indulged in any form of intoxicants. But at that moment I gratefully accepted his offer of the hard liquor. I took a long draw from the bottle to help calm myself. As it traveled down I immediately felt the deadening affects of the warm liquor on my nerves as it passed down my throat and into my system. Truth be told, I rather enjoyed it. After returning the bottle to the table I asked him, "How can I help you in this?"

He said, "You can help me by listening. For I have no one to talk to. I've tried talking to God, but he's not fucking with me anymore. I tried talking to my people, the Blacks, but they only pretended to be listening. You see, they hate me because I love them, yet more so because I'm black. But they love you because you gave them nothing! You can help me by taking this story to the press and joining in the fight against injustice. You see, they'll believe you because you're white."

If it wasn't for the presence of those two guns I might have walked back to my office and called the police. Instead, I sat there and listened for what turned out to be eight hours. It was a story of tremendous struggle, hardship, and sacrifice. A story of drugs, sex, murder, and betrayal. He told me in those eight hours of The People; sOmEThInG 2 DiE 4!!!

This, in his words, is what he told me...

CHAPTER 1

It was a very cold winter morning in December when Arthur Cruz stood outside the gates of Terre Haute United States Penitentiary. It had been nine years since his lungs had inhaled fresh air, minus the stench of prison bodies emitting fear and a false sense of courage.

Standing there he inhaled deeply. Deep enough to fill his entire 5'9", one hundred ninety pound frame with the cold winter air. "Free at last," he thought to himself. Years of exercise had kept Cruz sane and in tremendous shape. Preserving his youthful appearance.

Cruz had been incarcerated at the age of twenty-six for a conspiracy to possess and distribute cocaine in the Southern region of Florida. A BadLand (Miami Housing Project) native, Cruz was in no way a saint. Yet he explained that his crimes were not against the United States and its People—for which his indictment read. "The United States vs. Arthur Cruz." His crimes were economical crimes—very much like those of the Europeans at Enron—against a gross psychological economic system. He learned in prison that his true crime was being born of color and remaining loyal to his hood.

Being reared by a single mother, but ultimately raised by the streets, Cruz had taken one for the team. A team that he eventually learned did not hold the same loyalties towards him. In the nine years he had been away, the only people that had been there for him was his mother, the mother of his son and his cousin Dirt. The thought of it all left a bad taste in his mouth, causing him to spit as he approached the waiting cab.

"Where to, sir?" the cab driver asked.

"The airport. And please turn up the radio."

As the cab made its way, Cruz looked back for the last time at what had once been his home. A home that served as an institute of higher learning, a place of religious refinement, and self reform. Indeed he had learned many of life's most valuable lessons in the belly of the beast. Lessons that cut and tore like a double edged sword. In the last nine years he had seen that sword produce some great men, and in turn reduce and break some of the greatest.

That morning he had risen before sunrise, after a sleepless night. He brushed his teeth, showered, shaved his bald head, and dressed; all for the last time in anyone's penitentiary. That he swore!

"So what you gon' do out there whoadie?" asked his celly, Nate.

"Shiid homie, it's too early to call. But one thang's for sure, I ain't gonna forget this shit. I gotcha, homie," Cruz said.

Happy to be leaving, but all the while he was crying inside. Nate was a dear friend and comrade. Then there was Kunta, the epitome of struggle; Mr. Muhammad and Brother Captain Ali, both soldiers! And how could he forget Boo Baby, Arthur X and Pop?

They were closer than brothers. Cruz truly hated to leave them behind.

He and Nate had met about a year and a half into his bid. Nate was 5'10", brown-skinned, and of medium build. A good dude. He had been convicted and sentenced to life in prison for C.C.E. (Continuing Criminal Enterprise).

"You stay up out there, nigga. Can't stop, won't stop," Nate said as they exchanged hugs and pounds.

"Can't forget, won't forget. First Family, homie," Cruz replied as the C.O. called his name.

"Arthur Cruz! Inmate Cruz to R and D!"

* * *

As the cab's radio wailed some popular European song and crawled along the highway, Arthur Cruz knew that he had a long, hard trip ahead of him. Not so much as the trip itself, in distance, but life's travels. He had come a long way, yet he still had so far to go.

"Can't stop, won't stop," he said to himself as he wiped a single tear from his eye and prepared himself for whatever.

When the plane landed at Miami's International Airport, there were no marching bands or news reporters, though Arthur was a soldier. For nine years he had been at war, kidnapped and held against his will. Cruz considered himself a P.O.W. and since everything happened for political reasons, he was indeed a political prisoner. No one really gave a fuck about justice, right or wrong, or the actual victims of crime. "Justice," Cruz mouthed to himself as he exited the plane, "Everybody knew that the bitch was blind."

No one knew that Cruz was out. Hell, it was hard for him to believe it. As he walked along the airport in awe of all the different people. People walking around as if they didn't have a care in the world. Beautiful people from every walk of life. Some stared, others offered warm smiles and greetings. Cruz merely nodded in reply as he continued on towards the line of waiting cabs at the airport exit.

"Where are you headed, man?" the cabbie asked.

"103 and P," Cruz said with a smile. It had been a long minute since he had said those words. "103 and P, that's where the G's be."

The old ragged cab cruised along through the busy traffic. Cruz could not believe how much shit had changed. The remodeling of old hotels and new buildings were in place of vacant lots. Everything seemed all the more busy and crowded. This was not the Miami Arthur Cruz had left nine and a half years ago.

"Right here will be fine," Cruz informed the cabbie as they turned off of 103rd Street onto 12th Avenue. "How much do I owe you?" he asked.

"That'll be $28.20," the cab driver told him.

Cruz withdrew a roll of money from the pocket of his white linen slacks, which he wore with an expensive cream colored silk shirt and matching cream colored Bally casuals. He handed the driver $30 and made his way towards the Cuban Store entrance.

"Poppy," Cruz called out with a smile on his handsome face.

The old man looked as if he were trying to recall the face of the younger man. Then, all at once, Poppy's expression went from puzzlement to shock as he recognized his old friend. A wide smile tore across his wrinkled face. Poppy ran around the counter to embrace Cruz. He was so happy to see the man that had once been like a son to him.

"Arturo! Where have you been? It has been so long!" Poppy exclaimed in his heavy Spanish accent. "Why haven't you called? It has been six or seven year, no?"

"I've been away, ole man. Nine and a half years...conspiracy, Poppy. But it's all good because I'm home now."

"How long have you been out?" Poppy asked, gazing delightfully at his handsome young friend.

"I'm fresh out, Poppy. Nobody knows I'm out. And I wanna keep it that way for a while. I have some lookin' around to do. You feel me?"

Poppy read the expression on the younger man's face and also sensed the venom in his words. Someone was in trouble. Poppy had known Cruz since he was a child. Back when Cruz and his friends used to come into the store to buy and steal candy. That is, up until they started hanging around outside of the store, selling their own form of candy—bass, butter and sinse. Of course Poppy never minded the little guys hanging out around his place of business and doing their thing. After all, they were only doing business, very much like himself. Not to mention the fact that these kids and their parents made Poppy lots of money by patronizing his market. Furthermore, as long as they were outside peddling drugs to desperate nickel and dime customers, it diverted the attention of any onlookers away from Poppy and the large amounts of cocaine that he'd been moving out of the back room and the apartment above the store. Poppy had been importing kilos of cocaine from his homeland even before he'd purchased the store on 103rd Street and 12th Avenue. And though the store operated at a large profit it was merely a front for the old man.

No one, with the exception of young Cruz, knew about this. Because, of all the youngsters that hung around the store, Poppy had taken a special interest in Cruz. Early on he had noticed the way that all the other youngsters and a few older dudes seemed to just gravitate towards the serious young man. Cruz had a special leadership quality about himself as well as a superior hustle. So

Poppy took Cruz off the block at the age of seventeen and taught him the weight game. He showed Arthur Cruz where the real money was, in weight. Even after Poppy had supposedly left the game himself, he still acted as partner, friend and advisor to Cruz. He taught the bright young man everything he could, and the one thing that he could not seem to get him to see ultimately became his downfall—his friends.

"So how's business and the world been treating you?" Cruz asked the old man.

"Okay I guess. I got a few houses rented out. A lot of my old bonds have matured. I'm what the European call financially stable. So I don't see any of our old friends anymore. You understand?"

He knew that Poppy was referring to the old cocaine connect— his people in Cuba.

"Yeah, I understand. I understand that you're caked up now!" Cruz replied.

"Well, you know. But the store is not the same like when you left. The neighborhood is changed. Many of my customers now shop at the bigger stores. Better prices I guess. And even the customers I still have are poor and always need credit. But I don't mind. It's the damned robberies! At least two or three a month. These youngsters are real crazy now! Nothing like you all were. Shit, I just don't know," the old man said sadly.

"It's that bad, huh?" Cruz asked.

"Yeah, it's really that bad," Poppy answered.

"But you look good, ole man," Cruz told the old man while playfully slapping his shoulder.

"Yeah, yeah, but you. You still look like when you left. But only more fit, bigger," Poppy said.

"Thank you Poppy, but I gotta be out. I'll see you around, aiight."

"Yeah, make it soon. You hear me? Because I see those eyes. You have something in that head of yours. So we talk before you do it. You understand?" Poppy said, excitedly.

"Okay Poppy, we'll talk. Always, we'll talk," Cruz answered over his shoulder, walking out of the store.

Arthur Cruz had grown up in a fairly nice middle-class neighborhood. It was set with many fruit and Palm trees, chain link fences and nice lawns. He smiled as he walked up 12th Avenue to 100th Street. There it was! A lovely tan and brown house on the corner. It was the house that Cruz had grown up in. His mother had always worked extra hard to make sure that Arthur and his older brother Tyson had everything they needed and most of the things that they wanted. It had been hard for the three of them, but Dorothy "Ma" Cruz had always managed to make ends meet.

Walking up the steps onto the porch, Cruz rang the doorbell.

"Who is it?" a voice demanded from the other side of the door.

"It's me, Ma. Arthur!"

The door flung open at once and there stood Ms. Cruz, smiling with open arms. It had been nine and a half years since Cruz had seen his dear mother, let alone hugged her. For Cruz had forbade her to visit him; caged and treated as some kind of worthless animal. Then again, maybe he was. But he would never allow his mother to see him that way.

"Son, you are so big! Why didn't you tell me when you were getting out? I could have done something special."

Breaking their embrace, Cruz told his mother, "I wanted to surprise you."

"Well, that you did," she replied with a beautiful smile, revealing pretty even teeth.

She had aged some over the years that he had been away. Her hair was now heavily streaked with grey. Yet she was still as beautiful as the day he had left.

"I see that your timing is still good. I was just cooking ribs, greens and cornbread. It should be ready in a little while."

Cruz acknowledged what his mother had said by smiling brightly and rubbing his hands together like a starved construction worker. While the truth was, he did not have the heart to tell his mother that he had long since given up pork and the plantation diet. Yet after seeing her beautiful lovely face, Cruz decided that he would eat a plate of shit if it would bring his mother joy.

As Cruz walked along the long hallway that led to his old room, he looked at all the family pictures that adorned the spotless white walls and polished shelves. There were school certificates and football trophies that he and his deceased brother had collected many years ago. To him it seemed like only yesterday. Uneasiness gripped him as he entered his room. It was as if he were stepping into a time machine. There stood the bunk beds that he and Tyson had shared. On the nightstands were their high school football pictures. Tyson wore the number 44 and Arthur sported the number 33. They both played running back and would have definitely changed the game with their unique style of running had they only been able to avoid the lure of the streets.

Near the closet sat boxes upon boxes of books. Books that Arthur Cruz had read and studied over his incarceration period. Kneeling, he began to unpack the books and look them over. There were books there that he did not remember reading, while others he had vivid memories...Make Me Wanna Holla, special housing unit in F.D.C. Miami. Holy Bible, Noble Quran, and the Moorish Circle Seven Koran, Terre Haute U.S.P. Black Gangster and Black Girl Lost, his first meeting with the late great Donald Goines. The Mind of Hitler, The Autobiography of Malcolm X, and The Naked Soul of Ice Berg Slim. There was Brothers of the Struggle by Stacey Culburt, Blood in My Eye by George L. Jackson and The Destruction of America by the Honorable Elijah Muhammad. The titles and range of subjects were endless. He simply could not believe that he'd read all of those books. Because in prison inmates were only allowed five books at a time. So Cruz had never been in one room with all of his books at once.

"Son!" his mother called from the kitchen. "The food is ready!"

Setting the books aside, Cruz prayed that he might be able to stomach the pork.

"The food smells good, Ma." Cruz lied as he took his place at the table.

"Thank you son," she beamed. "Now let's pray and thank the Lord for your safe return home, and for this meal He has blessed us with."

As they held hands and lowered their heads in prayer, Cruz could not believe how long his mother held the prayer. His neck had gone stiff and his palms were sweaty from holding hands so long. He thought that his dear mother would never say Amen.

They ate in complete silence for about eight minutes, then the questions finally began. "So son, what are you gonna do?"

"About what, Ma?"

"About your life, about your son, about God!" Ma Cruz quizzed. "Are you coming to church with me? Bishop would love to see you. The whole church has been praying for you all of these years."

Cruz demurred for an instant. "Um, I really don't know, Ma, I just got home. I'll probably do some lookin' around tomorrow. But I ain't gettin' no job. I talked with Poppy today and we gon' set something up, so that I can make my own job."

And that was all that it took to set things in motion. At that very moment, all hell broke loose. Ms. Cruz was on her feet and slicing at the air as she spoke. "What the hell do you mean, son? No job! How do you expect to live without a job? What about Desmond? Is Poppy gonna look after him like he looked after you? You're so stupid! You'll end up back in prison and I'll end up looking after that poor child, because his poor mother sure can't do it alone. Poppy?!" Ms. Cruz snapped. "He will continue using and ripping everybody off, while you will be back in jail."

"Ma, come on, please. We're supposed to be enjoyin' this, not arguing. I promise, I am not goin' back to prison. I have a lot of beautiful ideas. A lot of them you may not agree wit', but they're ideas I formulated and I believe in them," Cruz said softly, staring into his mother's worried eyes. "Don't you think it's about time that somebody stood up around here and actually helped or at least tried to fix some of what we've fuc—, I mean, messed up around here? 'Cause I do. And I don't see why it shouldn't be me. Didn't you read any of my letters? I'ma make my own job and hopefully create some for other people."

"Son," Ms. Cruz said calmly. "Are you crazy? Because you sound like a fool, right on. What have you been reading? The only way you can help our people is to pray. The only answer to our problems is Jesus! You need to build a real relationship with Him and forget about this foolishness you are talking."

"Ma, what's foolish about believin' in somethin' other than religion? I don't need religion to show me that Jesus was only a perfect example of myself. He didn't wait for change, he went out and changed it. So what should I be waitin' on? Somethin' to fall outta the sky? Ma, ain't nothin' foolish about havin' your own. What's foolish is duckin' your responsibility as a man and lookin' the other way instead of facin' the problems. That's childish ma, and your son has become a man."

"You're just gonna end up dead, son!" Ms. Cruz continued in tears. "Just like your brother! Do you wanna die, son?"

Cruz sat there as if he was in deep thought before finally answering. "Ma, I died a long time ago...wit' my brutha."

Chapter 2

As Cruz laid soaking in the spacious tub, he carefully thought out his first move. He knew that he would have to relocate his love ones before he could implement any aspect of his plan. This would require money; and lots of it. You see, he had read and learned from past experiences that no change could come about without suffering and bloodshed—war. And one of the fundamental rules of war was to get your finances in order, and only then could you effectively go to war and expect to win.

These thoughts brought him to think of Smash. Smash was an old associate of Cruz. He was very shrewd and calculating as far as business was concerned. It was just a shame that his business-sense would not allow him to see beyond the streets.

It had been Busta, now deceased, that had introduced the two. Next to Poppy, Busta had practically ran the neighborhood. Busta was Cruz's first supplier. In fact, he supplied everybody until Poppy took Cruz under his wing. It had always been rumored that maybe Poppy was the reason those 63 AK projectiles met Busta head on in his front yard.

Cruz thought, if Smash had any deficiencies, besides his limited vision, it would have to be his inability to resist women. This had been the downfall of many great men (Adam, Solomon, Sampson, O.J. Simpson, Bill Clinton, Mike Tyson, etc.). And in this instance, it would be Cruz's window to the money and information that he now needed.

After bathing and dressing, Cruz decided it was about time he started to put the pieces in place. Picking up the phone as he sat down on the bottom bunk, the bed that had once been occupied by his big brother, Bryan "Tyson" Cruz, he lit a Double-O and waited for the other party to answer the phone. After the 8th ring an individual with a high-pitched voice answered, "Yeah?"

Recognizing the voice as the person he was seeking, Cruz blew out a gust of smoke and replied, "What up, gangsta?"

"Chillin' family! Damn, when you touch-down?" Breed said to his friend.

"I just hit the bricks 'bout eight minutes ago. So what's the business?"

"First Family! Ain't shit changed. We just been maintainin' until you finally upped and jumped. The nigga Wheat just flew back to D.C. two days ago. He was up here in the Chi' for about a week," Breed informed Cruz.

"Oh yeah? I hope yall niggas been about family business. Did yall get the shit that we're gonna need? Because the lawyer ain't givin' us shit until he sees some fuckin' work. You feel me?"

"Fosho'! It's all in pocket. The trucks are lined up on a bogus account, and the house is paid-up for a year. We're just waitin' on you, my guy," Breed answered.

"Okay, cool. I got a few loose ends to tie up, say, about eight days. Then everything will be set on my end. Call Wheat and give him the business, aiight," Cruz instructed.

"Aiight, I'ma do that now. See ya in eight," said Breed.

"Okay nigga, one!"

Arthur laid back on the bed and thought about the first time he and Breed had met. It was the year 2000. Cruz had been working in the prisons' industrial complex patching mail-bags. A job that he very much hated but desperately needed as a means for economic stability. After he had befriended Kunta, through Boo Baby, and came into the teachings, he saw no sense in him taking money off of the streets to survive in jail. It was on this job that the two of them had met. Over a period of time, both good and bad; serious and most often hilarious conversations, the two built a very strong bond. Cruz saw a lot of potential in the younger man. Strengths and ambitions that just needed to be guided. Breed was the little brother that Cruz never had. He was also the little brother that Cruz himself had never gotten a chance to be. And after six years together in hell, Cruz could honestly say that he loved Breed and trusted him with his life.

* * *

It was Arthur Cruz's first night on the bricks in nine and a half years, and he'd be damned if he intended to spend it alone. Putting on a solid black cotton Polo sweat suit and all black Reeboks, Cruz called himself a cab. "Ma! I'm headed out! I'll call you if I decide to come in tonight," Cruz yelled as he headed out the front door.

"Where are you going?" she asked.

"To see an old friend," he said while putting his ski mask under his shirt front.

As he sat out front waiting on his cab he decided to fire up a Double-O. Blowing out a cloud of smoke he thought to himself, "I wonder what ole Nate is doing?" Looking at his Kenneth Cole

Reaction watch, he knew it was now exactly 8:08. He figured that Nate was probably playing poker or scheming on a pack.

The lights of the cab broke his train of thought. Flicking the butt of his cigarette on the ground, Cruz stood and climbed inside the cab.

"Where to buddy?" the cabbie questioned.

"36th Street and 27th Avenue."

They rode along in silence for about 20 minutes before arriving at the corner of 36th and 24th.

"Right here, bruh...How much do I owe you?" Cruz asked.

Checking the meter the cab driver told him that it would be $17.25. Cruz handed the driver $20.00 and exited the cab. He then began walking towards the apartment complex. Not seeing the black Maxima in the parking space marked 1-B, he serpentined around the back and checked the rear window. To his dismay it was locked. Using a brick, Cruz broke the window. Reaching inside he flipped the latch and lifted the window before sliding inside. He was in the master bedroom of the small apartment. Walking down the hall and into the living room, Cruz found a spot on the floor, between the couch and an overstuffed Lazy Boy to await his prey.

* * *

Hearing a set of keys being placed into the lock, Cruz awakened and pulled on his ski mask. He must have dozed off, because the clock on the wall facing him now read 9:45. He could feel his heart rate quicken as the adrenaline began to flow. The door swung open and a lady with a petite but very shapely frame stepped into the living room. She was about 5'4", 123 pounds, with a short stylish hairdo. After closing and locking the door, she placed her purse on the coffee table along with a small stack of mail. She then began checking her answering machine. The attractive young woman wore a nice navy-blue skirt that revealed her shapely light brown legs and punctuated her immense posterior. Her shirt was a white silk button-down. The top three buttons were undone, exposing just the right amount of cleavage. Cruz could feel his erection growing. It had been nine and a half years since he'd had intercourse with a woman, and this one was so beautiful and so perfect in every aspect. Hanging up the phone the woman turned to enter the kitchen. She was totally unaware that there was a stranger in her house. Lifting himself, Cruz decided this was indeed the perfect time. He moved with cat-like agility. Cruz quickly closed the space between them. By the time she heard or sensed his presence, Cruz had applied and locked a vice-like 'L' on her while covering her mouth. He then began to drag her to the bedroom through which he had entered.

Once inside, Cruz roughly spun her around to face him. And before she could muster a scream, with the swiftness of a prizefighter, Cruz delivered a vicious open backhand that would have made old Pimpin Boo Baby sour with envy. Blood splattered from her lip onto her shirtfront. Deepening his voice, he said, "Bitch if you scream you're dead!"

He then caught her with an open left hand and ripped her shirt and bra open with one smooth motion. Spinning her again to face the bed, Cruz pulled the shirt off of her and used it to tie her wrist over her head. He then tore the zipper at the back of her skirt. She had been wearing G-Strings, which he simply ripped off.

Spreading her legs, Cruz inserted his index-finger into her vagina. He could feel her body tense up as she quietly wept. He slowly worked his finger in and out while removing his shoes and sweats with his free hand. Leaning in behind her, he began to lick her from her sex-spot to her anus. The excitement of it all caused

Cruz to climax prematurely. *Damn!* he said to himself. Still performing cunnilingus, Cruz used one hand to stroke himself to attention. He was now hard as penitentiary steel.

Maybe it was the perversion of his lower-self playing tricks on his higher-self, but at one point it seemed that the sobs had turned to moans. At that instance he licked her up her spine and began to insert himself. He could not believe how wet she was.

The woman still continued to cry as Cruz slowly long stroked her from behind. In a deep drawl Cruz asked her, "Do you like this dick, bitch?" She closed her eyes even tighter and cried as Cruz drove himself deeper into her sex-spot. Looking down at himself going in and out of her, he noticed the thick white creamy film that covered his love organ. *Damn!* he said to himself, *this freak is gettin' off on bein' raped.*

Removing the mask Cruz leaned over and kissed her ear. Then he stuck his tongue inside. "Who pussy is this?" he now asked in his regular voice.

Tamika's eyes shot open and she began to shout, "Oh Cruz! This is yo' pussy, baby! Oh Cruz, I missed you!"

He silenced her with a passionate kiss. As his tongue ran in and out of her mouth and he sucked at her lips, he could taste the blood from her busted lip.

"Oh daddy! I missed you sooo much! I missed you loving me. Oh please, daddy! Love yo' pussy! Please, fuck me!"

Cruz continued to drive himself deeper and deeper. Tamika was now struggling to free her hands. So Cruz reached up and removed the shirt. Unable to hold himself any longer, Cruz quickened the pace and Tamika matched him stroke for stroke.

"Tamika, I'm about to cum!" Cruz moaned.

Tamika in turn rolled over from under him onto her back and said, "Cum in my mouth! I wanna taste you!"

Moving her head back and forth in a rapid-fire motion, she performed fellatio on Cruz using only her soft lips and wet tongue to apply pressure.

"Oh shit! Damn, baby!" Cruz moaned as he exploded in her mouth.

She continued to perform until she had drained him completely.

Cruz rolled over and laid next to Tamika. She then raised herself from the bed and started towards the kitchen. "Cruz, you want something to drink?" she asked.

"Yeah, what you got?" Cruz answered.

"Water, juice, and Seagram's 7," Tamika yelled from the kitchen.

"Give me some Seagram's 7! No ice!" Cruz said as he sparked up a Double-O.

When Tamika returned from the kitchen she passed Cruz his drink and laid down beside him.

"When did you get home?" she asked, cuddling up next to him and rubbing his chest and well defined stomach.

"I got out today. Where is Desmond?" Cruz answered and asked.

"He's probably at a game or something. They made the playoffs. He'll probably be in 'round 1:00. He usually calls me if he's staying out," Tamika informed him.

"Staying out? What do you mean? He's runnin' the streets now?" Cruz was somewhat shocked.

Tamika had given birth to Desmond Bryan Cruz at the age of twenty, six years before Cruz was sent off to federal prison. He had not seen his son in person in nine and a half years.

Desmond was now a sophomore at Miami Central Sr. High, and just like his uncle and father, young Des was an absolute beast out of the back-field. Here it was, only his second year, and he had taken the Rockets to the playoffs.

"Cruz, have you forgot, Des is 15. A big ass 15, too! I cannot treat him like no little boy," Tamika answered.

Cruz thought to himself for a moment. "I guess you're right," he said, shrugging his solidly built shoulders. "I'm still gonna rap with him when he gets in," Cruz added before he turned to go to sleep.

"Cruz, baby," Tamika called, raising herself to sit up right. Cruz turned, lifting himself to face her and met a clean closed right to the mouth.

"Damn! Girl is you crazy?" Cruz yelled while wiping the blood from his lip.

"Nah," Tamika calmly continued. "That was for slappin' me, nigga, and rippin' my shit."

Almost laughing at the expression on his face, she kissed him deeply, now tasting the blood running from his busted lip. "Good night, daddy," she said and laid cuddled under him to go to sleep.

Chapter 3

Cruz woke up early the next morning and made prayer. Afterwards he prepared a small breakfast for Tamika and himself–Des had yet to come home. As he sat and ate his grits, eggs, and turkey bacon, he thought his day out. It felt damn good to be home, however a tremendous responsibility loomed over his head as a result of his freedom–both physical and mental. For life was anew for him. Everything he'd experienced before prison was absolete–void and of no further use in his new life. His old life and former way of thinking had been a joke. Arthur X had told him, *you are only responsible after knowledge.* Well he now had a profound knowledge of God and self, so there was no more room for excuses. As it stood, and from what he'd seen, the streets hadn't changed for the better; they were worst and his responsibility to them was greater.

Drinking the last of his coffee, Cruz washed the dishes and put Tamika's plate in the microwave. He could hear her in the shower.

"Tamika!" he yelled.

"What?"

"Yo' food's in the microwave!"

"Okay!"

"I'm takin' yo' car!"

"No you not!"

"Bye!"

"Boy! How I'm s'posed to move 'round?"

"As best you can...and I got yo' phone!"

"Boy!"

"Love you!" Cruz yelled out, laughing as he exited the apartment.

* * *

Cruz drove slowly down 79th Street and turned onto Little River Drive. It was still early so he decided to stop by Arcola Park and get in a good workout to begin his day. He felt safe doing so because even though it was a neighborhood park, nobody he'd been dealing with before going to prison ever got up before 10:00 a.m. Parking Tamika's black Nissan Maxima in the parking spaces near the handball courts, he hopped out and filled his lungs with Robbin Hood air. He'd done a lot on this park—played football, sexed chicks, drunk and got high.

There were two Spanish dudes playing handball and a few older couples jogging and power-walking on the large half-mile track. Cruz took his sweater and shirt off before walking over to the pull-up and dip bars. He began the merry-go-round with twenty pull-ups, twenty dips, twenty-five push-ups and ended with fifty crunches–set one. He then repeated this; arms, chest, and wings expanding with each set. By the time he'd done seven sets he was spent. *Goddamn!* he thought. *This shit ain't never bite like this in prison.* Deciding to get a few sips of water, Cruz started a slow jog across the park to the water fountain.

Tamika wore my ass out, he said to himself as he bent and began drinking the cold water. It was cool and soothing. He sipped long and let the cold stream run over his bald head. Feeling better, he looked up and inadvertently gasped. "Damn!" slipped from his drooling mouth.

The fire-red-bone whose ass he was looking up into looked back over her shoulder—still bent over at the waste, legs spread wide apart, stretching.

"Excuse me?" she questioned, having heard something but wasn't quite sure what it was.

"He-hello... I said hello," Cruz responded, staring lustfully at the cleft that hung between her pretty red thighs.

"Oh, hello," she said and continued stretching.

She wore some little cotton Nike jogging shorts, a tight Nike T-shirt and Nike Cross Trainers. The shorts exposed the plump dark palms of her big ass. Cruz felt his nature rising. He could think of a million different positions to put her in.

Cruz decided to hurry off and complete his workout before he embarrassed himself.

Back on the bar, he pulled-up, pushed-up and dipped; although his mind was back at the water fountain with Red—the stretching beauty. Just as he finished his tenth and final set she rounded the track. Her big D-cups bounced as she strided along. He stared until she'd floated beyond him.

Man, fuck this shit! I'm fresh out! he told himself and sprinted off behind her. The view was so lovely. The way her 42" ass flared out from her 26" waist and bounced with each step she took. It was a thing of beauty. Not to mention the fact that she was bowlegged and pretty as pie—a young red Angela Basset. *Lord! You sho' know what I wanted*, he thought as he finally ran up beside her.

"Pretty nice pace," he said, smiling at her.

She smiled back. "Thanks, I try to get it in at least four days a week. Three miles."

Three? Damn! I gotta quit smoking, he told himself, for his lungs were on fire.

"You from 'round here?" she asked.

"Yeah. I played for this park as a jit."

"Mmm, I've never seen you here before. I come out here at least four times a week."

"Been…a…way…on…business. I just… got back… in town… yesterday…" he said, sucking in air.

She nodded and continued pushing the pace.

Cruz cursed himself for jumping-out-there with her. He'd never been big on road work, mainly because he smoked Kools like they were going out of style— even though as a member of the Nation of Islam he was not supposed to be smoking. *I shoulda just waited 'til she finished*, he thought.

They finished the three miles in silence. They then walked a lap together to cool down. Cruz took that opportunity to pick up the conversation.

"So, did you say you were from 'round here?"

"No, I did not," she remarked and smiled at him. "I'm from Carol City. I just handle a lot of property around here."

"Oh, so you're into real estate?"

"Amongst other things."

"Such as?"

"You FBI?"

"What?!" Cruz asked, stopping.

She bussed out laughing. It was a cute laugh. So cute that he laughed himself.

"I'm just kidding," she said as they continued walking. "I also do accounting and handle a few marketing accounts for small businesses. I make ends meet."

Okay, brains to go with the beauty?! He was quite impressed. "I might be able to use you," he said, his Mr. Mischievous smile in place.

Her thinly arched eyebrows furrowed. "You might, huh?" She looked him over real good for the first time and had to admit to herself that she loved what she saw. "For what, might I ask?"

"For a few things," he capped back, unwittingly allowing his eyes to sweep her legs, cameltoe, and breast.

She laughed again. "You're a trip."

"Why you say that?"

"Because for one, you don't even know me, nor do I know you."

"You're right. But let's change that…" he said and extended his hand. "My name's Arthur Cruz."

She shook his hand. "I'm Ronni," she replied. "You said earlier that you'd just came back from out of town. What exactly do you do, Mr. Cruz that would lead you to believe that *you might be able to use me,* as you put it?"

"Umm, I'm a business consultant. I put things together for people. However, I'm thinkin' about opening up a few new fronts."

"Is that what you were doin' out of town?"

"Well, something like that."

"Where were you?"

"Are you FBI?" he asked and they laughed their asses off.

"You got that," she said, her perfect smile in place.

"Nah, I was in Terre Haute, Indiana."

"Oh, really? Did you like it? I have family up there. I usually visit twice a year."

"It was aiight," he half-lied. "But I ain't never goin' back."

By then they reached her car. She drove a silver Lexus. Opening the door she grabbed a white towel off of the seat and began toweling herself. Cruz loved her mannerism. She seemed to be a real girly's girl.

"Maybe you could give me yo' card or something and we could hook up."

Again she furrowed her eyebrows. "Hook up for business, right?" she asked.

"Of course," he shot back.

She handed him a card with her office number and address on it. "I'm there from around 11:00 to 3:00. After that I'm usually out showing or closing on a property. Even still, my secretary can always find me until 6:30."

"Cool, I'll be in touch."

"Fine," she said and got into her car.

"That you are," he capped.

"Excuse me?"

"I said, it was a pleasure meeting yo' acquaintance."

Ronni licked her suckable lips. "Same here," she replied and pulled off, leaving Cruz to wonder about their encounter.

Cruz jumped in the Maxima feeling good about himself. He cruised up Little River Drive until he hit 95th. Bussing a right, he U-turned and took 95th Street heading west until he reached 17th Avenue, turning right at Miami Central Senior High—his old school. He wanted to ride through Silver Blue Lakes and see what he could see.

Upon entering the gated entrance, he realized that the morality of his neighborhood had been greatly decimated. It was sad. Not only were the same old rundown whores and sack-chasers that had ran the block in his hay-days still out there, but some of them had their daughters with them. Sisters as young as thirteen were out in hotpants and sheer skirts. Filthy crack-whores were running to cars. Young boys stood on stairs pitching the bomb and watching for the cops. It looked like something from a horror movie. On the verge of tears, Cruz remembered the ills that he'd once brought to his people. He knew inside that he'd contributed greatly to the organized chaos that he now faced. *Can I fix in this life time what has been buildin' in my people for the last 430 years?* he asked himself. *If by chance I can't, I'll die tryin'... because my shamefully beautiful people are something to die for*, he thought and slowly drove away.

CHAPTER 4

BadLand Miami, a place of fresh attitudes and distinctive energy. A place where the world's rich and famous come to find luxurious bungalow suites amidst clear blue oceans and long green championship golf courses. They come from afar to escape, seeking warmth from the cold gray, days of winter. South Beach, Bay Side, Key Biscayne, and Bal Harbour provided this warmth. Yet right across the bridge in Overtown, Liberty City, Brown Sub, Carol City, and Little River, though it was hot as hell, it always seemed to be snowing.

These areas were where Cruz had grown up. In Little River, on 103rd Street, sat the Silver Blue Lakes apartment complex. It was Little River's version of the Match Box Housing projects, which made the Carter's look like a resort. What some of the most harden criminals might consider tragic was just another day in the life on 103rd. Whole families were lost! Victims of blood investments. New families were formed, the results of blood investments. Lose a child, make a stack. It was give and take. You see, nobody cared, so the hostages of these hellish social conditions took what they needed and gave the block hell for everything that they wanted.

"Two stacks up there, boy! Who tryna get money?" Headquartaz yelled as he shook the three dice. "Twenty-five or betta...money on the wood! Dice play off big money bettas, no sweats."

Everybody in the circle began putting their money beneath their feet. All hoping that Headquartaz might dickroll, or at least give them a low point to shoot at. Cee-low was a big pastime for Moehead, Bluey, Smash, DaDa, Boe Pete, Shorty and of course, Headquartaz. Everyone, with the exception of DaDa and Shorty, had grown up with Arthur Cruz. They had been like brothers at one point, and had shared everything from hardships to money, to women.

"Dice comin' out! Four, five, six for 'em!" Headquartaz yelled.

The dice showed two, six, one. Nothing! DaDa, Headquartaz's little cousin from Tennessee, gathered the dice and kicked them back to Headquartaz. Bluey, Headquartaz's best friend in the world, took this opportunity to drop some more money on his bet.

"Keep droppin' it, my nigga! That slick shit gon' getcha head hit! Dice go deep and let a real nigga sweep... headcrack for 'em!" Headquartaz yelled.

"Head! Headquartaz!" Peaches yelled as she approached the circle of men.

Headquartaz paid Peaches no mind as he released the dice. They tumbled to a halt right in front of Shorty. The two red dice showed sixes, and the lone green dice displayed a bitch.

"Damn!" Headquartaz yelled. "Hold the dice, my nigga. Bitch, what the fuck you want?"

"Head, I know you saw me textin' you. Lil' Head need some pampers and milk," Peaches said.

"Pampers and milk? You come 'round here fuckin' wit' me 'bout some pampers, bitch? Didn't you get yo' check! Bitch you better get the fuck on, fuckin' wit' me!"

"Nigga! You 'round here gettin' it, gamblin' and takin' care of these niggas, but you won't do shit for yo' son…. You a real fuck-nigga, Head!" Peaches spat back.

And that was it! Headquartaz punched Peaches square in the mouth. *Whop!* She fell on her back and began scooting backwards, trying to avoid being kicked by Headquartaz. The more she scooted, the further her skirt crawled up her body, exposing her reddish-brown bush.

"Whup that pussy-hoe, Head!" Smash yelled.

Everybody except DaDa and Ole Bluey were egging Headquartaz on as he dogged poor Peaches, the mother of his child, in front of the entire complex. Ole Bluey, disgusted, finally walked over and grabbed his friend.

"Damn, Head, baby! Come on, man… this is Lil Head's mom, man. Slow down!" Ole Bluey said.

DaDa walked over and helped Peaches up. She was crying and her mouth was dripping blood onto her shirt. Peaches was clearly embarrassed. She buried her face into DaDa's chest and held him as he walked her back to her car.

"Get yo' muthafuckin' hands off me, Blue! Fuck is wrong wit' you? Fuck that bitch, DaDa! Pussy-ass…" Headquartaz raged. "Where them dice at? Shoot, Blue!"

"Man, I'm up…I'ma head upstairs," Bluey returned.

"Nigga, I gave yall a point. You gon' shoot my money," Headquartaz said.

"Head, keep that lil' shit, my nigga. I'm gone."

"Fuck ya then! Shoot at Cola, DaDa. That's my point. Cola, nigga!"

DaDa just waved his big cousin off. He gave Peaches a hundred dollars and went upstairs with Ole Bluey. DaDa loved Headquartaz and appreciated him putting him on, but he was nobody's yes man. DaDa often followed Ole Bluey, who was more laid back. Bluey taught young DaDa about saving and staying humble.

Boe Pete, Moehead and Shorty were altogether different. Right or wrong, Headquartaz was always right in their eyes. It seemed the three of them loved trouble more than they loved money, or even life for that matter. Clubbing and thugging! Bitches and money! Headquartaz and his boys was 'bout it.

Smash on the other hand was a business man. It was always business first with Smash and Headquartaz was his business partner. Ever since Arthur Cruz had gotten jammed up and Busta had gotten killed, the two of them had grown close, though they were nothing alike.

"I punish hoes, my nigga! I'ma raw-dog bitch killa!" Boe Pete yelled as he released the dice.

Boe Pete was the last in line to shoot at Headquartaz's point. And he was also the last to see the two armed men run up from his blind side.

"Lay down nigga! Lay down!" the smaller of the two robbers yelled.

The other armed robber brought the butt of his AK down on Boe Pete's head, *Whop!* Causing Boe Pete to fall unconscious. Smash tried to run, but thought better when one of the robbers fired a shot. *Bocka!* the gun sounded. Smash laid down beside Headquartaz, Shorty, Moehead, and an unconscious Boe Pete.

"The next one of you pussy-niggas try somethin', I'ma kill ya! Now lay that dope money out...my nigga, find they dope while I get this bread."

In less than three minutes the two men had collected close to twelve thousand in cash and drugs. Plus they got Headquartaz, Smash and Boe Pete for about another twenty thousand in jewelry.

* * *

"Get me a beer, my nigga," Ole Bluey yelled from the couch.

DaDa passed Ole Bluey the beer and began putting the flames to a freshly rolled lace-joint. Inhaling deeply, the flame from the lighter disappeared as the end of the blunt glowed like the sun. Exhaling, the room filled with smoke. Sweet smoke. Raw cocaine and weed smoke.

"Damn boy! Smell like you got a whole ounce on that shit," Blue exclaimed.

"It is what it is, my nigga..." DaDa continued speaking as he blew out more smoke. "You wanna hit this?"

"Yeah, let me hit that." Bluey took the blunt from DaDa.

The two smoked in silence as Chuck D brung the noise...*Bass!/ How low will you go? Deathrow ...What a brutha know? /Once again, back! Is the incredible. The impeccable/ rhyme animal/ thee Public Enemy number one...Five-O said freeze! And I got numb/ Or should I tell 'em that I never really had a gun?/ Back on wax is the Terminator X One...*

"Blue, my nigga, that's some bullshit you playin', man."

"Nigga you crazy! P.E. classic...Hold up, you hear that?" Bluey asked.

"Hell yeah! It sound like a gun shot," DaDa answered.

"Maybe Head done shot Big Shorty stupid ass."

They both fell back laughing at the thought. Then the door flew open all of a sudden. Bluey came up with the Minnie-14 before he realized it was Headquartaz carrying Boe Pete.

"Damn Head, what happened?" Bluey questioned.

"Some fuck-niggas robbed us! While you and this nigga up here bullshittin'."

Ole Bluey looked over at DaDa, realizing that that was the gun shot that they had heard. The three of them took Boe Pete to the bedroom and laid him down. He had a nice little lump on his head for his problems. DaDa got him a bag of ice to put on it, and gave Boe the remainder of the lace-joint that he and Blue had been smoking. When he walked into the living room Head had an AK-47 laying on the couch while he checked and loaded another one.

"My nigga! I'ma kill that pussy-ass hoe, Peaches, and her fuck-ass bruthas," Headquartaz said.

"Head, Head, listen to what you sayin'...Peaches, man?" Blue questioned.

"My nigga, don't no nigga come up in my 'partments and take nothin'! 'Specially not from me! Them fuck-niggas got a problem wit' me for fuckin' up they shone-ass sista, then we gon' handle it."

"Head, man, where Smash, Shorty and Moe at?" Bluey asked.

"I sent 'em to get a car and some more heat. Dog, I'ma crush them muthafuckas!"

"Say Head, you 'bout to really fuck up, dog," Bluey told his friend.

"Nigga, how?"

"Head, I'll bet everythang that I got and everythang I'm gon' get for the next ten years, to a half a cup of piss, that that damn girl ain't even made it home yet...Bruh, think about the shit. This shit had to happen as soon as she got in the car and left...Now, if you just wanna killa innocent muthafucka, let's ride up to Sarasota and kill the fat ass nigga Mike-Mike about that lil' bread he owe," Bluey reasoned.

44

Headquartaz sat there and thought for a minute. Blue was right again. It seemed that Ole Bluey was always right. That's what Head loved and hated about him.

"You right, my nigga. Damn, them fuck-niggas got me in my buildings. I swear boy, I'ma find out and I'ma kill them bitch-ass niggas."

"Yeah, aiight...Yo, DaDa, call Smash and 'em and tell 'em to forget that. Tell 'em it's all good," Bluey instructed.

This was not the first time that Ole Bluey had saved the day. Every other day Headquartaz and his Three Musketeers were at the brink of war. It was clear to Bluey that Headquartaz was no general. Yet he had been Cruz's number one hammer. He had put in more work than anybody, so he sort of unofficially became the head when Cruz got jammed up. And poor Head spent every waking moment trying to come from under the ever present shadow that Cruz had casted. Bluey had no desire to try to fill Cruz's shoes. It was impossible! Yet he reasoned that he'd help Head keep the boat afloat until Cruz returned.

* * *

DaDa and Cola sat cuddled on the sofa in their den watching Scarface as a monsoon fell from the heavens outdoors. DaDa was smoking heavy-lace and Cola had taken her an X-pill. Everytime the thunder rumbled above, Cola trembled inside, causing her to cling even tighter to DaDa.

"You know you scary." DaDa laughed. "Do you be shakin' like that when you be stealin' them folks shit?"

"I ain't stuttin' you, DaDa!" Cola said, punching him in the arm.

Then all of a sudden, there was another loud rumbling at the window. Only this was not thunder. Cola jumped at the sound of it and held DaDa. They both looked in the direction of the window as DaDa removed his .32 from beneath the pillow.

Boom! Boom! Boom! Boom! The rumbling started again.

"DaDa! Boy, get yo' scary-ass up and open the door!" Bluey yelled over the sound of the heavy thunder and rain.

DaDa walked over to the window with his gun in hand, he looked a bit nervous.

"Blue, that you man?" he asked.

"Yeah, it's me, open the damned door," Bluey answered.

"Ayyyyyha!" Cola laughed. "Now who scary?"

"Hoe, shut up," DaDa said and went to open the door.

When DaDa came back to the den Ole Bluey was with him and was soaking wet. He was wearing black jeans, a black windbreaker, black Tim's and black gloves.

"Hey Blue, what's up witcha?" Cola chimed as he walked into the den.

"Ain't a whole lot, pretty baby. How 'bout you?" Bluey returned.

"I'm cool. I got some stuff. You need somethin'?"

"Do you have some shit for one year olds?" Bluey asked.

"Yeah, I got some Tommy, Guess, Polo and some lil' Nike stuff."

"Aiight here," Bluey said, reaching into his pocket. "Give me three hundred dollars worth of shit."

"Okay, but Blue, this is three-fifty you gave me," Cola said.

"Yeah, I know. The fifty's for yo' time. I'ma need you to take it to Headquartaz's BM tomorrow...Say, DaDa, baby, I need you man."

"Aiight, what's up? Whatcha need?" DaDa asked.

"I need you to come take a ride wit' me."

"A ride? Bluey, it's rainin' cats and dogs out there, my nigga."

"Yeah, go figure...here, put these on and let's go."

46

Ole Bluey handed DaDa some rubber black gloves and they were off. Blue was riding in a dark-gray Impala SS. They rode along without saying much at first. Bluey handed DaDa a lace-joint and a lighter while he took a two-on-two at the red light.

"Fire that up, baby. You look a bit nervous." Bluey smiled, his fourteen gold-teeth shined even in the dark.

"Where we goin' Bluey, my nigga? 'Cause this weather fucked up, can't see shit out here."

"This is the best time to ride, lil' homie. Ain't got to worry 'bout the poe-poe, and shouldn't be no ridas out. It's just us...My nigga, Arthur Cruz taught me this, ya dig. This is a serious game we in, DaDa. So we gotta stay on top of everything and everybody. Me and Cruz used to ride all night on nights like this."

"Who is Arthur Cruz?" DaDa asked.

"He was my main man before he got knocked. He jive ran the whole hood. Business back then wasn't on a scale as large as it is now, but times were better, and a whole lot smoother when he was around. He's a real 'G'."

"You don't get at him no more? I mean, what's up wit' him?"

"Shiid, about a year after he got jammed I sent him a grand through my ole lady. Then 'bout a year later I got a package on my birthday. It was a book. The Prince, by Machiavelli."

"You talkin 'bout Tupac?" DaDa asked.

"Hell nawl! Niccolo Machiavelli. Man, I didn't understand it at first, but I kept reading it. DaDa, man, that book was the best thing anybody could have ever given me."

The two of them rode around for hours. They cruised Biscayne, past all the hotels and then rode by Headquartaz's house, Moehead's house, Boe Pete's crib, and Shorty's momma's house. Coming off of 22nd Avenue, they caught 103rd Street and came through Silver Blue. Smash's car was parked outside of the trap apartment. Bluey picked up his cell phone and texted Smash twice. After about five minutes the phone rang back.

"Hey baby, what's up?... Yeah, where you at? Okay, yeah... I'm at the pad, I just thought about you... Yeah, aiight... Stay outta trouble, baby... aiight, fuck her for me too... Yeah, one love." Bluey hung up.

DaDa was sitting there looking sleepy and confused.

"DaDa, baby, you can't trust nobody! I check everybody out. I like to know everything. I wanted to see if Smash would lie about his location... 'Cause if a nigga will lie, he will steal. And if he steals, he will kill. Ya dig?"

"Yeah, but you lied. You told him that you was home," DaDa stated.

"Exactly! You see DaDa, hypocrisy is the tribute which vice pays to virtue... meaning, hypocrisy works only because the majority of men are not hypocrites, and therefore not suspicious. When you stop being suspicious, you lose your edge."

"You learned all that from a book?"

"Yeah man, it's a bad muthafucka... But you can't just know it, you gotta live it."

The rain was still falling very heavy! And showed no signs of letting up anytime soon. Yet Ole Bluey continued to patrol different hoods. Sometimes stopping and calling the occupants of the residence he was watching. It was now about 3am.

"Hey DaDa, get yo' ass up!" Bluey shook him.

"What's up, man?"

"Look, reach back there and hand me that stick."

DaDa got the AK-47 off of the backseat and handed it to Bluey as he'd asked him to. Confused, he waited for further instructions.

"Look DaDa, take the car and ride to the end of the block. It's some lil' apartments down there. Just park and wait. I'ma signal you when I want you to come back..."

Bluey began to get out of the car. But before he could, DaDa stopped him.

"Bluey, where you goin', my nigga, and what's the signal?" DaDa asked, nervously.

"I'ma be right over there in them bushes...I been peepin' dude for a minute now, and he usually comes in 'bout four, five o'clock. So when you hear the AK go off, you know he home. Come get me..."

Ole Bluey got out, AK in hand, and walked over and squatted in the bushes. The rain fell even harder as DaDa drove off to the apartment on 63rd Street and 17th Avenue. He sat there, scared to death, listening to the slow blaze on 99 Jamz. The radio's clock read 4:18 when DaDa dozed off.

Bocka! Bocka! Bocka! Bocka! The AK-47 called.

"Oh shit!" DaDa said to himself as the shots woke him up.

He started the car and headed back to where he had left Bluey. The radio's clock was now reading 5:30. He had been asleep for over an hour. The rain had finally stopped. But Bluey had to have been laying on this dude, in the rain, for a long time before it had stopped.

Bocka! Bocka! Bocka! The AK went off again before DaDa got to the house. As he neared the house Bluey came out and jumped in the car.

"Drive, DaDa!" was all he said.

DaDa did as he was instructed, but not before looking over at the house where the two dead bodies lay. They were both face down with most of their heads gone. One was right next to the car. The other was outside the fence. The AK-47 was lying beside him.

"Damn Bluey, man! Why you leave the choppa?"

"Why not?" Bluey calmly continued. "I bought it for 'em. It's only right that I left it wit' 'em...and make sure you keep that under ya hat."

"Yeah aiight, I ain't seen shit," DaDa responded.

It was the first time that he had actually been involved with a murder. Of course, it would not be his last...

* * *

The next day it was business as usual in the Blue. Of course, DaDa was late. When he finally arrived around 2:30 pm, everybody was already out and bullshitting as usual.

"What's up, niggas?" DaDa said after paying his cab.

"Ain't a whole lot, jit...Why the fuck you just gettin' here?" Headquartaz asked.

DaDa looked at Ole Bluey who was just putting the finishing touches on an EL-PO full of cocaine and weed. After flaming up, Bluey blew a gust of smoke and answered for his little buddy.

"Give him some slack, Head, 'cause it seems that hoe of his ain't givin' him none. Look at him, eyes all red, the boy tired! Probably been up all night wit' Cola's muff in his jib," Bluey capped.

Everybody got a good laugh out of that, everybody except DaDa. Taking the lace-joint from Ole Bluey, he wondered how in the hell had he managed to be up and in good spirits after being up all night in the rain? Bluey was a cold-blooded dude he reasoned.

"I see you fresh, big cuz!" DaDa said.

"Hell yeah! Niggas got me yesterday, fuck-niggas...I couldn't even sleep last night! So I hopped up first thang today and fell through the flea..." Head said as he lifted his new Cuban-link and displayed his four-link bracelet with the diamond incrusted plate. "I dropped a light ten stacks. Nothin' too heavy."

Bluey just shook his head. Headquartaz would never learn it seemed, always flossing. Always willing to take or exceed what had already been taken. And no sooner than Bluey had gotten the thoughts out of his head, up walked another problem. Another one of Head's problems.

"Hey Head, I don't mean to bother you, but I was wondering if I could get somethin' on that," Fran asked hesitantly.

"Get somethin' on that? Bitch, what is you talkin' 'bout? I don't owe you shit!" Headquartaz snapped.

"Nawl Head, I'm sayin', you don't owe me nothin'. I was just sayin', you said the other day that you was gonna look-out for what we did."

"Bitch, I don't pay for no pussy. So you got me fucked up."

"Ut'un Head, I ain't trippin' off that, I'm talking about when I let you and DaDa use my apartment and I helped yall bag up that work. I'm sayin', you could..." Fran pleaded before Head cut her off.

"Fran, I'm fucked up. Niggas got me yesterday for some change. So I'll holla atcha a lil' later on," Head lied.

"Aiight Head, I'm not trippin'. And I wouldn't have asked you, but I need to get my daughter."

"Bitch! Didn't I say I'll get you later? Now I ain't givin' you shit! Pussy-ass-hoe...get the fuck on!" Head went off.

Fran dropped her head and walked off. Which was the right thing to do, because she had a no win with Head. Whereas Fran was a very nice, sincere type of chick, with a body that demanded attention from everyone that witnessed it; Head was an uncaring show off that really did not give a fuck about anyone but Head.

Bluey, being of sound mind, pulled DaDa up and had him take Fran two hundred and fifty dollars. Meanwhile, Big Shorty, Smash and a few other dudes from around the complex had a nice dice game going in the back. Bluey figured that this would be the perfect time to talk with his friend.

It was about thirty minutes before shift change. Bluey, Headquartaz and Moehead were in the apartment going through some money, they had been counting for the last hour and a half. The trap ran 24-7, two shifts, each bringing in close to twenty thousand. They were just about finished when Big Shorty walked in.

"Yeah, my nigga! Raped 'em!" Shorty yelled, holding nothing but fifties and hundreds in each hand.

"Boy, who you robbed?" Ole Bluey asked.

"My nigga, I just roped the dice game off! Raped them niggas...Here Moe, take me off the books. I'm payin' all mine off, and I'm 'bout to get grilled up, and drop me a Chevy, my nigga."

Big Shorty was ecstatic! He gave Moehead a grand in crispy hundreds and still had about six thousand left. Moehead took the money, but after looking closely at it, he began to frown.

"Big Shorty, where you get this money?" Moehead asked.

"The dice game," Big Shorty answered.

"I mean, who was droppin' all these honeybees and fifties?"

"Oh, the lil' nigga Wease and his brutha Mike. The two niggas stay on the end."

"Muthafuckas! Head, look at this shit. Man, this my money. The money the niggas touched me for yesterday," Moehead exclaimed.

Head jumped up and came over to where Big Shorty and Moehead were standing. He took one of the bills and looked at it.

"Moe, this is money, man. But how you know it's yours? It's a big face hundred! Everybody got 'em," Head said.

"Nawl, Head, not like these. Man, look at the serial numbers. They the same, they counterfeit! My lil' partner Mal, up in Liquordale, sold 'em to me for fifty on the hundred," Moehead said.

By now Head, Big Shorty, and Bluey were eyeing the queer government notes. Moehead was right! The money had the same serial numbers. Other than that, it looked like the real deal.

"Moe," Headquartaz finally called.

"Yeah man?"

"They got this off of you yesterday?" Head asked.

"Yeah, at the dice game," Moehead answered.

"So, let me get this right...Nigga, you was playin' me with counterfeit money?"

"Oh, dog, it wasn't like..."

"I should kill you! Get the fuck outta here nigga and grab them two niggas," Headquartaz yelled.

Moehead hauled ass out of the apartment, because he knew that he had fucked up. Still, he had helped find the dudes that robbed them yesterday. Approaching the dice game he looked but could not find Wease and Mike.

"Smash, where Wease and Mike?" Moe asked.

"I don't know, nigga. Shorty broke 'em, ask him," Smash returned.

They had gotten away for the moment, but only for the moment. The cat was now out of the bag, and street justice would soon run its course.

Chapter 5

I'm a muthafuckin' pimp-pimp! Come on, say it...Yous a pimp, baby, yous a pimp, baby.... Cause I'm a pimp-pimp! Come on, say it... Yous a pimp, baby, yous a pimp, baby.... The system blarred as Trick Daddy, JT Money, and Buddy Roe traded verses over a Righteous Funk Boogie track.

Cruz was at the wheel of the black Max' breezing through light traffic. Him, Tamika, and Des were headed to South Miami to pick up Des' girlfriend, and then they were all going to the county fair.

"Okay, that's enough of this mess," Tamika said, turning the radio off.

"Hold up, Ma! Why you cut it off?" Des pleaded.

"'Cause ain't no hoes in here, so I know it ain't no pimps in here."

"Oh, I don't know 'bout that, Ma. 'Cause I'ma pimp-pimp, for real," Des returned.

"Boy puleez! Mesha got yo' butt wide open," Tamika said.

"Straightin' that, Dad!" Des yelled.

Cruz laughed. "He might be a lil' pimp. I heard him gettin' his lil' thang off the other day."

"Cruz, are you crazy? Des ain't no pimp! Pimps are low-life nothings! I can't believe yall two," Tamika spat.

"All pimps ain't bad, baby. Some just run the title, but are actually good people. For real, a pimp saved my life," Cruz said.

"How daddy?" Des asked.

"By pushin' me in the right direction. And even when I wanted to give up, he encouraged me to stick with it and do what was right.... Yeah, if it wasn't for Pimpin Boo Baby, I'd still be doin' the things that got me locked up the first time."

"Well tell me 'bout this Pimpin Boo Baby," Tamika said.

"It's a long story," Cruz returned.

"Well we got a long ride. Tell us!"

"Aiight, dig... I was in prison and we used to get high together. So one day I'm layin' in my bunk and Pimpin Boo Baby comes in like..."

* * *

"Say, baby, what the fuck is goin' on in this funky muthafucka, lil' mac?" Boo Baby asked as he barged into the stuffy little cell.

Arthur Cruz looked up sheepishly and saw his pal. "Pimp, what the fuck is wrong witchu, man? Why you always runnin' up in a nigga cell all early?"

"'Cause the early pimp gets the hoe! And a good hoe is the only thang that getta pimp his dough...now get up, let's rap a taste."

Cruz wanted to kill Boo Baby! But being as he looked up to Pimpin Boo and enjoyed getting drunk and high with him, he simply had to roll with the punches. Wiping some of the sleep from his eyes, Cruz sat up.

"Is my cellie down there?" Cruz asked from the top bunk.

"Lil' mac, pimpin' raised me, not crazy," Boo popped. "Do you thank I'd be in here if yo' jive ass cellie was in here?"

"Whatever, nigga." Cruz jumped down from the top bunk and opened his locker. After removing his toothbrush and toothpaste, he quickly polished his grill and washed his face.

"You got some money, lil' mac?" Boo Baby asked.

"Yeah why?" Cruz shot back, searching his living quarters for a cigarette.

"'Cause, lil' mac, them boys over in M-block got sacks as fat as hoe pussy! And I ain't gotta tell ya how fat a hoe's pussy is...do I?" Boo capped and passed Cruz a Newport from the pack he had in his pocket.

Firing up the Newport, Cruz sat down and blew big smoke. It was a bad habit that he'd picked up on the inside. Every morning he had to have a cigarette as soon as his feet touched the floor. He was now halfway finished, the room smoky and dead quiet. Boo Baby broke the silence.

"Say baby, is you smokin' or is you jokin', 'cause niggas runnin' gettin' them bags like them boys got parole papers in 'em, and I'm tryna get high, jack." Boo Baby stood up to leave.

"Hold up, man!" Cruz said and grabbed his sweat pants. Digging through the pockets he came up with five books of stamps—$25 in money terms.

"My man!" Boo Baby said with a smile. "I'll be right back, killa!"

* * *

With Boo Baby gone, Cruz got dressed and straightened up the room some. He didn't know where his cellie was. The two were real close but moved in two totally different circles.

He quickly put three spoons of Taster's Choice in his plastic Miami Dolphins mug and stepped off to the hot water dispenser, which was downstairs at the far end of the cell block. After filling and stirring the thick black liquid, Cruz took the steps back up to the second tier. He saw Pop, the grumpy old store man that over-charged everybody for everything, sweeping out his cell. Cruz stepped in, strewing the small pile of trash everywhere. The old man looked up with pure unadulterated murder in his eyes.

"You lil' stupid fucka! Why you always gotta be so foolish?" Pop exclaimed.

Cruz laughed at him. He loved to make the older man mad. "My bad, Pop. I just want two packs of Kools."

"Here!" the old store man said, rushing to get the cigarettes out of his locker. "Now get away from my cell."

"Damn, Pop, I said my bad." Cruz continued laughing. "What I owe?"

"You can have 'em for free if you promise to stay ya ominous ass way from here...besides, you know them's Cad'llacs. Cost thirty stamps a pack."

"I ain't know they had Jews in Omaha, old-tight-ass nigga!" Cruz shot back, giving Pop three books of stamps.

Pop gave Cruz the evil-eye. His bottom lip trembled as he spoke, "I done told you 'bout that nigga shit! I ain'tcha nigga, boy."

"You old niggas kill me...yall the reason why so many young niggas is locked up. Yall old niggas is confused and fucked up in the head. One minute you Ron O'neal, the next minute you Martin Kang...you need—"

"Get out, boy! Get out! You gon' drive my pressure up!" Pop yelled, pushing Cruz out of his cell.

Cruz walked out laughing his ass off. Pissing Pop off was always the highlight of his day.

When he got back to his cell Boo Baby was already inside, turning up a quart of prison made brew and holding a joint of refeer. Cruz quickly stepped in and snatched the smoking stick of dynamite from his main man. For the next twenty minutes not a word was uttered. Only an occasional cough was heard as the two passed joints back and forth, filling the small cell and their lungs with a thick haze of weed smoke. Cruz was high as a muthfucka! His mouth was dry and his head was spinning.

"Damn!" he murmured. "You wanna smoke another one?"

"Hell yeah!" Boo Baby fired back without a moment's thought. As Cruz twisted the weed Boo Baby glanced at his prison Rolex (a gold Citizen's Quartz) and sighed. "Damn! You needs to hurry up, baby...I gotta make this next move."

"For what?" Cruz asked, sparking the joint.

"Gotta hit the chapel...my main man out-the-sky is speakin' today and I can't miss it, jack."

"Chapel?" Cruz questioned and sucked his teeth. "Fuck is a nigga in prison speakin' on in the chapel?"

"On our plight, baby." Boo Baby took the joint and pulled it hard. He loved weed! Not as much as he loved cocaine and pills, yet he loved it nonetheless. "I mean, really, you've never gotten really-really high and listened to the bruthas talk that black shit?"

"Bruthas? Mmaaann, you talkin' 'bout them niggas wit' the bow ties?"

"Yeah, exactly!" Pimpin Boo hit the weed again and passed it. "I absolutely love to get extra-loaded and dig on 'em! It's really-really out-of-sight, maann."

"Nigga, you trippin'! I ain't no muthafuckin' Mausoleum, my nigga...my ole-g Baptist...Bishop Curry," Cruz shot back, pulling on the roach.

Boo Baby laughed his ass off. Real tears fell from his eyes he was laughing so hard.

"What's so funny?"

Pimpin Boo looked at his young, ignorant partner. "It's Muslim, not Mausoleum, lil' mac buddy. And the truth of it is, you are Muslim. We were all born Muslim, which simply means, *one who surrenders and submits to God.* Anything else that we as a foolish and downtrodden people *claim to be or adhere to,* we made ourselves. I mean, baby, it was three *super-fast-steppin'* whores that made me a *foot-in-they-ass pimp.* Just as something or someone in yo' life made you a *drug-dealin-gangsta.* Can you dig that?"

"Nigga, you high!" Cruz shot back.

"As e-muthafucka! And I make no secret of it...nonetheless, lil'mac, it don't change the truth...so, umm, do this for me. Come on down to the chapel, hear my main man *out-the-sky* talk that talk, and if you don't righteously dig it, I'll get you super-high for the rest of the month and I'll never ask you to come down again...what's up?"

Cruz thought for a minute. "The whole rest of the month?"

"Right on, jack."

"Let's go, nigga."

The two stood and made their way to the chapel.

* * *

When they entered the large chapel it was standing room only. Rows and rows of chairs were filled and brothers were standing all around the large room. Before Boo Baby and Cruz could find a spot along the back wall to stand, a cool brown skin brother of medium build, baldhead and wearing razor sharp beige Dickies, approached

59

them. He smiled brightly and escorted the two to two reserved seats near the front. Then a dead silence rushed over the room as a short, barrel chested man stood and approached the rostrum. His face was set in a serious expression. As if he were an elementary school principle about to reprimand an audience of troubled students. The pitch black flesh on his shiny baldhead glistened like the full-moon on a dark starless night. After clearing his throat a deep booming baritone filled the room. His voice was exciting and everyone seemed to be sitting on the edges of their seats in anticipation. Cruz looked around the room at their faces and wondered, *who the fuck is this black ugly nigga 'posed to be?* His answer came booming...

"Who am I? A lot of you bruthas want to know! What am I talkin' about and who gave me the authority to speak on *what I think I know?* That's what you're thinkin'. Who this nigga *think he is?*"

The speaker had his piercing eyes locked on young Cruz as he asked these particular questions. *Damn?!* Cruz thought, *this nigga read minds?* The forceful orator had his full undivided attention.

"I'm the truth! And the truth is—"

"God!" the brothers in the audience and around the speaker's rostrum yelled in response to the question.

The coal black orator wiped his mouth with a snow-white handkerchief and continued.

"For what *He is I am!* In spirit and likeness. For the Gods came together and had a talk..."

"What they talk about, bruh?" someone in the audience asked.

The speaker chuckled slightly and answered. "They talked about makin' a man!"

"What kinda man, Bruh Minister?" another member of the audience yelled.

"They talked about makin' a man in their own image and likeness...the Bible says it this way, *God said, Let us make man in our own image, in the likeness of ourselves, and let them be masters*...the definition of *master* is *one havin' authority over another*...Genesis 1:27 says *God created man in the image of Himself, in the image of God He created him, male and female He created them*...So who gave me my authority?"

"God!!!"

"And if I'm created in His image and His likeness, what am I?"

"A God!!!"

"Okay, then." The speaker wiped his mouth and face again before neatly folding the handkerchief and scanning the crowd. He locked eyes with Cruz again, whose attention he had in a vicegrip. The youngster was now on the edge of his seat like everyone else. He'd never heard a man, any man, speak about God and himself in such a manner.

"The Holy Quran says it like this, *The likeness of Jesus with Allah is truly as the likeness of Adam. He created him from dust, then said to him, Be and he was!* That's chapter 3:59, talkin' about the creation of Adam and our brutha Jesus. Chapter 2:30 starts like, *thy Lord said to the angels, I am going to place a ruler in the earth.* This is God (Allah) talkin' to the Gods, that *'us'* from earlier in Genesis. Only now we get to hear what the *'us'*, the other gods had to say. Listen now, they said: *Wilt thou place in it such as make mischief in it and shed blood? And we celebrate Thy praise and extol Thy holiness*...You see, haters! The gods didn't want to do it. But check out what God said, *He said: Surely I know what you know not.*"

The man paused and gauged the crowd. The room was quiet as a cemetery. Young Cruz could hear his own heart beat. He felt his pulse quicken in anticipation of the speaker's next words. *Come on, bruh. Say it! Kick that shit!* he wanted to yell.

"God then taught Adam all the names and gave him authority. Made him a ruler in the earth…you see, you see, God gave you, the so-called American Blackman, dominion over everything! He said, *Be fruitful and multiply! Fill the earth and 'subdue' it!* Now who could *'subdue'* but as master, a ruler, one of authority, a god!"

"Say it then, Blackman!"

"Teach, Bruh Minister! Teach!"

The weed, alcohol and mastery of words had Cruz gone! *This nigga a beast!* he thought, looking around at everyone clapping and pumping their fist.

The speaker raised his hands to quiet the audience. He then continued. "But with every positive there's a negative. Remember the haters? The ones that questioned your authority? Well, with power comes responsibility. You gotta be tested! God gave you something. And in return He said *be faithful and believe.* What did we say? *We believe…* God smiles and said, *Oh you who believe, enter into complete peace (Islam) and follow not the footsteps of the devil. Surely he is your open enemy…*"

The handsome brown skin brother with the creased up Dickies on approached the rostrum, handing the speaker a bottle of water. He drank and quickly passed the bottle back before continuing.

"Now who is the devil? I know that that's what I woulda asked. I'd say God, who's this devil cat you're talkin' about?" A few muffled laughs erupted from the spectators. "He said in so many words that the devil was the *disbeliever.* He was made contrary to our, the gods, nature. You see, we the Muslims submit to God's divine authority whether we like it or not, because Muslim means *one who submits to God…*Well, God said to the angels, *Be submissive to Adam.* They submitted… the one, Iblis did not. He refused and was proud, and *he was one of the disbelievers,* a devil!"

"Teach! Blackman!"

"Take 'em there, Bruh Minister! Point that cracka out!"

"That's right! Teach on that!"

The brothers all around the room began screaming and yelling.

Cruz looked around expecting the police to run in at any moment. *These niggas trippin',* he thought nervously. Then he looked to his right, Pimpin Boo Baby was smiling at the beauty of the moment, a Blackman standing tall and teaching the unadulterated truth to his people. The moment alone was *something to die for.*

"Are you a believer?! Do you submit?! Are you fit to rule in the earth as it was ordained by Allah your God?" the speaker asked, now pacing the make shift stage like a caged lion.

Brothers pumped their fists and replied yes. Cruz wanted to stand up and pace with the smooth talking nigga with the black bowtie firmly placed on his shirt collar. But instead he just listened.

"Oh you who believe...or say that you believe. *Do you think that you will not be tested? For surely we tested those before you...*We-were-tested-and-we failed! But not of our own doin'... no, no, no...through the trick knowledge of our open enemy, the devil-white-man, we've fallen from God's grace. The Holy Qur'an says it like this, *But the devil made them slip from it, and caused them to depart from the state in which they were...*Qur'an still talkin', *And We said: Go forth, some of you are enemies of others. And there is for you in the earth an abode and a provision for a time!*

"You see, you see, but for a time! Bible talkin', *Far from the richness of the earth and the dew of heaven above, your home will be. By our sword you will live, and your brother you will serve...* but! But when you wake up, Blackman! When you come into the knowledge of yourself and your God! When you make the connection between you and God. When you start to live in His likeness and reflect His image in you! When you give that cracka back his drugs, guns, tobacco, liquor, and adulterous livin', you will find freedom from this mental bondage that has been placed on our minds. The scripture says, *But when you win your freedom, you will shake his yoke off your neck!*"

"Say that then, Blackman!"

"Expose the cracka, Brutha! Expose him!"

People were now on their feet.

"We have been open prey to our enemies, the devil-white-race! In fact, all nations of the earth have taken advantage of the poor Blackman and woman... we have been beaten, robbed and subjected to our slave masters and their children's lustful and wicked deceitful teachings! Thus, we have been reared today from the soil of corruption and from the very seed of their hate! Their violence! Their evil influences and practices have been our life-blood for the last 430 years! We are now the product of our enemy's makin'! Where we are, here in prison, lost in the inner-city ghetto's, trapped in the drug house; what we are today, criminals, dead beat fathers, no account husbands, enemies to our own kind; it is the work of our enemies—the white race!

"Today they hate and despise us, the very product of their murderous hands! Our laziness, our ignorance, our drunken and filthiness!

"But God has a plan! He wants and has chosen the once powerful, masterful people of the earth, the gods that were made in His likeness and image, God desires to make us *a people for Himself!* If we will submit to Him, He will give us back our own—complete mastery of the Universe...so teaches the Honorable Elijah Muhammad. And it is in his name that I greet and leave you in, peace!"

Everyone came to their feet again, clapping and shouting. Cruz just looked on in complete awe. Something inside of him connected with the speaker's words. Something inside of him wanted what the speaker had: a knowledge of self and God. Something he'd never before desired.

After shaking hands and speaking with a few people, he began making his way over towards Boo Baby and Cruz.

Cruz nudged Boo Baby in the side upon seeing him coming. "Say Boo, my nigga, who is that nigga?"

Boo Baby smiled brightly, showcasing a solid ten pack—four gold teeth to the top and six to the bottom. "That's the nigga I was tellin' you 'bout, Kunta! My main man out-the-sky!"

Just then Kunta walked up. "Peace, Brutha Boo."

"Peace be unto you, baby! You really said a mouthful today, jack. I mean, I really liked to have claimed my own, baby."

Kunta laughed and shook Boo Baby's hand.

Boo turned and introduced Cruz. "Say baby, this is my lil' mac buddy, Cruz. Cruz, this is my main-man-out-the-sky, Kunta."

"Please to meet you, lil' bruh," Kunta said, shaking Cruz's hand.

"Nah, man. The pleasure's mine...I mean, damn! You a bad muthafucka, man! Where you learned that shit at?! I mean, who the fuck taught you how to talk shit like that?"

Kunta couldn't help but to laugh at the youngster. "God, lil' brutha. And He'll do the same for you, if you submit."

"Submit? Whatchu mean?"

"I'm speaking again next Friday, come down. This time, come sober," Kunta said and walked away.

Cruz did return the next Friday, the following Friday, and the Friday after that. Each Friday he learned a little more and was drawn closer to the teachings. Then, one Friday as he sat listening to the strong message of truth, he saw himself standing outside of himself saying, "my name is Arthur Cruz and I'd like to claim my on."

His bid, his life, his way of thinking really changed after that. The teachings and the lessons that led to them became his life-line. Every minute of his days were dedicated to reading and studying. The law library became a second home. He read book after book. All of which were given to him by Arthur X, the handsome brown skin dude that had seated him and Boo Baby at the service.

Arthur X was also his tutor and mentor. They began spending a lot of time together. Which Cruz loved but hated, because Arthur X really drove him to excel. Partly because he liked the youngster, but mainly because they were homeboys—not a lot of brothers from Miami chose to accept the teachings, so those that did had to be razor sharp.

* * *

"Say, baby! A pimp gotta ultra-fantastic line on some green. After all beautiful, you're unemployed, disenfranchised, and loathing away in disillusion. Some fine green would really set us right, kinfolks," Pimpin Boo Baby said.

"Pimp, don't come up in here poppin' ya collar and talkin' crazy every morning. A nigga ain't even brushed his teeth and drunk breakfast; and here you come bullshittin'. Man, get the fuck outta my cell!" Cruz said, raising himself from his bunk.

"Say, baby! Did a pimp somehow disturb your groove? Because a pimp definitely meant you no harm," Pimpin Boo Baby capped.

"You right, man. A nigga just tired. Arthur X been pushin' the shit outta me. He give a nigga a book, over 300 pages, and want an oral and written report in four days! In the past six months I've read damn near 30 books. I don't know where the nigga keep gettin' 'em from." Cruz continued, "I think the nigga tryin' to make me quit. Then I gotta meet this nigga at 1:00 in the law library, so I can't do nothin', Pimp."

"That is so disheartening, sweetheart. My pump's really tender for you right now. I mean, a pimp almost dropped a tear. Especially seeing as how your new found misfortune is a result of my folly," Boo said with a genuinely sad expression.

"Whatever nigga," Cruz quickly countered and they both fell out laughing.

Before leaving for the law library, Cruz had to wash up, clean the cell, and complete the book "Last Man Standing." He had about 63 pages left. It seemed crazy that the government would knowingly take 28 years of a man's life, knowing that he was innocent, just to persuade others to disassociate themselves with a party that stood in their best interest. A party, The Black Panthers, that had never lynched a white man, never enslaved a white man, and never stopped a white man from pursuing any endeavor that he'd chose to pursue, be it legal or illegal. Yet they, The Black Panthers, had been deemed, by J. Edgar Hoover, the greatest threat to national security; while racially sadistic groups like the Ku Klux Klan and the C.I.A. continued to function with impudence. "It was a cold world, dirty game!" he reasoned.

While finishing up his lessons, gathering a few last thoughts, and preparing to leave for the library, his cellmate walked in.

"What it do, lil' one?" Nate asked in good spirits.

"Nothing. Just chillin'," Cruz answered.

"The sun don't chill, it shine! Look alive, young nigga," Nate said with even more excitement.

"I'm feelin' that. A nigga just a little tired," Cruz responded.

"Yeah, I see you was up late as shit last night. You really serious 'bout this shit, huh?" Nate asked, now more serious in tone.

"Yeah, man. After just listenin' a little, and doing some serious readin', man, I see how fucked up I was. I see how fucked up we all are! Man, I'm tryin' to right a few of my wrongs, help a few folks, and make moms and everybody proud of a nigga," Cruz said.

Nate just smiled. He really had a genuine love for Cruz and was happy to see him striving for something in life.

"Say, lil' one. I'm proud of you right now. You heard me?" Nate continued. "Now go got 'em."

* * *

The library was packed. And why shouldn't it have been? The Feds were passing out time like they were giving away candy. Brothers were walking around with 50 year and life sentences. Who would ever have thought that a time would come when a man with a 20 year sentence would be considered blessed by his peers?

Making his way through the sea of hopefuls, Cruz spotted Arthur X at his usual rear table holding court with two of the brothers from the Sunni Community. Upon seeing Cruz, they both greeted him and left.

"What's up, big homie?" Cruz said while sitting his stuff on the table and taking a seat.

"Same struggle, different day, homeboy." Arthur X continued. "I just spent the last two hours debating with them niggas. Tryin' to show them how much we all—Nation, Christians, Moors, Hebrews, and Sunni—have in common. Yet all they care to focus on is the differences. While the Qur'an says that *man is but a single nation. We made you into tribes only that you may know one another*, and it says ultimately that God alone would judge that in which we differ. It's crazy. Did you finish the book?"

"Yeah, I finished it. I also wrote somethin' and I was hopin' that you might read it," Cruz said.

"What is it?" Arthur X asked very casually.

Of course, he had already known beforehand that it was a speech. Cruz was not Arthur X's first student, and like all of the rest, he was very eager to command the rostrum. Very much like himself when he first came into knowledge. Ambitions were a beautiful thing when they were properly nourished and guided. Yet impatience or immaturity was altogether a horse of a different color.

He reflected on his first experience of speaking to an audience. It was his third year in prison when he'd came into the knowledge. He had been one of Brother Khalid's top students, mainly because of his thirst for the lessons and his afore knowledge of the Bible. Arthur X had studied, rehearsed, and studied some more. He was going to make them all bear witness to his knowledge and stage presence. He was on fire, chest out and his head held high as he took the rostrum. After looking into the eyes of all those people and opening in prayer, he could not remember one word of his speech. He stuttered out some words and fumbled on until the reality of his impatience had humbled him. Coming down off of that rostrum was like walking the Green Mile. All eyes were on him. He exited the rostrum deflated; his head hung way-low.

"Lil' bruh, lil' bruh, let me share a word with you," said Raja. He was an elder from the Sunni Community.

"Yes sir," Arthur X answered in a very humble tone.

Raja looked him in the eyes and gave him a lesson, in words that he would never forget. Raja said, "son, if you hada went up yonda like you come down, you might coulda came down like you went up."

With that he smiled at the younger man, slapped him on the shoulder and walked off.

For that reason X pushed the young man and did his best to keep him humble and prepared. For that reason Cruz had to be catechized.

"Okay, just hold on to it. Maybe I'll look at it next week!" X said without looking at it.

"Say man, what's up? You got a problem with me? 'Cause I ain't really feelin' this shit," Cruz said, snatching up the papers.

"Pardon me?" X said, somewhat shocked by Cruz's outburst.

"Man, you heard me! I ain't feelin' this masta-grasshoppa shit. You been workin' the shit outta me. Every morning my cellie gotta turn the lights out and pick up the book I done fell asleep readin'. I've done everything you've asked of me, and all you've done is pushed harder. And you ain't even considered me speaking or how a nigga feel," Cruz spat in anger.

"Are you finished?" Arthur X calmly asked.

"Yeah, I'm finished," Cruz answered.

"I commend you on your hard work. But let's get a few things straight. Jit, I could give a fuck less about you and your celly's arrangements. And I really don't give a fuck about your feelings. I'm your instructor, not your baby sitter. I'm supposed to push you! I'm doing this, tutoring you, as a favor to Kunta. He sees something in you. Well, he thinks he sees something special in you, because personally I don't see shit in you. So it would probably be best if you got your shit and fell back, 'cause the next time you get outta pocket I'ma fuck you over," Arthur X said, looking Cruz square in the eyes.

Cruz just sat there. He had never witnessed that side of the humble man. And even now, he was not scared, he was shocked. He respected the man he was facing and realized that a lot had been said. Maybe too much. All he wanted now was to fix things. If they could be fix.

"Say, brutha, I'm just a little tired. I have been really tryin', man. And ain't nobody ever pushed me like this before. I mean, shit always been easy for me, and all of this is kinda hard on me. I would 'preciate if you would continue to help me. And if it's at all possible, somehow forget what I said."

Arthur X sat and looked at him for a moment before he spoke. "Yeah, we'll see. But for now, get ya shit and leave," he coldly replied.

"Well, aiight. Do you have an assignment for me or somethin'?" Cruz asked.

"Yeah, I got one for you. I want 500 words explainin' what it is that you expect to get out of this, and why I should spend anymore of my time fuckin' with you."

With that said, Cruz nodded his head in agreement and gathered his stuff to leave. For some reason he was hurt. In that brief exchange more than words had been expressed. He knew now that he loved the teachings, and feared that he might lose them. He knew now that this was all he really wanted to do in life, and he would use every one of those 500 words to express it as best he could.

* * *

Back on his cell-block after the confrontational meeting with Cruz, Arthur X went straight to his room to relax. A little quiet time would do him good. But before he could find the rest that he very much needed, Kunta walked through the door.

"Saleem, brother," Kunta said with a smile.

The two were very good friends and had been cellies for most of their bid in Terre Haute U.S.P. They'd both came up through the ranks together, under the leadership and guidance of Brother Minister Khalid Muhammad and Brother Captain Ali Muhammad.

Kunta ibn Ali was the half African half Arabian son of Algerian Prime Minister Ali Ruholla Mussaui. Kunta, at the age of eight, had been sent to the United States to learn English and economics. It was the hopes of his father and the 17,000,000 people of Algeria, that Kunta, schooled by the top scholars on the West and armed with the greatest minds of the east, would bring Algeria back to prominence.

It was for this reason that Kunta studied unceasingly for his first seven years in America. He far surpassed all of his peers academically. This caused Kunta to somewhat deviate in his studies. With much academic freedom Kunta drifted from public to private institutions and from one academy to another. Not only was he mastering science, mathematics, language, and economic; military tactics and history had become favorite subjects of his. At the age of 13 he could tell you the exact number of shots a machine gun fired in a minute; whether it was light, medium, or heavy, and where it was made; rotations of aircraft engines and fuel; the lightest and best armor available at the best price, and what armament would be needed to counter its advantages.

However, at the age of 16 his whole young world came crashing down around him. Exactly two days after his birthday, he received confirmation that his father, Prime Minister Ali Ruholla Mussaui, had been assassinated in a bloody coup d'état on his regime. This changed everything in his young life. His sole purpose became to avenge his father and regain what was rightfully his. It was in this light that the A.P.L.A. (Algerian Peoples Liberation Army) was born.

Kunta understood that the only way he could beat his enemy, the devil, was to climb down into the mind of his enemy. Taking lessons from the life of Adolf Hitler, he began to build the instrument of his revenge. At the time of his arrest for conspiracy to distribute a number of controlled substances, conspiracy to murder, possession of firearms and explosives, extortion and racketeering, the A.P.L.A. was numbered at about 275,000. Always quoting Hitler he vowed that "no amount of persuasion, coercion, sacrifices, or unpleasant duties could persuade him to alter his course."

"How is our little project coming along?" Kunta calmly asked his partner, Arthur X.

"Shiid, it almost blew-up. But as far as I can tell, he's in pocket," X answered.

"Well, turn it up! We got him in the fire, now it's time for the beating. If I am right about him, we shall make us a man in our image and likeness."

"Yeah, if you are right," X responded.

"I'd better be right. I'm going to put him with the lawyer. The whole lick will be in his hands. My freedom, our future, and $250,000 of my money. Yeah, I'd better be right," Kunta said, rubbing his baldhead.

* * *

"Say, baby?" Boo continued smiling. "How is life treatin' the future of our people?"

Cruz looked up from the paper he had been working on for Arthur X. He was sure enough tired and seriously contemplating giving it all up.

"Ain't nothin', Pimp. Another day, same shit," Cruz answered.

"Say, lil' bruh? Why the hound dog eyes and broken spirit?" Boo Baby asked.

"Man, I'm a lil' fucked up. X trippin'! Man, I'm 'bout to say fuck this shit."

"Look bruh, befo' you do that, come and take a walk wit' me. You got enough time to put yo' paperwork up and get ya hat and jacket. 'Cause it's cold as a black bitch's heart out there. We gon' hit the big track and rap-a-taste," Pimpin Boo said.

Picking up the papers and books he had been using, Cruz took them to his cell and returned with his hat and jacket on. Walking along in silence, the two finally reached the Rec yard, wherein they proceeded to walk onto the big track. Once they were far away from everybody Boo Baby pulled out a Black & Mild cigar filled to its capacity with marijuana. Lighting it and taking a righteous pull, he passed it to Cruz.

"Nah, man I'm cool," Cruz said.

Blowing out the smoke Boo Baby capped. "Baby, what's the deal? You 'bout to burst my ticker, man. Square business! Get ya mind right wit' me, and let's hear it. Shit, it can't be worst than all this time they gave a nigga."

Thinking for a second, Cruz took the weed. Following suit, he took a righteous pull himself. The weed instantly began to soothe him.

"That's right, baby boy!" Boo continued smiling. "Now what's the deal?"

Cruz passed the joint back to Boo Baby and began explaining all that had happened with X and his desire to quit. As they walked and he talked, Boo just listened to his young friend. He had learned over the course of his incarceration that sometimes all one really needed was someone to listen. After about the third lap Boo finally spoke again.

"Look baby, I truly feel you, but you got it all wrong. I've known that dude X for years. He's a real pal, very much like yo'self. He's pushin' you to get the best out of you." Boo Baby hit the weed and then continued. "Do you righteously like what you're doing? Do you really feel that this is what you are, and that this is yo' purpose?"

"Yeah, I righteously believe this is my purpose," Cruz answered.

"Then let me tell you a little story. Once there was these three hookers down in Minnesota who belonged to this pimp name Sweets. Say, these were three righteous mudkickers that humped fast and hard. Ole Sweets was checkin' about eight to ten a day. Long story short, some sadistic funky hearted muthafucka laid on Pimpin and took his life, along with his money, diamonds, and his Rose. A hoe that had been on the scene doubled back to the whore house where Pimpin had put his three foxes down. Burstin' through the door the hoe cryed 'Pimpin dead! Pimpin dead!' And ran off in haste. The three whores looked one to the other and asked 'well, what are you gonna do, baby?' One said, 'I'ma get me a few grams of blow and lay-up with some fine man, child. That'll be my way out'. The second said, 'I'ma go get me a nice dress and go to church. I'ma get saved! That's what I'ma do. How about you?' She asked the last girl. After only a moment's thought, the girl smiled and said, 'I'ma finish the game. That's what I shall do, ladies. I'ma finish the game'. And she walked away towards a potential trick who had been sittin' on the couch alone." Boo Baby smiled at the beauty of it all before he continued. Patting Cruz on the shoulder he then said, "Go finish the game, baby."

Cruz just smiled. Boo Baby was truly a pal at heart.

* * *

After a long hot shower to sober him up and help to clear his mind, Cruz finished the 500 word paper and prepared to meet with X. Arriving at the law library he quickly spotted him at his usual rear table.

"How is the brutha?" Cruz asked with his best smile in place.

Surprisingly X greeted him with a brilliant smile of his own and answered. "Fine. Very fine and you brutha?"

"I'm straight," Cruz answered while taking his seat.

X began putting up the papers he had stacked in front of him. Cruz on his part removed the 500 word paper he had completed and handed it to Arthur X. After reading in silence for about 15 minutes, he handed the papers back to Cruz and smiled.

"That was beautiful," he continued. "I want you to keep that paper with you always. And whenever it gets rough, because it will get rough, and you start to question why you're doing what you're doing, I want you to read your own words. That is why I had you to write it."

"Thank you, man. That means a lot coming from you," Cruz said.

"Save your thanks until you've finished hearing me out. You may wanna take it back." X took a deep breath and then continued. "I've spoken with one of the homies out at Unicore. He said he can get you a job next week. I think it would be a very good idea. That way you can save, take care of yourself, and stop taking your people's money to spend in here. And every day when you get off, after 4:00 count, I'll be waiting for you on the yard. You're my new workout partner. This, along with your studies, will help you to stay focused, it'll help your time pass, and it'll help to build our camaraderie."

Before the young man had a chance to protest, he stood and extended his hand to seal the deal. All Cruz could do was stand and receive the hand of the man he admired.

"Shit!" he thought to himself. "I gotta finish the game."

And finish he did. In the next eight and a half years Cruz would work his way into a top position at both Unicore and in the Nation. During this time he and Arthur X became inseparable. And though he hated his Unicore job, it was on that job where he built many lasting friendships.

* * *

Between work, studying, and working out, there was not much time for anything else but eating and sleeping. Time flew by! And when he finally looked up from his days' activities nine and a half years had passed.

"Cruz! Yo Cruz!" Nate yelled from the lower teir.

"What's up?" Cruz answered as he walked to the cell door.

"Ya man X said come up to the library, it's important," Nate told him.

"Aiight, bet that up, homie," Cruz said, walking back into the cell.

All he had was a wake-up and he was out of this hell-of-a-place. He had learned a lot and he knew that a lot was to be expected of him. He could not lose. After all, there were no excuses after knowledge.

Making his way through the library he spotted Arthur X at his table. Only, he was not alone. Sitting there beside him was that black esoteric bull of knowledge, Kunta.

"What's up, brutha?" Cruz said, shaking X's hand. Then turning to Kunta he smiled and shook his hand also. "What's going on?" he asked.

Kunta cleared his throat and began. "Do you believe all of the things you say? Do you really want to make a difference out there?"

"Yes sir," Cruz answered without a moment's hesitation.

"Well, I've watched you over the years, and I'm very proud to say you may be the best that's ever come from under me." Kunta stopped to gauge Cruz's expression before continuing. "Son, in order to make a difference you gonna need finances and a helluva lot of support. That, I can help you with, if you really want my help."

Sensing the seriousness of the conversation, Cruz looked to Arthur X for a hint as to what was going on. All he received was a blank stare. It was now obvious that it was Kunta's show and all answers would come through him alone.

"Of course I would like your help. But what's the angle?" Cruz answered.

Kunta smiled. *Ignorance was indeed bliss.* Here the future of a nation was being decided and Cruz made it seem as if they were running down some cheap two dollar Murphy con.

"There is no angle, little brutha. It's a simple proposition. I have all of the necessities to make your visions a reality. I have what it takes to build a nation! What I don't have is my physical freedom. I need someone I can trust to handle a large sum of money, a very large responsibility, and to stand-up when the pressure comes down," Kunta said.

"So that's what it's been all about? Me helping you get out?" Cruz asked, looking back and forth from X to Kunta.

Kunta chuckled before answering. "Cruz, do you know who the fuck I am?" But before he could answer Kunta continued. "Nothing I've done since the age of eight has been for me! Here I am doing life in an Amerikkkan prison, over 9,000 miles away from home, for simply trying to regain what was taken from me. Unlike you, my lost Amerikkkan brutha, I'm going to do more than talk and write songs about the wrongs done to me. I agree with Frantz Fanon when he says, 'the majority of black people do not realize that someone has taken something from them, because when a man realizes that something has been taken from him, he will take it back'. I'm offering you an opportunity to take yours back! In turn, I'm asking that you help me."

After thinking about what the man had said, he knew that he was absolutely right. And he intended to take his back.

"What do you need me to do?" Cruz asked.

"Okay! No notes. You must remember everything that I tell you, and everything that you have from us, because you will need it all! Every book that you was given by X, 104 all together, contained an aspect of what you will have to deal with...None of my people are able, or willing to come down here. By you having been here for over eight years, you know the institution like the back of your hand. I need for you to go and give this information to my people. Shift change, number of guards on duty, the distance from the main highway to the fence, from the fence to the chow hall. Number of towers and what they're armed with. They will need to know all of this...You will have to secure, with your own money, a house within eye-sight of the yard. You will also have to rent a few dump trucks and a heavy machine. This will show good faith. Upon turning over the receipts and the information, the lawyer will transfer $250,000 to your account...My lawyer's name is Tylson. William E. Tylson. He probably will not see you, but will deal with you through his secretary, who's quite stunning to be a white woman. You, on your part, will be the go-to between her and my associate Zoe...The project is Holiday Styles, and after your little good faith investment, the lawyer will handle all financial responsibilities...I have people working, right now as we speak, to replace the Prime Minister of Algeria. So time is of the essence! My man could be in place any day now. I could have left here long ago, but I feared extradition. With my people in position there will be no treaty. The U.S. will have no jurisdiction. There will be no extradition! Are you in?" Kunta asked.

Extending their hands to seal the deal, the two shook hands. Looking Kunta square in the eyes Cruz repeated the question and answer to the Lost Found Lesson No. 1, question 11.

"Have you not learned that your word shall be bond regardless of whom or what?" He paused then continued. "Yes! My word is bond and bond is life, and I will give my life before my word shall fail."

Kunta could see that the man was 100% in his corner. "Thank you, brutha. One struggle, one family, one love! Now I'll leave you two to your business." Kunta then departed.

Opening an envelope X produced a picture of a little girl. Handing it to Cruz, he leaned back in his chair. Taking the picture, Cruz just smiled. Judging her facial appearance this had to be X's daughter. Though he had never seen her, Cruz had heard a lot about her. Never mentioning a name, Arthur X always spoke of his daughter and how she meant the world to him.

"You asked earlier was this all about me getting out. No man, it's about her. It's about you. It's about every child growing up like you and her, without a father in the house, because he's locked-up, dead, or simply unwilling to shoulder his responsibility. As men we've been poisoned with a sinister mind-state. A mind-state that's destroying our families and our people as a whole...I love my daughter to death! And she loves me right back. I do what I can to be active in her life, but the fact remains, I'm not really in her life. I left her momma straight, but it's still not like doing it myself. Shit, me and her, my daughter's mother, we've fell so far apart that it's ridiculous...Shorty, for what it's worth, I believe in you. You're driven by something special; Kunta has that same drive. He calls it 'taking back' what was his. When in truth, it's simply a need for redemption. Go redeem yourself, lil' homie. And don't let anything stand in your way." X finished. "Here, this is for you. Every great leader had a book or some sort of scripture to rally around. Moses had the commandments, Muhammad had the Quran, Noble Drew Ali had the Circle Seven, the Black Panthers used The Red Book, The Nation has A Message to the Black Man, and etc...Lil' homie, you need a book." Arthur X smiled and continued. "It took me three years to complete this. You'll see that all of the letters have been readdressed to you, all of the speeches and essays have been credited to you, and all of the copyrights are now yours."

With that said he handed Cruz the manuscripts for Black August. Cruz could not believe it. The moment alone almost brought tears to his eyes.

"I love you, big homie," was all he could manage to say.

"I love you too, man. Now remember, nothing stands in your way. Can't stop, won't stop!" X said.

"Can't forget, won't forget!" was Cruz's response.

CHAPTER 6

Laying in the king sized bed which was located in the master bedroom of his spacious, four bedroom, elegant two-story ranch estate, which was nicely nestled on two acres of prime land in West Broward. Cruz was awakened to the soft lips and warm tongue of the woman that had accompanied him to dinner that night. With more speed and pressure, the woman felicitously bobbed up and down with the precision of a high performance piston.

"Damn," Cruz moaned in pure delight. "Yo' head is felonious."

Stopping, she looked Cruz in the eyes while lightly striking the head of his love-muscle with her serpent-like tongue. Holding it, she took a moment to admire the girth of it, rubbing it along the side of her face and across her soft lips; again, she looked Cruz in the eyes.

"Do you love me, baby," she asked in the innocent tone of a child.

Rubbing the top of her head, Cruz answered, "I love what you do."

With a very sinister smile she assaulted Cruz, taking the full length of him into her month. Bobbing! Applying more pressure! At the brink of climax, Cruz called out to her, "goddamn, Ronni!"

At that very instance there was a colossal explosion beneath him, followed by the rapid three round burst of M-16's. Pushing the beautiful naked woman aside, Cruz slipped into his slacks and Bally casuals. Making his way over to the walk-in closet, he removed a piece of wall panel and retrieved an AK-47 semi-automatic assault rifle, two pineapples, and two extra reversible clips.

Standing with the bedroom door slightly ajar, he could hear the tremendous number of invader footsteps as they quickly approached, still firing in three round burst. There was an agonizing yip from one of the in-house guard dogs followed by the return call of an AK-47.

Wocka! Wocka! Wocka! Wocka! The AK barked as Breed walked it through the patio entrance leading to the living room. Recognizing friendly fire, Cruz, bare-chest, pocketed the pineapples and extra clips. Chambering the rifle, Cruz stepped out to join the foray. He stood on the inner balcony overlooking the gorgeous marble and granite living room, and quickly shouldered the ominous instrument of death. He fingered the trigger twice.

Wocka! Wocka! The AK exploded. Both projectiles found rest in the heads of two enemy invaders, causing yellow fluid, blood and brain matter to escape the confinements of their skulls.

With their attention now on Cruz, they proceeded with increased fire. Leaving Breed, who had been pinned down, free to circle around and take position.

Tac-tac-tac! Tac-tac-tac! Tac-tac-tac! The M-16's sounded. Cruz was now running to the opposite side of the house. His intentions were to divert their fire away from the master bedroom where Ronni was, and away from the second bedroom where his mother had been asleep.

Stepping just inside the bathroom, Cruz pulled the pins on the hand grenades one at a time. Holding them for a few seconds he then tossed them over the custom wrought iron banister. In mid-air the twin disciples of disaster cried out in consecutive explosions.

Boom! Boom! sending shrapnel to find its way into body and mind alike; destroying expensive marble, custom furniture, and the unwanted invaders simultaneously.

Those that had been fortunate enough to escape the explosions of the hand grenades sought to retreat. Only to run head-on into the barrage of fire that Breed was now laying down.

Wocka! Wocka! Wocka! Wocka! The AK-47 barked, catching one invader square in the face, the whole back of his head threw up, sending all that was inside into the face of the man trailing him.

Splat! the brains and blood sounded as they hit. The man stood frozen for a second before he vomited all over the dead man that laid before him.

"Officers down! Officers down, goddammit! We need fucking help! Please! Officers are down!" cried one invader into his walkie-talkie.

Mother Cruz and Ronni had worked their way down the stairs by then and were headed for the front door. Cruz was still up stairs laying down a heavy wave of fire to keep the men pinned down. He and Breed had them in a serious cross fire.

Right as Mother Cruz rounded the corner at which the door had once stood, a few more paces to freedom, she ran head first into the incoming policemen. Had they not been so afraid of what they had been hearing over the radio and in the near distance as they ran up, they might have seen that the ladies were unarmed and merely trying to escape the perplexing situation. Had the officer only taken a split second longer to evaluate the situation, he might not have killed an innocent woman.

Boom! The 12 gauge went off, releasing a single round of double charges into the face of Ms. Cruz. Cruz watched from the second floor as the explosion sent what was left of his mother's head in one direction, and her lifeless body in the opposite direction. Seeing the horrifyingly grotesque look come across his friend's face, Breed spun around in the direction of the gun blast just in time to see Ma Cruz's body drop. Without a moment of hesitation he began firing his weapon. This gave Ronni time to change directions and head for the patio exit. Cruz changed clips and came down the steps firing. He made it downstairs just in time to see his friend's head disappear.

Tac-Tac-Tac! Came the three round burst. One round landed in Breed's neck, the other two found refuge in his head, sending his decapitated body flying into the incoming officers. This gave Cruz the time he needed to spin in the direction of the fire, squeeze off four rounds, one of which silenced the invader that had killed his friend, and escape in the direction that Ronni had taken.

Making their way through the guest house, Cruz stopped and opened up all of the kennels, releasing seven man-eating Bullmastiffs. He and Ronni then continued along the wall until they reached the end of his property. Helping her over the wall they both continued running until they reached the main highway. Then, out of nowhere, a man stopped and told them to get in. It was a white man and he was wearing a black suit and a collar like priest often wore.

"Who are you?" Cruz asked as he leveled the AK in the man's direction.

But before the man could answer a stream of bullets came out of nowhere, tearing through Cruz's chest and stomach. Just as his wounded body was making contact with the pavement, Cruz woke up out of the nightmare in a cold sweat.

"Damn!" he said to himself while simultaneously checking his body for injuries. His entire body and bed was soaking wet and he was out of breath. The dream had been so real! After catching his breath and calming down a bit, Cruz noticed Tamika laying fast asleep.

"Damn!" he said again. "What the fuck was all that about?" He drank a glass of water and tried to go back to sleep.

* * *

Finally able to summon the strength to rise, Cruz reluctantly prepared himself for another day in the concrete jungle of Miami. After using the toilet, showering, and brushing his teeth, Cruz sat alone and drunk breakfast. Gathering his thoughts, he figured that today might be the day that he visited the woman of his dream, Ronni. And what a hell of a dream it had been.

Dressing in a charcoal colored linen pants and jacket set, with a white button down shirt and charcoal Bally slip-ins, Cruz took a large priority mail envelope and was off to Miami Lakes.

When he entered the cozy little office, Cruz noticed a cute dark-skinned receptionist, whom upon seeing him, greeted him with the loveliest smile.

"How are you doing today, sir?" She beamed. "Is there anything I may assist you with?"

Returning her smile, Cruz stepped forward and asked the beautiful lady was this the office of Mr. Ronni Sims. After the receptionist had assured him that this was indeed Ms. Sims' office, she asked his name and picked up the phone to notify her employer that someone was here to see her.

"Mr. Cruz, Ms. Sims says to come right in."

Thanking her, Cruz walked past the woman and into the adjoining office. There she sat behind a huge mahogany desk. Her skin radiant, even down to her exposed cleavage. Her hair was now styled in honey colored micro braids. Smiling, she transmitted confidence and happiness. How cute, she wore braces. How could he have not noticed that before? Maybe it was her legs and other shapely assets that had caused him to overlook them.

"And how are you today?" Ronni asked him in a jubilant tone.

"I'm fine. You have a very lovely office," Cruz said, looking around and admiring all of the African and Asian art that adorned the walls. She was definitely black, yet the office was very impersonal. So all business. There were no family pictures or plants of any sort.

"Thank you." She paused, then continued. "But I gave you my phone number," she emphasized the word phone as if questioning his sudden appearance at her place of business.

"Yes, of course you did. And yo' address was right above it," Cruz responded.

"Oh yes, my business card," she remarked, now remembering the exchange.

"Yeah, yo' business card, as I am here to do business," Cruz stated while coming closer to the huge desk.

"What kind of business?" she asked with molasses dripping from each word.

Cruz, still standing, was now in a position overlooking the desk. With his glance fixated on the smooth skin located on her inner thigh, Cruz asked her, "What kind of service might you recommend?"

Slowly closing her legs, she forced Cruz to meet her stare. Freeing just the tip of her tongue, she lightly glazed her lips before speaking.

"Real-e-state and accounting. Which do you need?"

Unable to get last night's dream out of his head, Cruz thought how that same tongue had made him feel so euphoric. Barely able to focus on the business at hand, he fought to compose himself.

"I'll take both and simply hope that there's more," he smoothly capped.

Removing the papers from the priority mail envelope, he laid them on her desk, along with a government check for $38,000.

"I need for you to set up two corporations. One for profit, Familiar Press, Inc. The second a non-profit, First Family Foundation. I'll need checking accounts for both no later than 1:00pm tomorrow. Also, please look into a restaurant, preferably in the black community, and a large building that I can use to set up office spaces, a pressing plant and a storage facility," Cruz stated.

"Will that be all?" she asked, still smiling.

"Yes. And please take your fees out of that check. Whatever is left, divide it between the two accounts."

"Anything else, sir?" Her words now contained more sarcasm than molasses. Yet, the smile remained in place.

"Not now, but when you finish with that, I'm sure I'll be able to find you something to do with that body of yours."

"Excuse me?" she said, raising an eyebrow.

"Here's my number. Call me when time permits." He handed here the number, totally ignoring her last remark, and walked out of the office.

Situated in the black, all leather, cockpit of the Maxima, Cruz jumped on the Palmetto Expressway headed south. Jamming the accelerator, Cruz sat back and listened to the purr of the small twin cams as they performed. Doing 89 mph in a 65 mph zone, Cruz effortlessly breezed through the light traffic. He could not afford to miss his appointment with the lawyer. And the sooner this whole thing was over, the better it would be for all parties involved.

After parking the car Cruz made his way into the all glass space-age new construction that served as a base of operations for prominent, yet highly overrated, doctors, lawyers, and professionals of the like. Cruz had never had the occasion to visit the building before, because it had not been erected some 114 months ago. There had been immense change from a decorative stand point. Millions had been spent since he had left. But no one had seen it necessarily important to invest one penny in building a more pleasing character in the people. This was asinine in Cruz's assessment of the situation.

Finding the register just inside the corridor, Cruz looked under the letter T and found Attorney William E. Tylson. Taking the elevator Cruz found Tylson's suite in an eighth floor corner. He entered the suite without first knocking, and at first glance he knew that there had to be a God. Standing wide-legged and bent at the waist, the receptionist had her head submerged in a lower file cabinet. Her tiny little skirt had found its way up to her waist, leaving nothing to the imagination, but much for the eyes to behold.

"How beautiful!" He thought to himself. "No panties!"

If she had not been wearing tan pantyhose, which barely concealed anything, he might have been able to see what she had eaten for lunch. She possessed the kind of muff that Cruz loved! It was situated in the back. And judging by the way it hung it had to be ripe for eating.

Her legs were long and muscular. Standing erect, which Cruz had found himself, she had to be at least six feet tall. Finally, clearing his throat, Cruz made his presence known. The big beautiful receptionist quickly turned to face Cruz and immediately began fumbling with her tiny little skirt, which surprisingly covered her upper thigh. She was totally embarrassed. Her cheeks were almost beet-red, merely enhancing her ornamental appearance.

"Ple-ple-please excuse me! I had no idea you were back there. You, you didn't..." The receptionist tried to continue.

"Notice you weren't wearing any undergarments?" Cruz said kind of child-like, as if he might have been embarrassed himself.

Her cheeks reddened even more. Of course now she wasn't embarrassed, she was upset. Squinting her seductive water-blue eyes at Cruz, she childishly crossed her arms over her voluptuous mounds, which Cruz had been admiring.

"Those must have cost a fortune," Cruz said in an even tone.

"How dare you?" the receptionist said, standing back on those long beautiful legs.

"I was talking about the diamond bracelets," he lied.

"Of course you were. What do you want?"

"Excuse me?" Cruz chuckled and held up his hand before continuing. "Did I catch you at a bad moment? Would you like for me to maybe leave and come back in so we can start this over from the beginning?"

He then began walking towards the door which he had entered. But before he could reach it the lady spoke up.

"That won't be necessary," she spoke now in a more acceptable tone. "I'm sorry for my behavior, my name is Summer. I'm Mr. Tylson's secretary, how may I help you?" She then extended her hand to Cruz.

He accepted it. Her hand was soft and sweaty. Obviously nerves. Cruz smiled.

"My name is Arthur Cruz. I also apologize for what transpired earlier. It was truly my fault. I should have knocked… At any rate, I have an appointment to see Mr. Tylson concerning one of his clients. A Mr. Holiday Styles."

Eloquent, important and handsome, maybe he isn't a complete ass, she thought to herself before locking the outer door to the suite. She then gestured for him to follow her through a partition, which brought them into a small room with a couch, table and two chairs. She gestured for Cruz to take a seat.

"Would you like something to drink?" she asked.

"Maybe some water," Cruz answered.

Turning, the woman left the room, leaving Cruz alone with his thoughts.

That got to be a body by Christian, he thought to himself. He had seen many brilliant European women exceed the limitations of perfection, but they had all been on 'Nip Tuck', a show he watched in prison.

When she returned she handed Cruz his water and seated herself directly in front of him. For the first time he could smell her perfume. Pleasant. Sweet. Obsessive! She wore Obsession for Women. Her skin was flawless. It was hard to imagine her running the hills and cave sides of the Caucasus Mountains with a tail, covered in hair.

"Shall we begin?" she asked, lifting her pencil to pad.

"Yes, of course," Cruz answered, taking a sip of his water.

For the next 45 minutes they engaged in a tantalizing series of questions and answers. She asked, he answered. Sometimes she wrote, other times she drew. On both occasions he watched. Admired! There was constant conflict involving her silk blouse and perfect breast. She wore no brassiere! Her nipples were alert, watching. Still the war waged on. Pressing! Those courageous twins had a will to be free. And Cruz was rooting them on with wanton enthusiasm.

Following Cruz's eyes to her breast, she looked up into his eyes and asked, "bothering you?"

Cruz unflinchingly replied, "not at all."

Summer noticed Cruz still lusting over her voluptuous mounds and stated, "Would you please stop that, Mr. Cruz?"

"Can't help it," he smiled. "Besides, they started it."

"Listen, we have work to do."

Cruz relented and focused on the questions and not on the ivory goddess that sat before him. It was difficult but they finally finished the interview, at which time Ms. Summer Rose gave him Zoe's phone number and address.

"That's Mr. Styles' partner. Also I'll need a number to contact you directly, I'll need the receipt for the rental property in Indiana, and last I'll need the account where you want your money sent."

After handing the woman the aforementioned receipts, Cruz wrote down the number to the cell phone that he'd taken from Tamika and passed it to Summer.

"I'll have someone to contact you with the account information," he told her, standing.

"That'll be fine," Summer Rose said, her blue eyes sparkling. "And thank you for your time."

"It was indeed my pleasure...and umm, you contact me if you need anything."

"I might just do that, Mr. Cruz," Summer finished, licking her delicate lips. "My text ID is 69."

"Lady, I was thinking the same thing."

With that Cruz turned and left. He had one more stop to make before he could officially bring his day to a close. He stretched the Max out headed north on I-95. When he reached the 125th Street exit he slowed and got off. Now headed east toward West Dixie Highway, Cruz pulled into the parking lot of Advanced Books & Brochures. He grabbed his trusty priority mail envelope from the passenger seat and sprinted to the building's entrance. A light drizzle had begun to fall and he could not afford to get his papers wet.

"How are you, sir?" a little pimple-faced white man asked as he approached Cruz.

"I'm good, sir." Cruz extended his hand to shake the little man's outstretched hand. "I spoke with someone yesterday about gettin' a book manufactured. I need it done fast and I need it done right."

"Well sir, you came to the right place," the man stated and babbled on about their state-of-the-art printing process, color separation, perfect binding, and short-run efficiency. He went on for 15 minutes before Cruz cut him off.

"Hold up, man! Hold up." Cruz had heard enough. "Look, here's the book. I don't want any editing. I know this book by heart, so I'll know if you so much as change a comma to a period. Do you understand?"

"Yes, sir," the little man responded.

"Make the bill out to the Familiar Post, all of my information is inside, along with $12,000 cash. When you call me all I need to know is the balance of my bill and where to pickup my 50,000 books."

"You want 50,000?" the little man asked.

"Can you handle that?" Cruz asked, a little concerned.

"Yes, sir!" the man answered with more confidence.

"Aiight then. You call me." Cruz smiled and gave the little man a crisp salute.

The man blushed childishly, but with very little hesitation he straightened up and saluted right back. Cruz turned and headed back to the car.

* * *

Between setting up his base of operations, the restaurant, and convincing his mother to move into the new three bedroom house he had purchased, all through Ronni's agency, six months had flown by in almost a blur. Though very tiresome, the days had been very uneventful.

The most gratifying thing to happen was the success of Black August. Advanced Books & Brochures had taken just two months to produce an extraordinary product. With a letter from Kunta inside of the book to give it his stamp of approval, and a ceaseless mail and internet marketing campaign, he watched all 50,000 books fly out of the doors of his office and restaurant. People were joining the foundation and the restaurant was already operating at a small profit. And with an order for 100,000 more books, it was time to shift the plan into overdrive. All of the offices had been set up, and there was now enough money to put a very sizable down payment on the equipment he would need to run the Familiar Post. From now on he would be able to press his own books, produce the foundation's newsletter, and provide a vehicle for all of the brothers behind bars with a story to tell.

With all of this in mind, he sat down for the first time to write Kunta.

* * *

"Mail call! Come get ya mail!" the C.O. shouted as countless convicts filed in, hoping that today would be the day that society acknowledged their existence.

"Roberson!"

"Which one?" an inmate yelled.

"074!"

"Shorts! Gladden! Culbert! Tensly! Pless!"

"Pass it back!" someone yelled.

"Evans! Humphries! Okori, 034! Bloodsoe!"

"Man, that's Bledsoe. Gimme my shit!" the little dude yelled.

"Yo Kunta! You got mail, man! From somebody named Bishop," one of his homies informed him.

Kunta just smiled. For with that information came a great sigh of relief. Removing himself from the game of chess that he and Boo Baby had been playing, Kunta took the letter from Hump and headed to his cell. True to his word, Cruz had touched down with his old teacher. Bishop was an alias that he would use to correspond with his friends and comrades still behind the wall.

Opening the letter he found these words:

Greetings Brother,

I hope that all is as well as can be expected under the current circumstances. As you see, I've made it, and I did not forget my responsibilities to my people (friends). As far as my position, or role in this whole mad human drama, not much has changed. As I am sure that hell is still hot (in there)! Another day, same struggle.

I trust that the sister (she is stunning to be a European-smile) told you I came by—as you asked. She handled her end of the deal like a true professional. It was only with your letter and her assistance that I was able to make Black August a success!

I also talked with your man in Little Haiti. Though everything is on schedule, he is quite a character. I don't know how you deal with him.

I met this other chick, a very special lady! She has been very instrumental in setting up everything from the corporate structure down to the letter and internet campaign.

Familiar—meaning guardian spirit. Post—meaning to be fixed firmly in an upright position. "Familiar Post," can you dig that? We all feel and agree that a newspaper bearing the afore name and an article by you in each publication would be very conducive in reaching our aim. The first issue will be rolling off the press in eight days. So please! Send any article, speech, letter, or essay that you wish to have published to: The Familiar Post, c/o Elijah Glaster (the address is on the envelope). Elijah is a very courageous and gifted brother! I met him over at Advanced Books, where he had been working for the past 13 years. He was invaluable in the process of creating Black August. With his knowledge and connections, I have been able to secure countless speaking engagements. Book sales are up, consciousness is on the rise, and Foundation membership has largely increased.

Without a doubt you are the Big Homie, I would still be so lost if not for you. Please stay strong, for the scent of change is in the wind! Tell Ole Pimpin Boo to get at me. Also, Arthur X should have gotten a very handsome political contribution from the Family. Tell him he'll be hearing from me soon.

Give my love to Pop, Boobie, E-4, Nate, crazy ass Eastwood, Brown-Bey, Young Gunner (Mollette), and all the homies.

One Family, One Struggle.......

One Love,
Bishop

"Say, baby," Boo Baby smoothly capped as he slid into the cell and took a seat. After a few seconds' pause to evaluate the rotation of the ethers, Boo continued. "Was that damn kite from the undertaker, or ole Tom himself? Because you look like you're about to open those forsaken floodgates of destitute."

"What?" Kunta asked.

"Nigga, you look like ya 'bout to cry," Boo said rather frankly.

Kunta had to laugh. Boo was his main man out-the-sky! Intellect and philosophy aside, it had been Boo's humor, his ability to laugh in the face of despair, and his ability to bring out the most in others with his classic wit and familiar smile, that had helped Kunta stay sane over the course of his bid.

"No sir, I'm not about to cry. But if I was I'd most certainly be crying tears of joy. This letter is from Cruz," Kunta said.

"What'd he say about a pimp?" Pimpin Boo Baby asked in obvious excitement.

"He said what's up and to get at him," Kunta informed Boo Baby.

"Get at him? He didn't say that I should check my account for some long scratch?" Boo Baby asked despairingly.

"No Pimp, he didn't. I'm sure he meant to though! But as long as I'm here, or alive, I'ma make sure you are always straight."

"Say, baby. A pimp ain't choosin', but if I had to, it would surely be you, beautiful." Smiling, Boo continued. "'Cause you are my main man out-the-sky."

"Pimp, before it's all said and done, you gonna deny me like ole Peter did Jesus. But you won't be alone. Many will choose. And it won't be the wrong choice; it'll be the necessary choice. Because that'll be the way in which it was written."

Pimp did not agree with his statement, nor did he question it. He just took it for what it was and decided that when the time arose he would rise to the occasion.

CHAPTER 7

...if I don't do nothin, I'ma ball...I'm countin' all day like a clock on the wall/ So go and getcha money little duffle-bag, boy/ Go and getcha money little duffle-bag boy...Cause I ain't never ran from a nigga/ and I damn sho' ain't pick today to start runnin'... Player Circle's hit single 'Duffle-Bag Boy' blasted from the radio in the trap apartment as Headquartaz, DaDa, and Ole Bluey ran through the money from yesterday.

"What we lookin' like, Bluey?" Headquartaz asked.

"This here thirty-six thousand."

"What we got left at the warehouse?"

"I ain't sho'. It's somthin' like six kilos in there."

"Aiight, make sho' you give Boe Pete two for six-o...Blue, man, can you believe that shit Moehead tried to pull?"

"Of course I can believe it. Head, baby, men injure either through fear or through hate. In yo' case, it's both. Everybody hates you, Head. And from where I sit, they have good reason," Bluey stated.

"Fuck is that supposed to mean, my nigga?" Headquartaz yelled.

"Head, to be a boss nigga, you gotta have the love of the niggas that surround you. 'Cause if not, you ain't gon' have no resources in times of trouble. Take for instance the shit you did to Fran or Peaches, even… Then last week when you and Shorty stupid ass took that quarter fare from lil' T-man. Not to mention when you and Boe Pete shot Tall. What you doin', man?"

"My nigga, I'm handlin' my business!" Head yelled.

"No baby, that ain't business. That's a bunch of bullshit! You can only effectively fight one war at a time. If somebody came at us right now, we wouldn't know who it was. 'Cause you and yo' flunkies pop shit with everybody."

"Oh yeah, so now you're the boss, huh? You gon' run shit for me?" Headquartaz asked.

"Nawl baby, but you wildin'. We gettin' too much bread for you to be treatin' people the way you do. You gotta stop shinin' on broke niggas like you do! Give somethin' back Head, or they gone take it all!"

"Niggas ain't gon' take shit from me, my nigga!"

"Head, niggas just laid you down two days ago. Then niggas just hit the house in Carol City for three bricks. Niggas really hate you, man."

"Do you hate me, Bluey?" Headquartaz asked slowly.

"Nawl baby, I love ya."

"Then fuck 'em! We'll kill everybody else."

Headquartaz was hopeless. Injury was always his answer to a problem, when most problems could be avoided altogether. He simply did not understand politics. Therefore, he did not understand war, because they were indeed two in the very same.

* * *

The next day, about 1pm, Ole Bluey picked DaDa up in his '76 four door Chevy Impala. Dolphin green, beige guts and top, chrome and gold 22" French Fries in between fresh blue-cheese. And even though he had bronze tints, dudes still couldn't see him.

Yes! The rhythm, the rebel/ without a pause/ I'm lowerin' my level...The hard rhymer/ You want styling? It's time to get deep! The Enemy, tellin' you to hear it...Last year they played the music/ this time they play the lyrics... Chuck D exploded from the Chevy's trunk.

"Gotdamn, Blue! You sound like you got T-Rex and King Kong in the trunk!" DaDa managed to say over the music.

"Yeah, that's ten rubberbands in 'get-down' back there. Three JBL 12's in the deck, three JBL 15's in the trunk, a 1200 surfboard on every two woofers, and a Precision Power 1000 on my mids and highs. Shiid jit, I got over a grand in wires alone," Bluey capped and turned it up some more.

The two rode all over Miami. The route was similar to the one they had taken that late rainy night. DaDa was only hoping that it did not end the same way. Bluey pulled into the marina right off of Biscayne and delivered a big army duffle-bag. From there they stopped in the Matchbox and then hit the apartments on 183rd. Both times Ole Bluey picked up two gym bags.

"Here boy, fire that up," Bluey said.

DaDa fired up the lace-joint as Bluey brought the '76 through Opa Locka and stopped on the Bah. Again he returned with two gym bags. It seemed that every corner the two turned, someone was blowing their horn and flashing headlights, or hollering for Ole Bluey's attention.

"Hey Blue! Holla at me, Blue. You know you know me!" they'd yell.

Bluey would simply hit his horn in return and chuck up them deuces. But for some, the lucky ones, he would hold his cell phone out the window. And no sooner than he could bring the phone back inside, it would be ringing.

"Yeah boy... I see ya! Yeah, nineteen-five all day...Yeah, a light somethin'...Get at me later. I'ma drop you somethin' on the strength..." he'd rap over the pipe.

And though the conversations were brief, Blue stayed on the phone. They loved Bluey! It seemed for every gym bag he collected, he gave away five hundred to a grand out of his pocket. Dudes, women, children, they all knew and respected Bluey.

Catching 27th Avenue going south, Bluey gave the four-barrel carburetor an extra dose of vaporized fuel and air in an over explosive mixture. The Corvette cam kicked in, the rear struts dropped, and the small block 400 put on a show! The glass pipes sounded like a motorcycle gang coming through.

Bluey dropped off two kilos to Boe Pete on 60th and 14th, and had the Chevy back on 95th Street and 17th Avenue as Miami Central Senior High was letting out. There were a lot of pretty young ladies making their way home and all of them seemed to know Ole Bluey.

"Hey Blue!" they yelled in groups.

"Hey babies!" Bluey returned while Teena Marie's "Square Biz" kept the JBL's vibrating in the trunk.

Still pushing up 17th Avenue towards 103rd, Bluey brought the '76 to a creep.

"Hey, Daddy Blue!" the three pretty girls said in unison.

"Hey babies! What yall learn today?" Blue asked.

"A lil' somethin'...Daddy Blue, when you gon' let us ride witcha?" the tallest of the three girls asked.

"When them lil' pussies get some hair on 'em," Bluey capped.

"Blue, how you figure ain't no hair on our shit now?" the dark skinned one with the beautiful light-brown eyes asked.

"'Cause you too eager to give it away. And anytime somebody's too eager to give somethin' away, it can't be no good. Ya feel me? Now by the time it get some real hair on it, you'll have learned how valuable it is, and how important you all are. Then maybe, I'll let yall ride. But until then, get this Reebok money."

Blue gave each one of the girls a hundred and fifty dollars and pulled back into traffic. They were all smiles as they walked along.

"Who was they, Blue?" DaDa asked.

"Oh, them my lil' babies. The tall brown skin one is Lil Moosie. The lil' black one wit' the pretty eyes is her sister. They stay on 103rd. The other one is Lil Mesha. She stay on the 17th side of Silver Blue."

"How you know 'em?"

"They 'round the way girls. And I'ma OG 'round here. It's my job DaDa, to 'look out' for 'em and tell 'em somethin' good. You feel me? I tell 'em what I'd want a nigga to tell mine if I wasn't here. I break 'em off about twice a week."

DaDa was impressed. He could see why everybody loved Ole Bluey, he really was a loveable guy.

* * *

Boe Pete and Headquartaz were turning into Silver Blue after a long night of partying and bullshitting. They were riding in Boe Pete's steel-gray Cadillac STS. After dropping off the three animals, Lil Annie, Pinky and Lotto, that they had tamed last night, it was now back to business.

"Boe, my nigga, slow down! Ain't that that lil' bitch-ass nigga, Weasel?" Headquartaz asked while taking the MAC-11 from under the seat.

"Where?" Boe Pete questioned.

"Right there! Sittin' on the crate talkin' to Pookie Boy."

"Yeah, that's him!"

"Pull over there."

Head chambered the gun and as Boe Pete stopped the car Headquartaz opened fire. *Tat! Tat! Tat! Tat! Tat! Tat!* Bringing the passenger side window crashing down as the projectiles exploded through it.

"Gotdamn, Head! My window, man!" Boe Pete yelled.

Pookie Boy dove to the street, but Weasel was off to the races. Both Head and Boe Pete gave chase. Firing in rapid succession as Weasel made a beeline for his old Dodge station wagon parked at the mouth of the gangway.

Pop! Pop! Pop! Pop! the little 9mm called.

Weasel managed to get those four shots off, shooting over his shoulder as he ran. He was about five yards from his wagon when bullets riddled it. The front driver side tire exploded! Then the window came crashing down. Weasel, still running, took this cue and dove through the opened window like a seasoned half-back leaping for the goal line.

Tat! Tat! Tat! Tat! Tat! Tat! The MAC-II screamed unceasingly.

Boe Pete stood next to Head, unloading his .40 caliber as the two Swiss-cheesed Weasel's Dodge wagon. He had to be dead! They had cut the car from bumper to bumper with over sixty rounds. When both guns locked up, they walked all the way over to the car and looked in.

"Damn! Got-damn-it!" Headquartaz yelled.

The passenger side door was open, leading to the gangway and Weasel was gone! Head and Boe Pete ran around back hoping to find him laying injured, but to no avail. Weasel proved to be just what his name implied; he was as slick as he was slimy.

* * *

The episode that had transpired between Headquartaz, Boe Pete and Weasel left nobody hurt, but it sure brought a lot of undesired heat to the trap. So they decided to close up that portion of their business until it cooled off. That meant more responsibility for Headquartaz, Boe Pete and Smash; while it afforded Ole Bluey some much needed down time.

With this at hand, Bluey went to holla at Jahhead. Jahhead was his man. They had gone to high school together. Jahhead was no square, but he really was not a street dude either. His people, himself included, were Arabs and owned over thirty stores and a hotel on Biscayne. Ole Bluey, at one point, could always depend on Jahhead for firearms. But after that 9-11 shit, you couldn't get Jahhead to sell you a sling shot. No bullshit! They even took the cap guns out of the stores.

Bluey had a nice little baby with a sure head on her shoulders and a desire to attain great things. The most important being him. Her name was Tosha, and she attended Florida Memorial College. Jahhead was messing around with her partner Twalla, so the four of them would often get together and just disappear for a spell.

Today was one of those times. The two couples both had suites at the El Palacio Sports Hotel on 214th and 27th Avenue. After watching the Dolphins get killed on the eight-foot video wall in the hotel's Legend Bar, Jahhead and Bluey broke to return to their rooms on opposite sides of the exquisite hotel.

"Don't you eat too much, boy," Bluey said, leaving the elevator.

"Shit, all the money that I paid for the books this semester, I'ma eat plenty!" Jahhead laughed.

Ole Bluey entered the suite to find his petite red-bone laying on her stomach reading a book. Tosha had on some white and black boy-shorts with no top. And from where Bluey was standing, it was hard to figure out how in the hell did she get all of that pussy and ass in those cute little panties.

Bluey walked up to the bed, removing his penis, he laid down on top of Tosha and began kissing her ear and neck. Tosha turned her head to meet Bluey's mouth. The two began swapping tongues. Bluey slid Tosha's panties to the side and penetrated her moist vagina.

"I missed you, Blue..." Tosha moaned.

"Then cum for me," Bluey whispered.

"Oh, Blue, I'm about to... yes, right there."

And Blue kept it right there too! Tosha began throwing it back harder. Bluey's love stick continued to swell as Tosha's suction-hole got richer. Long gentle strokes turned into violent spasmodic thrusts; as her candy walls fell Bluey exploded and the two laid shivering, holding each other like lovers meeting for the last time.

Tosha got up after catching her breath and went to clean up. She returned with a warm soapy rag and a fresh towel. Bluey really liked Tosha, she was a real woman. She took pride in pleasing him and smiled as she cleaned and dried his private areas.

Back in bed she picked up her book and began reading. She was really very pretty and mature to be so young. Tosha was nineteen years old, only two years removed from high school. Blue had known her since she was fourteen, but had refused to mess with her until she did something with herself. That something was to go to college. He did not see her much, but when he did it was always worth the money that he deposited into her bank account every week. Bluey really liked her and if it were not for Keta Black and the children, Tosha would've been his main squeeze.

"What you readin', Red?" Ole Bluey asked.

"Oh, Black August. It's by this dude who just got out of prison. He did like ten years. He came out to the college and spoke. He was the bomb! I had to buy one of his books. His name is…it's right here…yeah, Arthur Cruz."

Bluey jumped up and snatched the book from Tosha. Maybe he had heard her wrong. Or maybe it was a different Arthur Cruz. There was no picture in the book.

"What did he look like, Red?" Bluey asked.

"He was cute, brown-skinned, bald head, about your height. Why?"

Ole Bluey did not answer her. It had to be Cruz! But what was he doing talking at colleges and writing books? And why hadn't he hollered? These were the thoughts that ran through his mind as he got dressed.

"What you doin'?" Tosha asked.

"I gotta go! Tell Jahhead to take you back."

Ole Bluey threw her five one-hundred dollar bills and left to go find Head.

* * *

When Bluey got the SS Impala on I-95 southbound, he noticed that he had missed some calls. The calls were Headquartaz blowing him up from the apartment in the Blue. Bluey was now nearing the 103rd Street exit, so he would just see Head when he got there.

Entering the apartment, the sweet smell of weed and lace filled his nostrils. Ole Bluey took a quick survey of the room and saw that everybody was there. They had a three blunt rotation going, which Bluey immediately interrupted by taking the joint from Big

Shorty. After righteously inhaling he added his smoke to the already congested haze.

"What's the national emergency?" Bluey asked.

"Man, where the fuck you been? Shit happenin' 'round here and can't nobody find you!" Headquartaz barked.

"Well, I'm here now, baby, what's goin' on?"

"Me and Boe ran into that hoe-ass-nigga Weasel and..." Headquartaz began.

"And you jumped the gun and let him get away. Now you can't find him. And I'm guessing, maybe the other nigga Mike, done contacted somebody tryin' to cop a plea...am I right?" Ole Bluey spilled.

Headquartaz just shook his head. "Man, how the fuck you know that?"

"'Cause, it's what I would do if I was him...Head, you always gotta put yo'self in the other fellas' shoes. And thinkin' logically, you can just about predict his every move...now what did you tell 'em?" Bluey took another pull of the joint.

"I ain't told 'em shit! I been waitin' on you...So what you wanna do?" Headquartaz asked.

"Tell 'em we want all of our shit back. And from here on, they ain't to never be seen 'round here," Bluey stated.

"That's it?" Headquartaz questioned.

"Yeah, that's it. In fact, I'll handle it, have 'em call me."

Ole Bluey began negotiations that very next day. Some chick named Nikki called him claiming to be Mike's cousin. It took a day and a half, and a helluva lot of diplomacy, but Bluey was finally able to get a direct line to Mike.

Passing off both numbers, Mike's and Nikki's, to a little police broad that he was fucking named Pam Gram, Bluey got two addresses. He put DaDa on one and he took the other. All the while, he assured Mike that he was safe, and that all they wanted was the money (in the value of what had been taken), and for him and his brother to stay out of Silver Blue.

Now, the problem was, Mike was broke! And Weasel was missing in action. This was a major problem! Because as Machiavelli stated in The Prince, "injuries should be done all together [at once], so that being less tasted, they will give less offense. [But] one should never allow a disorder to take place in order to avoid war...[because] deferment was to the advantage of your opponent."

For those reasons, Bluey and DaDa were working overtime to locate Weasel. Bluey also kept the pressure on Mike to hurry the payment. Mike assured Ole Bluey that he had a sweet lick lined up, and that he would soon pay him. But Bluey did not trust Mike. He felt that Mike was stalling for time. Why? Because that's exactly what he would do himself.

Headquartaz was going crazy! And he was about to drive Ole Bluey crazy in the process. The situation was real ticklish. But then, that's why Bluey made the big bucks. For situations like this.

Come to find out, Mike was stalling for time, but he was not lying about the sweet lick. Bluey followed him to a house in North Miami Beach and watched as Mike and a stud named Goon, out of Brown Sub, ran up into a house and came out with two large duffle bags. Five minutes tops! The two scored without firing a shot.

Bluey continued following them. He called DaDa and instructed him to pick up Headquartaz and be ready to meet him. He called Boe Pete and Shorty and sent them to Nikki's place. Moehead and Smash were sent to the other address, which turned out to be Mike's and Weasel's parent's house.

Mike and Goon finally stopped at a little house on Bunch Park Drive. Bluey immediately called DaDa with the address. He then slipped around the back of the house and peered through a window, hoping to see Weasel in there with them but he wasn't. Goon and Mike were sitting at the table with some slim dark-skinned dude counting the loot.

Seeing some lights flash near the direction of his car, Bluey knew that DaDa and Headquartaz had arrived. Wasting no time, he jogged over to meet them.

"What's up, my nigga?" Headquartaz questioned.

"They just came off. It's three of 'em in there," Bluey informed him.

"Weasel wit' 'em?" DaDa asked.

"Nawl, it's Goon and some black ass nigga…yall ready?"

"Yeah!" Headquartaz answered.

"DaDa, come wit' me. We gon' hit the back. Head, you know what to do."

"No question! See yall inside…"

DaDa and Ole Bluey both had MAC-11's. Headquartaz, on the other hand, had an AK-47 and a 12 Guage. They all began jogging towards the little house. Head stopped in the front yard and walked up to the front door. DaDa and Bluey kept on towards the back door. But before they could reach the door the 12 Gauge sounded. *Boom! Boom! Boom!*

The blast knocked the locks off, giving Headquartaz entrance. Goon was the first to jump up, gun in hand, and he was the first to get gunned down. The shotgun blast hit him in the stomach and blew his entrails onto the table behind him.

Mike ran! The nameless dark-skinned dude came up hitting!

Boom! Boom! Boom! Boom! his .45 called.

The first shot hit Headquartaz in the shoulder. The impact spun him and caused him to drop the shotgun. Hit, he dove for cover.

Boom! Boom! The dude fired his last two shots. *Click!*

Headquartaz came up barking. *Bocka! Bocka! Bocka!* The AK-47 cut the nameless man down.

As soon as Mike came through the door DaDa and Bluey grabbed him. After a very brief scuffle, he was subdued and brought back in the house.

"Damn fellas! I was just about to call yall. You, you see I got the money," Mike managed to say.

"DaDa, get the money," Ole Bluey commanded.

"We, we good now, right?" Mike pleaded.

Bluey said nothing. He simply pulled out his cell phone and called Boe Pete.

"You at Nikki's place?" Bluey asked.

Mike's eyes grew to the size of baseballs. He knew exactly what time it was. How? Because had he been Bluey, he would've done the same.

"Kill everythang in there..." Bluey calmly instructed.

At that instance a very vile odor filled the room. It was terrible! DaDa and Bluey checked their shoes.

"What the fuck is that?" Head yelled.

"I, I, done messed up my pants, man... please don't kill me!" Mike begged.

Again, Ole Bluey said nothing in response. He simply made another call. This time to Moehead.

"You at his mom's crib?" Bluey asked.

"Come on man, please! Not my ole girl, man, please!" Mike begged.

"Damn, Blue, my nigga. You ain't gon' do his moms, is you?" Head asked.

"Kill everybody in there..." Bluey calmly instructed.

"No!" Mike cried out.

Tat! Tat! Ole Bluey silenced him with two to his head.

DaDa could not believe this shit! Bluey was really cold-blooded. Even Headquartaz seemed a little thrown by Bluey's actions. They truly did not understand, but how could they? If they did not understand politics, they would never understand war.

* * *

The next day, Headquartaz, Ole Bluey, and DaDa were riding in Headquartaz's Suburban; going to meet the connect. They had been riding, each man in his own thoughts, listening to 'All Eyes On Me' by Tupac. The lace was in the air as always, but today was different.

"Hey Blue, my nigga, you cool?" Headquartaz asked.

"Of course. Everything's copasetic with me," Bluey answered.

"You know somebody killed Big O and Dave the other night?" Head sort of stated.

"Yeah, killed 'em right out front they shit...Fuck 'em," Bluey answered.

"Yeah, saved us some problems," Head said, trying to read Bluey.

"Nawl, man. Saved 'you' some problems. 'Cause I ain't have no problems wit 'em."

DaDa remained quiet. It dawned on him that Big O and Dave were the two men that Ole Bluey had killed that rainy night. But why had Bluey killed Weasel's whole family?

"I got a question, Blue, my nigga," Headquartaz said.

"Fire away," Bluey answered.

"You a real laid back dude and all. You ultra-smart, and I really respect yo' mind. But why you 'do' they whole family like that? And what we gon' do 'bout Wease?" Head asked.

Bluey hit the lace-joint before speaking. "Fuck Wease. We ain't gon' do nothin' concerning him. You see Head, 'men will avenge themselves for small injuries, but not so with great ones. So when I ride, I leave afflictions that I need not fear vengeance.' We clear, Wease a bitch."

"But what about puttin' yo'self in the other nigga's shoes. If you was him, would you let it go?" DaDa asked.

"Of course not! But Wease ain't me. It's one thang you gotta always know, and that's yo' opponent. If Wease ain't killed himself, he's long gone and happy to be livin'."

DaDa reflected on what Bluey had just said. He then put himself in Weasel's shoes. Bluey was right, because had he been Weasel, he'd be long gone and just happy to be living...

Part 2wo

Hit 'Em Up!

A Prince should have no other aim or thought, nor take up any other thing for study, but war and its organization and discipline. For that is the only art that is necessary to one who commands... never let his thoughts stray from the exercise of war; and in peace [fairtimes] he ought to practice it more than in war...

[The Prince]
Niccolo Machiavelli

Chapter 8

Like a charm, the first three bi-weekly issues of the Familiar Post had been highly successful. So-much-so that they decided to make it a weekly publication. With that decision subscriptions tripled. Ronni increased her workload by taking full charge of the company's internet and mail campaign. Thereby, adding greatly to her company's portfolio. Kunta contributed an article in each issue, and with the connects and hard work of Elijah, Cruz held lectures at the University of Miami, Barry University, F.I.U., Florida State, New Birth Church – in both Miami and Atlanta, Howard University, FAMU, and Clark. He even spoke before the Board of Education in Dade, Broward, Orange, Clay, Duval, and Sumter County. Then with the success of Black August, Cruz and the First Family Foundation became a success in every sense of the word.

After arriving in Miami, Breed was placed in charge of all of the Foundation's security. Which not only included Cruz himself, but also The Familiar Spot (the group's restaurant and social club), and Mecca (the three story office and storage facility that housed the Familiar Post, Ronni's marketing, real estate, and accounting firm;

and other black owned businesses). All of this made Breed's job almost impossible.

"Look, Cruz, man," Breed said as they sat in Cruz's tiny cluttered office. "I know you got a lot of confidence in me, but man, I need some help! We have some good people, but I don't know these dudes. I need somebody I know and can trust."

Looking up from the papers he had been reading, Cruz asked Breed, "So what is it that you propose?"

"Just that you get me some help! I talked to Wheat, Palmer, and Captain Jack. They are all willin' to help," Breed said.

"Okay, bring 'em in," Cruz responded.

Breed smiled, leaping from his seat. "I knew you was gonna say that. Their plane lands at 1:00. So we got a hour to get to the airport."

"Incredible," Cruz said as he folded the paper he was holding and followed Breed out of the office.

* * *

"Are you sure they had a 1:00 flight?" Cruz asked impatiently.

"Yeah, I'm sure. There go them niggas right there," Breed said, pointing in the direction of the security office.

"Sshaawday!" Wheat yelled as they made their way towards one another.

They had all met in Terre Haute's U.S.P., working in the Unicore factory together. They'd really grown close. Wheat was the body builder, slash fake playboy of the group. He spent his every free moment on the weight-pile or looking in the mirror. Palmer, on the other hand, was a much smoother, rather comical, older dude. Make no mistake about it, he was no joke. He had spent the better part of his life in jail, or waiting to go to jail. So he was very adept at holding his own. Captain Jack was no different, minus the comedy. He had served as Brother Minister's Chief of Security in the Nation. Seeing them together, after so much time had passed, was a sight for sore eyes.

"Damn, man! Where yall niggas been? The plane outta D.C. landed at 1:08. It's 2:40!" Breed spat while exchanging pounds and hugs.

"Slim! This old nigga fucked up! The freak ass nigga almost got locked-up," Wheat said, laughing at Palmer. "Then his scared ass wanna run when the plane land."

"What happened?" Breed asked out of genuine concern.

"We on the plane, and this nigga done pulled his lil' dick out on the stewardess hoe. Slim! When we landed, security was everywhere," Wheat said.

By now everybody was dying of laughter. Breed was literally in tears.

"What?" Cruz asked, laughingly. "Man, you still on that?"

Diddy, as they called Palmer in prison, was notorious for masturbating on the female staff. Always respectful to others, Diddy limited his antics to the confinements of his cell. Nonetheless, it was what it was.

"Oh, so you wit' that?" Palmer asked in his usual tone. Which, no matter how serious he was, was always borderline comedy.

"Nah, Diddy, man! I'm just sayin'," Cruz replied, still laughing.

"I didn't do nothin' to that bitch," Palmer said. "She was on me, for real, for real."

"Palmer! So how ya dick get out in public?" Breed asked.

"Come on now...Yall know my skin fucked up, right. I gotta rash somethin' terrible on my joint. So I was puttin' some lotion on my shit," Palmer managed to say with a straight face. Of course, nobody believed him.

As they exited the airport, now en route to the vehicle, Palmer loudly exclaimed. "Ggooddamn!"

They all turned to witness a couple walking hand-in-hand. No one could see what all the fuss was about.

"What?" Cruz asked. "That chick ain't nothing."

"Shawdy, fuck that chick! That nigga jive phat as-e-muthafucka."

They all looked at Palmer and fell out laughing. He had not changed a bit.

"What!?" Palmer asked as if he were serious, but laughing all at the same time.

Wheat and Captain Jack just shook their heads.

"Slim! I told you this nigga was fucked up. Kill me! Let's go befo' somebody been done killed him," Wheat said as they all climbed into the truck.

* * *

Ronni sat silently, gazing out of the front window of her three bedroom home in Carol City. It had been some time since that day in the park. The day that her life had changed so much for the better. It seemed so sudden. So dramatic! It was so wonderful.

Not only had Arthur Cruz personally touched her life from a romantic and social aspect, but financially he had opened up so many doors. Doors that had been closed to her and so many in her situation. Single. Ambitious! Yet struggling to make ends meet. *A buoy!* That's what he was. Not just for her, but for the entire community.

She had accompanied him on the majority of his speaking engagements throughout the country. They had never been arid. Exciting! So passionate. To her delight they had made love in the most exquisite hotels. *News Day* labeled him esoteric. *The Times* called him a demigod. While the majority of white Amerikkka saw him as a demagogue. How did she see him? In two words, *flawlessly beautiful*.

She was brought back from her daydream by the voice of her daughter.

"Momma!" the beautiful eight-year old yelled.

"Yes baby?" Ronni responded to Arlexus. She was the spitting image of her father. Arlexus had never had an opportunity to bond with her father as a free man. He was sentenced to life in federal prison while she was but an embryo. But despite the distance and harshness of the situation, there was no antipathy in their relationship. What the two, Arlexus and her father, had ascertained was love. So close they had grown, while he and Ronni had drifted so very far apart.

"When you going to take me to see my daddy again?" Arlexus asked.

"I don't know, sweety. I have some things I have to work out first. Maybe we'll go for X-mas."

The phone rung, interrupting their mother-daughter conversation.

"Hello," she answered.

"Hey lady," Cruz said in his distinctive tone.

"I was just sitting here thinking about you. Where are you and when will I be able to see you again?"

"I'm just leavin' a speakin' engagement at Florida Memorial. I was thinkin' that maybe we could meet up at The Familiar Spot. What do you think?" Cruz asked.

"Well, I was thinking that maybe you could come over to my place."

"Oh, yeah?" Cruz said in genuine surprise. "So I finally get invited to the house? I was beginnin' to think that you were married. Or is it that yo' husband's out of town?"

"No, silly! I'm not married. But my eight-year old daughter will be here."

"Cool, I love kids. And besides, that'll give Big Breed somebody to play with."

"You are so silly!" she replied. "I'll see you at seven then."

"Make it eight," Cruz interjected.

"Okay, eight it is," she continued. "I'll see you then."

"Who was that?" Breed asked, looking to the backseat where Cruz sat in the big Excursion.

"You know who that in-love-ass nigga was talkin' to," Palmer said before Cruz could answer.

"Say it ain't so!" Wheat chimmed in. He loved to egg Palmer on.

"Yeah! I know, Wheat. That was that red hoe with the big feet. Slim! Shawdy got a sho-nuff set of dawgs on her." Palmer laughed before he continued. "That pussy must be on blast! Ya hear me, man?"

That was all it took. Wheat, Breed, and Captain Jack were in tears. Even Cruz could not help but to laugh.

"Is the head like that?" Wheat asked.

"Fuck you!" Cruz replied.

"I know you done sucked that lil' box for her," Palmer said.

"Hell nawl! I don't know slim like that," Cruz replied.

"See, that's the problem. You young niggas is fucked up, slim. I don't even want the pussy if I can't eat it. I sucked this one hoe pussy I met at my sista house, right. And I knew the bitch was burnin'."

"What?" Cruz asked.

"Hold up, Diddy, man. How you knew she was burnin'?" Wheat asked.

"Shiid! The bitch told me," Palmer said.

"Aah, Laawd! Diddy, you fucked up!" Breed said.

"I ain't tryna hear that shit. You woulda did it too! Slim, this bitch was fat as-e-muthufucka!" Palmer replied.

"You got the Big Breed fucked up! Nigga, what I look like to you?"

"What? What you look like?" Palmer asked, looking around the truck in disbelief. "Nigga! Ya look like a big-dumb-ass Coolio! That's what you look like!"

Everybody in the truck fell out laughing. Because indeed, Breed did look like a big ass Coolio.

* * *

After dropping Wheat, Palmer, and Captain Jack off at their newly acquired house in Miami Shores, which they had purchased through Ronni's real estate agency, Cruz and Breed were en route to their place in Miami Lakes to prepare for tonight's outing.

When they arrived there were five messages on the answering machine. Before checking them Cruz flipped on the TV just in time to catch a special CNN report.

"There is again civil unrest in Algeria. Earlier today, there was a bloody scrimmage between Algerian forces and members of the A.P.L.A. The group is believed to be headed by reputed terrorist and convicted racketeer Kunta ibn Ali. The son of ex Algerian Prime Minister Ali Ruholla Mussaui.

"The A.P.L.A. guerillas simultaneously set off explosives at the U.N. and the Courthouse, killing 27 people. While troops were busy trying to regain order in the streets of Algeria, the A.P.L.A. stormed the palace of Prime Minister Hamzah Yasir, killing 13 more people. The Prime Minister did escape, and is believed to be en route to the U.S. But for now the A.P.L.A. has gained control of the Algerian government. There will be more news on the situation as it arises."

"You see this shit?" Cruz asked, pointing to the TV.

"Yeah!" Breed said. "Ya man ain't fakin' one bit."

Cruz turned off the TV and turned his attention to the answering machine.

"...hello, my name is William Tylson. I'm calling in reference to one of my clients. A Mr. Holiday Styles. My number is 800-973-3397. Thank you.... *Beep!*

"Dad, this is Des. I was just holla'n atcha. Thank you for the money and all. Momma said you could come through, and if you gonna keep her car, at least you need to pay the note and her rental car bill. Anyway, I love ya. Peace!... *Beep!*

"Boss, this is Elijah. I just received this week's piece from Kunta. He's really talking that talk. We've also received another 300 orders for the paper. The majority came from overseas. Please stop by so we can go to press... *Beep!*

"I know damn well you seen all of those 69's text, you sexy dog! Mr. Cruz, will you please call me, or come by tonight? This is Summer Rose... *Beep!*

"...You will not be charged for this call. The call is from...*Arthur X*, Press five to accept. Press 7 to... *Beep!*

"You have no more messages," the machine said before rewinding itself.

"Damn Breed! We missed the big homie's call," Cruz said.

"Oh! I forgot. He called last week while you and Palmer were up in D.C. at the Black Expose. He said that he had received another check and that he was in the process of writin' the introduction for *Black By God's Demand*," Breed informed Cruz.

"Why didn't you let me know? He's very important! Not only to our progress, but to me! From now on forward the calls to the cell. That way we won't miss another one."

Arthur X was an idealist. He was also the mastermind behind Black August and the driving force behind the Foundation. It was him who had given Cruz all of the right books to read and opened his young mind to a whole new world. A world that was built around the people. It was him who made Cruz *The Peoples' Champ*.

* * *

As Breed navigated the huge Excursion to its Carol City destination, the two rode in complete silence. Cruz was going over tomorrow's plans in his head. It would be a long and rough day, he reasoned.

Pulling up in front of Ronni's house, Cruz could see her standing at the glass door talking on the phone. She opened the door for them and continued talking to whoever was on the other line.

"Listen, I cannot do this now. As soon as I'm able I'll be up there….No. Money isn't the issue. Just please bear with me, okay? I'll try to be up that way X-mas. Okay? Of course we love you…. Bye-Bye," she said hanging up the phone. She seemed to be upset. But Cruz was never one to pry, so he simply removed his coat and took a seat beside Breed, who had already seated himself on an overstuffed leather couch. Sensing the queerness of the situation, Ronni put on her best smile and played the perfect hostess.

"And how are you, Mr. Cruz and Mr. Moore?" she asked.

They both returned the smile and answered in unison. "Peaceful."

"Would either of you care for something to drink before we eat? The food is just about ready," she said, still wearing her million dollar smile.

"Sure, some juice," Cruz ordered and Big Breed agreed.

"Okay, two juices coming up," Ronni replied as she headed for the kitchen.

"Hello," Arlexus said, taking both Breed and Cruz by surprise.

"Oh, hello to you too," Cruz responded to the pretty little girl.

She then turned and walked off to join her mother in the kitchen. The little girl was beautiful. She looked nothing at all like her mother. Not that her mother was not attractive. The little girl just seemed to have so little of her. Looking. Thinking. Her cute little face seemed familiar. Puzzled? Okay, Cruz could not place it.

"Mr. Cruz," the little girl interrupted his thoughts. "The juice gone. You want some Kool-Aid?"

"Of course, I would love some Kool-Aid," Cruz smiled.

They all ate in relative silence. Everyone enjoying the meal. Everyone caught up in their own thoughts. Cruz could not figure out who this little girl reminded him of. And Ronni could not figure out how she was going to explain Cruz to the father of her child, the first and only man she had ever loved.

After dinner Arlexus asked Breed, "Do you wanna see my computer?" Her head cocked to one side with her hands on her hips. She looked to be sizing the huge man up.

"Yeah, come on," Big Breed replied.

"So how did the lecture go today?" Ronni asked in an attempt to break the ice.

"As always, we had a very good turn-out. It was a good cause. We're raising funds for a community center. Some real state-of-the art shit. We're plannin' to build it from the ground up. The problem is, niggas love to attend rallies, hear a good speech that fires them

124

up, and then go back home to do nothing…. Anyway, what's up with you? You look a little stressed," Cruz said as he hugged her around the waist and looked into her eyes.

"It's nothing serious. I just have to handle some unfinished family business in Terre Haute. It's nothing," she said. Again wearing her fake hostess smile.

* * *

"So what you gonna be when you get big?" Breed asked the little girl as they breezed through different websites.

"I'm gonna be a writer, like my daddy," Arlexus answered with pride.

"Oh yeah? Well, what you gonna write about?"

"I don't know. Something. About people and things," she continued talking as she walked to her closet. "You wanna see my daddy?"

"Yeah, where's he at?" Breed answered.

After retrieving the photo album she passed it to Breed, who in-turn opened it and began looking through the pictures. On the third page he spotted a beloved friend and comrade. Smiling, he pointed to the picture and asked Arlexus, "who is this?"

Beaming with pride, Arlexus said, "my daddy!"

With those two words she had turned his smile upside down. His whole world for that matter! Confused, he fought to catch his breath. Think! *Did Cruz know? He couldn't!* There was no way that he could have possibly known that Ronni's baby's father, and Arlexus' father was Arthur X. Dropping the photo album he rushed out of the room to inform Cruz.

Interrupting their groove, Breed told Cruz, "We gotta go man!"

Puzzled, Cruz rose from his seat. "What's wrong?" he asked.

"We can rap later, man. But right now we got-to-go," Breed stated as he made his way towards the door.

Still puzzled, Cruz kissed Ronni goodnight and followed Breed out to the truck.

"What's up?" Cruz asked as soon as they were in the confinements of the SUV.

"Man, please tell me you don't know who she is," Breed pleaded.

"Breed, are you losin' it, man? What the fuck do you mean, who she is? That's Ronni! Who she supposed to be? I know forsho' she ain't the police," Cruz said.

"Man, did you see that little girl? Where have you seen her before?"

"She looks familiar, but I don't know. Why? What the fuck is up?" Cruz asked. He was growing tired of the games.

"Homie, that's X's daughter," Breed said in a low tone.

Cruz's whole body went numb. The little girl's face. *Terre Haute!* It all flashed before his mind. *Yeah, man, my ole lady got people up here in Terre Haute. Can you believe that shit?* This was what Arthur X had asked him over four years ago. It all added up. *I have family up in Terre Haute. I usually visit twice a year for the family reunion.* Ronni had said that first day in the park. Sick! Cruz was so sick. How could he tell his man that he had been intimate with his people?

"Damn Breed. I think I really fucked up this time," he said with pain in his voice.

"Yeah, I can dig that," Breed replied as they rode home in complete silence.

Chapter 9

Up before sunrise as always, Cruz went about his normal regiment. After washing up and making morning prayer, Cruz completed his twenty sets of bar-work and stomach-work. He then completed three and a half miles on the treadmill. All of this by 8:08. After a quick shave and shower, he dressed and met Breed out front to begin their day.

"Where we headed?" Breed asked as they made their way into morning traffic.

"We got a full one today. Shoot down south to the lawyer's office. And make sure you have Diddy 'em to meet us at the Flea on 54th. Did that young nigga Steve from D.C. come down yet?" Cruz asked.

"Yeah, the dude Ralo. He came down yesterday. And E made it back from Boston," Breed said.

Stepping from the interior of the vehicle, Cruz left Breed to make the necessary calls. Entering the modernly decored office complex of Mr. Tylson, Cruz took the elevator to the eighth floor. He stopped at the suite's door, remembering his first visit and what he'd seen, Cruz smiled then knocked. Soon after the gorgeous receptionist opened the door and frowned.

"Hello, Mr. Cruz. How may I help you?" she asked in an even tone.

"I'm here to see Tylson."

"Do you have an appointment?" Summer Rose asked.

"No, I do not," Cruz said sarcastically.

She knew damn well that he did not have an appointment.

"Well, you have to make one..."

But before she could finish her statement Cruz just walked around her and entered Tylson's private office. The middle aged, handsome lawyer spun around in surprise. Placing his free hand over the mouthpiece of the phone, he asked Cruz in an angry tone, "May I help you?"

"William E. Tylson?" Cruz asked, looking at the man.

"Well, yes," Tylson replied, still holding the phone.

"I'm Arthur Cruz. Let's talk about the Holiday Styles."

By now the receptionist was entering the room angrily.

"Sir! I told you...Mr.Tylson, I'm sorry! I told this man..." the beautiful receptionist tried to explain but Tylson cut her off.

"Shut up! That'll be all. Please! Just leave us," he yelled, causing the young lady to jump as she turned and exited the office.

"I will have to call you back," Tylson said into the phone before placing it back onto its base. "Please have a seat, Mr. Cruz. I was expecting you to call."

"Well, I don't like phones. Especially when it comes to business of this magnitude. Now why am I here?" Cruz asked.

"You are here because there has been a change. The Holiday is now in jeopardy, and Mr. Styles is growing very impatient. I'm sure you're abreast of the recent bloodbath in Algeria. Because of that the institution has moved to transfer our man to A.D.X. as early as 72 hours," Tylson said.

"Excuse me, but what the fuck has any of that got to do with me?" Cruz asked. He had to see what was Tylson's angle. Sometimes you just could not tell who you were dealing with.

"You have everything to do with it! Let's not play games, Mr. Cruz. If Styles is not celebrating within 72 hours, there will be no holiday."

Cruz knew now that Tylson was indeed who he was supposed to be.

"Yes, I am aware. Is that the most time we have?" Cruz asked.

"No, it's not." After looking at his watch he continued. "We now have 71 hours, 59 minutes, and 35 seconds," the lawyer responded with obvious irritation.

Without saying another word Cruz left the office.

"What's up, my guy?" Breed asked as Cruz entered the truck.

"Shit is crazy. We gotta have Kunta on the ground in three days. Call them fuckin' Africans and tell 'em we're coming in."

* * *

Rolling up 12th Avenue en route to 54th Street they spotted the all black Lincoln with dark tinted windows parked in the Flea Market parking lot. Once parked all of the occupants of both vehicles emerged. It was Palmer, Wheat, E, and the new dude, Steve.

"What's up, man? Why the fuck you gotta nigga out here in a damn parking lot at 11:00?" Palmer asked.

"Bad news, we gotta go see the Africans. I hadn't planned on it, but I'ma need yall all day," Cruz answered.

"Oh! Hell nawl, slim! I ain't fuckin' wit' 'em, slim. Them muthafuckas fucks wit' me. I don't trust 'em! And I don't like 'em." Palmer was tripping.

"Wheat, did yall bring some heat?" Breed asked.

"Hell yeah! Three AK's, three 9mm's, and a MAC-11," Wheat answered.

"Okay, Palmer, get the nines and ride wit' us. Wheat, yall play the perimeter wit' them AK's. Give us 'bout 30 minutes. After that, come in humpin'," Breed instructed them.

"Slim? You must ain't heard me, man! I ain't fuckin' wit' them African muthafuckas. And I definitely ain't taking no nine! Is you niggas crazy, man?" Palmer asked. His eyes were bugged and his hands were flaring as he talked.

"Look, I'm not trippin' off whether or not you're going in, but what's wrong with the nines?" Cruz asked.

"Look, slim! One time me and this nigga, Bulldog, were getting high. Good muthafucka! Bulldog, ya hear me? Well, we run outta dope. Well, I thought we run outta dope. We get up to leave, me and Bulldog. We 'bout to go out northeast to get a half. When Bulldog get up, slim?! Kill me! A muthafuckin' whole bag of joint fell out the nigga pocket. Yeah! So I'm lookin' at the nigga. He lookin' at the dope layin' on the couch. Now you know! Slim? I'm mad as shit! I go to reach for the dope, and the nigga Bulldog snatched me up against the wall. Slim? In my own crib!" Palmer said as animated as ever.

"What the fuck that got to do wit' the nines?" Breed asked.

"Where you get this big dumb muthafucka from?" Palmer continued. "I'm 'bout to hip ya if you shut the fuck up! Anyway, I tell the nigga Bulldog, 'put me down man'. 'Cause he done fucked up. You hear me, man? Soon as he put me down, I up the joint, 'boom-boom'!"

"You shot ya partna, man?" Cruz asked.

"Hell yeah! Right in his muthafuckin' head. So look, slim? I drag the nigga down two flights of stairs, 'cause I was living out southeast on the third floor, end apartment. I went back upstairs to clean up the blood and shit. I get all the rags and shit, and I'm 'bout to dump 'em and move the body. When I opened the door! Slim? The nigga Bulldog stole me, 'boom!' Slid me clean cross the living room. Slim! The nigga Bulldog 'bout 6'3", 250, ripped! Ya hear me, man? If that nigga, black ass Toe Wilson, hadn't walked up, Bulldog woulda still been fucking me up right now! Slim? I ain't fuckin' wit' no nines. Fuck that shit!"

As serious as the situation was, everybody was dying laughing. Palmer was one funny dude. Wiping the tears from his eyes, Cruz stepped up.

"Dig man. You get the nines, Wheat. Palmer, can you handle the perimeter?"

"Slim, I'm like that! After serving three tours in Lebanon wit' 23 confirmed kills, this ain't shit," Palmer said, knowing damn well he had never been outside of D.C. as a free man.

* * *

Pulling up in Little Haiti at the Palm Gardens Projects, Breed, Wheat, Cruz, and Steve all exited the vehicle and headed for Zoe's second floor layer. They, Zoe and his Pound, occupied the entire 18 apartments on the second floor, with Zoe's living quarters settled in the middle of them all. Young and middle aged Haitians and Algerians loitered throughout the projects carrying AK's, M-16's, and a variety of small hand guns. Palm Gardens was similar to a war zone. Guns, drugs, and human-flesh was all being sold in an abundance. There was major conflict from major dealers from each section vying for control of it all.

"Damn! They don't do it like this in D.C.," Steve thought to himself.

Before they could mount the stairs the four men were stopped by Zoe's armed soldiers.

"What do you want?" the shortest of the group asked Cruz.

"I'm here to see Zoe," Cruz answered.

"Zoe don't want to see no one! Who are you?"

"Look man, I'm Cruz. Arthur Cruz! And I need to see Zoe about Holiday Styles."

The short man looked Cruz up and down with absolute scorn. It had never been a secret as to how the foreign blacks felt about the Amerikkkan born blacks. If hate, anger, and disgust did not exist, they would simply have no feelings at all towards their Amerikkkan born black brothers and sisters.

As everybody stood tense, each waiting, but hoping that no one would make the fatal mistake of upping their weapon, Cruz could see Palmer and the others taking up position.

"Turn 'round and let me search you," the man ordered.

"Ain't no need for no searchin'. You know for certain that we have fi' on us, just like you. And we're keepin' it! So please, either move aside, or pop ya toast. 'Cause I have business to attend, sir," Cruz replied.

The stare off grew even more intense. Every man mentally noting which one he would kill when the moment arrived. Steve could feel the weight of the Mac-11 pulling at the belt line of his Polo slacks. Apprehension. Perspiring! It felt like he had an oven around his waist. It seemed that hours had passed in the standoff between the two groups. Finally it ended with the short man yelling "go ahead!"

As they approached the apartment they encountered more armed men patrolling the hallway. Stopping in front of apartment 208, Cruz was informed by one of the heavily armed men to go on inside. Upon entering Cruz and his men witnessed very young girls walking around the apartment, nude. There were many men, some carrying firearms, other smoking marijuana and drinking while some indulged in illicit sexual acts with the underage women. The whole scene was very distasteful.

"How may I help you? Mr. Cruz, I presume?" a fat, very dark-skinned man asked from across the room.

"Are you Zoe?" Cruz asked.

"I am!" Zoe confirmed.

"There has been a change in plans. Styles has grown too impatient and has jeopardized the holiday. So we, no, I'm sorry, you no longer have two weeks, you have three days, which began this morning," Cruz told him.

"That is ri-dic-u-lous! I can have holiday in one week, tops!" Zoe countered.

Moving in closer, Cruz stood face-to-face with Zoe and spoke to him through closed teeth. "Listen man! And please listen good. If he's not outta there in 72 hours, there will be no holiday! But there will be a funeral. Would you like to know what the tombstone will read?"

Zoe spun away, obviously shaken. He began pacing the apartment, pounding his fist into his other opened hand. Then, stopping in mid stride, he turned and ordered everyone out except Cruz and his three men.

"I'm going to need another fifty men, two more trucks, one more heavy machine, and $125,000 now, and $125,000 more when the job is done. Whether he makes it or not," Zoe stated.

"Okay. I'll have it arranged," Cruz said and him and his men left the apartment.

* * *

After turning onto 54th and 7th Avenue, Cruz saw that Palmer and his men had finally rejoined them. The all black Lincoln was now only two car lengths behind them.

"Where we headed?" Breed asked.

"Up to Big Mac's on 79th and 18th. I think it's 'bout time I went to see the fellas," Cruz said with a smile.

Big Mac's was an old run-down strip joint where the neighborhood dudes hung out at, shot pool, made drug transactions, and drunk over-priced, watered down drinks. You would even catch some of white Amerikkkan's corporate bosses venturing down into this ghetto cesspool in search of the pungent, fireful splinder of funky black cunts. Crackas would fall-in Mac's like drones seeking pleasure, and often the pain of sexual punishment through debasement. Which in their fucked up minds could only be reached by amalgamating with society's dog-nigga-women. They came to Mac's to joyously and eagerly ram their little pink dicks and hooked noses into the funk of an unclean, sweaty, black pussy. To soil and punish themselves for their own unrighteous, devil, caveman existence. It was a mean scene.

Pulling up, Cruz saw that the place was full as usual. Taking full inventory of the variety of cars that filled the parking lot, Cruz knew that the people he needed to see were in attendance. There was Headquartaz's Suburban (off of 103rd), Smash's Harley truck (off 60th), BoePete's Cadillac STS (Out of Carol City), Moehead's 67 convertible (Out of Overtown), and Ole Bluey's Lexus Coup (Off Ali

Baba). These were the Dogs of Miami's drug trade. And these were the friends that Cruz had done nine and a half years for.

"Slim? What's going on in this raggedly muthafucka?" Palmer asked.

"Yall get that heat and be ready. Ain't no tellin' what might pop off in here," Cruz said.

"Look, man! I ain't ate shit all day. You done had a nigga running 'round since 8:00 this morning. I ain't on that one meal a day shit," Palmer complained as he checked the AK-47 and fell in line.

Breed was the very first to enter. Unarming the doorman, he was followed closely by Diddy, Wheat, and Steve. All three were leveling AK's at waist level. Positioning himself just inside the door with the Mac-11 that Steve had last carried, E signaled for Cruz to come in. By now everybody in the club was staring wide-eyed at the gun wielding intruders. Yet no one dared to make a move.

As if being cued in on a part for the silver screen, Cruz strolled in, gun visible on his waistline, putting the flames to a Double O. Looking up from the flames into the eyes of the shocked men and women, Cruz blew out a gust of smoke before speaking.

"Fellas, you don't look to happy to see me," he said through a most cynical smile. As Cruz ventured further into the room, his troops fanned out along the walls in strategic positions, leaving E alone just inside the door.

Still smoking his cigarette, Cruz took a seat and lifted a nice wad of bills from his pocket. Placing it on the table he called the waitress.

"Give everybody a taste on me. Cheer-up niggas, I'm just here to rap."

After the half naked waitress had accommodated everyone, Cruz, Headquartaz, Smash, BoePete, Moehead, and Ole Bluey settled in to talk.

"First off fellas," Cruz began, "that was real fucked up how yall left me out there. You niggas fucked me over and left my fuckin' family hurtin' while I suffered in prison. Yall boys was livin' and gettin' fat on these streets. If I was the same nigga that left here nine and a half years ago, I'd be lettin' them big guns that my 'real' friends is holding do all the talkin'. But I'm not. Even knowin' that at least one of you niggas played an active role in gettin' me snatched-up."

Everybody began looking one to the other, and then back to Cruz, who had paused to evaluate their expressions before continuing.

"Yeah, it's a fuckin' rat at this table. But I'm willin' to leave the past in the past. But for us to coexist in the future, shit, we gonna have to have some changes," Cruz spoke between sips of his cognac and pulls of his square.

"So whatchu want, my nigga? You want some work? You want yo' old spots back? Some bread? What the fuck is up, Cruz?" Headquartaz asked.

"Yeah, jack? Fuck is all the guns for, my nigga? We coulda rapped about shit wit'out that," chimed in BoePete.

Staring BoePete in the eyes, Cruz venomously spat.

"The guns is for you niggas! Fuck you mean? And Head, I wouldn't go to talkin' loud and movin' my hands all crazy if I was you. 'Cause them dudes wit' the guns might get nervous.... Now look, I don't want no work." Running his hand over his attire and then pointing about the room at his men, Cruz then continued. "Do it look like I need some work? Nah, I do need some long green, and plenty of it. And as far as my ole spots go, yeah, I'ma need them back, but not for illicit purposes. Fellas, we've known each other for years. And at one point I could've said I loved yall, and I've often wished that we could have those days back, but we can't. Not like this. Meanin', we gotta clean this shit up.... I know for a fact that all of you boys are sittin' on retirement money. But you just can't see past the grind! I wanna help you and me, to help get the community in order."

Again, each man looked from one to the other and back at Cruz. Moehead was the first to speak up.

"Hold up, my nigga," he chuckled before continuing. "Let me make sho' I'm diggin' you, 'cause it almost sound like you forcefully suggestin' that we stop hustlin'.... Is you?"

Everybody looked at Cruz. The tension in the room was now mounting. "That's exactly what I'm sayin'. Man look, I just left where you niggas is headed if you don't get hip. It's a million and one ways to score for grits and greens if you kats would just give it a chance.... Have you niggas ever took the time to just look 'round at the hood? At the lil' girls playin' dress up like they grown, fuckin' and tradin' sex for 10 karat jewelry and outfits? Yall niggas don't see the lil' niggas gettin' caught up and killed tryna imitate us?.... Maann, I just left niggas, good niggas, that ain't never comin' home, man. It's simple, bruh, the way I see it. You can be part of the problem or part of the solution, but either way, it goes down today," Cruz finished with a poker face.

Everybody sat silent before Moehead spoke up. "NIgga, you done gone plumb crazy! I'm up outta here," he stated, raising to leave.

At that instance Breed stepped forward to stop him, but Cruz waved him off.

"Nah, he good. Let him leave. Anybody else got anything to say?" Cruz asked, leaning back in his chair.

"Nothin' but, *what the fuck happened to you, my nigga?* Fuck is you been readin'? You did a lil' *light-ass-bid* and come home on some Donald Goines shit! Who the fuck is you, Kenyatta? Them white folks done really fried yo' skull, man. 'Cause you got it fucked up! I'ma sell dope 'til the crackas make it legal, my nigga. That's how I cop my grits and greens. In fact, I'm gettin' hungry just talkin' 'bout it. I'm gone," said Headquartaz.

"Yeah, this nigga crazy," BoePete stated, following Headquartaz's suit.

"What about you, Smash? What you think?" Cruz asked his old friend.

Smash had not said a word the whole time. Him nor Ole Bluey. They both sat facing Cruz even while the others had left.

"I don't know, dog. It's a tough call. You know I fucks witchu, but this shit gonna get crazy...gimme a few days. Either I'm witcha or I'm leavin'. You feel me?" Smash said, nursing his watery drink.

"Yeah, I'm right there too. I'ma holla at Headquartaz because you made a lot of sense, baby. I ain't gon' lie, I be thinkin' on that same shit. Especially when it comes to them lil' hoes," Ole Bluey said sincerely. "Give us yo' number or something."

"I can dig that. Yall just get at me," Cruz said before the two men gave him dap. After getting his information, they exited the run-down strip club.

* * *

"Breed, we gon' kill that nigga Headquartaz tonight. I swear befo' God and all that I've ever loved, if his bitch-ass livin' when the sun come up, I'ma kill my gotdamn self," Cruz stated as they stood outside of Big Mac's preparing to leave.

"So what now, slim? 'Cause you done fucked a nigga's whole day up," Diddy said.

Cruz just waved him off and jumped in the Excursion, leaving Big Mac's for the next episode.

Chapter 10

...First I'm gon' stack my dough/ And then what?/ Then I'm gon' stack some moe'/ And then what?/ Close shop and then make my count/ And hide the rest of them yams at my auntie house/ And then what?/ Get fresh and jump in one of them cars/ And then what?/ Hit the club and get me one of them broads.... the radio sounded through the still night air.

"You wanna hit this, my nigga?" DaDa asked Headquartaz.

"What is that, lil' nigga?"

"Lace," DaDa answered.

"Yeah, let me hit that, my nigga. A nigga don't fuck wit' that airplane," Headquartaz said, taking the joint from DaDa.

"Aye, Bluey! Yo Blue! Brang a nigga a beer when you come downstairs, my nigga," DaDa yelled up to Ole Bluey.

"Jit, I don't know how the G's carry it in Ten-a-Key, but 'round here, in this bottom, the jits run for the G's! The G's don't run for the jits," Bluey said, passing DaDa a green bottle, an El Poducto, some weed and cocaine.

"What I'ma do wit' this?" DaDa asked, looking crazy.

"You young, but you ain't dumb. Roll that shit!" Bluey capped.

"Man, can you believe that *hoe-ass-shit* that nigga was talkin'?" Headquartaz asked Ole Bluey as they stood in the parking lot of Silver Blue.

"Who, DaDa?" Ole Bluey asked.

"Hell nawl, nigga!" Headquartaz snapped. "That sucka ass nigga, Cruz."

"Oh, yeah. I been thinkin' on that shit. He made a lil' sense," Ole Bluey said.

"Oh, you wit' that sucka shit?" Headquartaz asked.

"Nawl, man, I'm just sayin'," Ole Bluey replied.

"You sayin' what? Fuck that shit! And fuck that *pussy-ass-nigga*, Cruz! I use to chump that nigga! Run that nigga! Now the *cunt-ass-nigga* come from the joint and you wanna get on his dick. Fuck that shit. M-O-B, nigga! I'm holdin' this shit down. I'ma end up smashin' the nigga. That's what I'm sayin'. Just like I smashed Busta soft ass," Headquartaz fumed.

"This nigga trippin'! Damn, DaDa, you ain't roll that yet, my nigga…. Damn that Chevy tight, look DaDa. Who shit that is?" Ole Bluey said, pointing to the blood-red 72 four door Chevy on twenty-four's.

"Yeah! That muthafucka drippin'. And he sound like he runnin'," DaDa replied.

"You niggas some grouples," Headquartaz said, laughing.

The rear driver side door opened and out emerged a medium built dark-brown skin dude wearing black Polo slacks with a black and red long sleeve Polo shirt, and black Reebok classics. He walked right over to Head, DaDa, and Blue.

"Yo, yall dudes got some weed?" he asked.

"Nah, man, this ain't no muthafuckin' weed-hole!" Headquartaz snarled.

"Nah, dude, but you can try down there by the stairs. They be havin' weed," DaDa told the baldhead man.

"Country-ass-nig-" Headquartaz started to say before the impact of the .41 slug crashed into his face.

Boom! the huge gun sounded, sending Headquartaz's lifeless body flying to the concrete.

Boom! Boom! Boom! Boom! Boom! Boom! Boom! Steve stood over his victim still fingering the Desert Eagle.

Click! The huge frame of the gun locked frozen, exposing an empty chamber.

"Damn! This bitch empty!" Steve said as he turned to run back to the Chevy.

Pop! Pop! Pop! Pop! Pop! Spat DaDa's 9mm as he backed off in a nearby cut.

Doom! Doom! Doom! Ole Bluey sounded his Mini-14. *Doom! Doom! Doom!*

If Captain Jack had not jumped out of the driver's seat with cover from the AK-47, Steve would not have made it to the car alive.

Wacka! Wacka! Wacka! Wacka! the AK called.

Two of the projectiles perforated Ole Bluey's abdomen and chest. But not before DaDa managed to squeeze off two more shots.

Pop! Pop! the little 9mm screamed.

One slug shattered the rear glass of the Chevy and the other one hit Captain Jack in the shoulder.

"Fuck! Oh shit! I'm shot!" Jack yelled as he fell to the ground.

Wheat jumped out of the passenger side to help Jack into the car. Cruz jumped out and laid down a heavy stream of AK fire to cover Steve.

Wacka! Wacka! Wacka! Wacka! went the AK-47.

"Come on, nigga, drive!" Cruz yelled to Steve.

Taking the wheel of the Chevy felt good after what he had just done. Feeling the power of the 400 rumble beneath him helped to settle his shaking hands. He had never killed a man before and hoped he would never have to do it again.

"Yall niggas hear them sirens? Push this bitch, shawdy!" Wheat said.

Jack was holding his wounded arm. It was bleeding badly and would need immediate medical attention. Rounding the corner of 102nd and 14th, Cruz had Steve to stop the car.

"Dig, Wheat, my aunt stay right there at 1427, the light-brown house. Take Jack over there and let her fix the nigga's arm. We gon' run these hoes!" Cruz said.

Gunning the big Chevy, they were off to the races. Steve whipped it onto 17th Avenue. They rode a block before Metro-Dade Police were behind them. It was one officer in his patrol vehicle. Crossing 103rd, they were two blocks from the 17th side entrance to Silver Blue Lakes.

"Dig, Ralo!" Cruz began speaking from the backseat. "Turn in up here. Turn in kinda slow. I'ma roll out on the turn, on yo' side so the cracka don't see me. You just keep goin' forward, hit the first shit you see, and lean on the horn. I got you!"

Turning in, Steve did as he was instructed. The first thing he saw was a Dodge Magnum. He pushed the Chevy forward and smashed that shit.

Crash! sounded the impact, followed by the horn. *Hhhoonk!!*

Steve laid still, slumped over the steering wheel like a dead man. The officer whipped his vehicle in and jumped out with his service revolver drawn.

"Get your hands up!" he yelled as he circled around to the driver side. "Get your fucking hands...."

Wacka! Wacka! Wacka! Wacka! the AK-47 barked, silencing the cop.

All four rounds perforated the officer's neck, severing his head from his shoulders. The sound of the gun blast caused Steve to jump. He turned just in time to see the man's head fall from his body.

"Urrrrrggg!" Steve threw up on the tinted glass of the Chevy.

"Nigga, drive this shit!" Cruz said, jumping in on the passenger side.

The Flow Masters roared loudly as the 400 performed down 22nd Avenue. They were on 119th Street before they spotted the first police car in the distance.

"You gotta mean engine in this bitch, Ralo," Cruz said, looking back.

"Thank you," Steve said. What else could he say? His car was his world. He had spent a lot of money getting it just the way he wanted it. Only to destroy it all in one night.

"Say, cuz?" Cruz spoke into the cell phone. "I'm 'bout to bring a few through there.... Yeah! I'm in a red Chevy.... Yeah! Bet that!"

The police were closing the distance between them. Cruz could see that it was no more than three cars.

"Turn in here!" Cruz told Steve. "And slow down."

Steve turned into the apartment complex as instructed and coasted along at a slow pace. The police came flying in behind him. Sirens blaring! They ran headlong into a boobietrap.

Tat! Tat! Tat!.... Doom! Doom!.... Wacka! Wacka! Wacka! Wacka!.... Doom!...Wacka! Wacka!.... Boom! Boom!.... Tat! Tat! Tat!.... Doom! Doom! an array of different gun blasts sounded. They were shooting from dumpsters, rooftops, and wrecked cars.

"Goddamn!" Steve yelled, not believing what he was seeing. He had never heard so many guns going off at once.

"Pull over here, Ralo," Cruz instructed.

Getting out of the car, Cruz looked, then tossed a pineapple inside of it.

"You betta get yo' ass outta there," Cruz said, laughing.

"Oh shit!" Steve said and ran away from the car.

Boom! the explosion sounded as the two walked off.

Chapter 11

"What up, Breed?" Cruz said, coming through the door of their Miami Lakes residence.

"Shiid, you! Everybody lookin' for you. Where Ralo?" Breed asked.

"As long as that everybody don't include the police, I'm cool...shit got ultra-crazy out there tonight. Ralo caught a cab over to Diddy 'em crib."

"Bruh, yall niggas been on the news for the last hour. They say the nigga Bluey gon' make it. But Head and two of the officers is outta here. Ain't no leads, but they askin' for tips," Breed informed him.

"What's up wit' Jack?"

"Oh, he straight. Yo' aunt put him in there. All them niggas at Diddy crib. Oh yeah, Elijah called. He say he hope you ain't forgot you speakin' in Americus tomorrow."

"Damn! I did forget that shit. Damn!" Cruz replied.

"You gotta red-eye flight to Albany. Tickets for three. So what you gon' do?"

"Call Jack, tell him to jump a cab to the airport. That way he can get his arm checked while we're up there. Then go and pick up Summer for me. I'ma make a phone call and pack," Cruz said, leaving the room.

"Hello?" Cruz spoke into the phone. "May I please speak to Summer, please?"

"It's been so long you've forgotten how I sound?" Summer sassed.

"No, it's not that. I, I jus...." Cruz stuttered.

"What do you want? It's late and I do need my rest."

"Look Summer, I'm sorry about the shit at the office earlier...."

"Are you also sorry about neglecting me? You became intimate with me, Arthur, then you just, you just.... You aborted our relationship! You never returned my calls, I haven't even seen you. You, you manipulated me!" she said in a woeful tone.

"I apologize if that's how I made you feel. But please know and believe that that was not my intent. And if it's at all possible, please allow me to make it up," Cruz capped.

"Cruz, I don't believe you."

"That's a shame," he said in an even tone.

"Why?" she asked, so wanting to believe him.

"Because I have an inexhaustible reliquary of reliance in you."

"What do you want from me?" she asked in a manner of a child.

"To be your best friend," he popped like Boo Baby, knowing his partner would be proud of him.

"I mean, now. What do you want from me? What do you want me to do?" There was frustration in her tone.

"Come with me on a trip."

"Okay," she answered without hesitation.

"The car is already en route to pick you up."

"What?" she asked in surprise.

"Didn't I just tell you that I believed in you."

She just smiled and hung up the phone.

* * *

Arriving in the small southern town of Americus, GA was indeed a monumental point in Cruz's life. To be invited as the keynote speaker of an event giving honor to the heroines who had been abducted and held for weeks without legal counsel, without medical attention, or even decent housing, during the civil rights movement, was one of the greatest things to ever happen to him. These heroic women had protested and fought the racist subhuman treatment of the local authorizes. This community, which was now giving them honor, had protested and fought in Albany, in Atlanta, and Alabama. He was here not only to pay homage, but in an attempt to somehow recreate that spirit which had gave way to dope dealing, womanizing, gang-violence and self-hate.

"I like this hotel. It's old and cozy. What's the name of it again?" Summer asked Cruz.

"The Winsler. This is the hotel that Oprah stays in when she's in the area," Cruz answered.

"I can see why. The people are so nice." Summer continued. "But you know I'm still mad with you."

"Is it because I'm black?"

"Stupid!" she said, throwing a pillow at Cruz playfully. "I'm going to kill you!"

They playfully wrestled on the couch until they fell onto the floor, with Summer landing on top. She kissed him.

"Do you take it back?" she asked.

"Of course not," he answered matter-of-factly.

She kissed him even deeper.

"Take it back!" she demanded.

"No!" Cruz insisted.

She kissed him longer and even deeper.

"I said to take it back, Arthur."

He could feel himself growing erect beneath her. Looking her directly in her pretty water-blue eyes, he mouthed the words "Fuck you, Summer."

"I thought you would never ask," she slowly said in a most seductive voice.

She covered his mouth again with hers. Their tongues fought and chased each other from one mouth to the other. Cruz began rubbing and squeezing the soft roundness of her hind parts. They continued to tongue wrestle while Cruz pulled up her dress. He then felt down in the area of her vagina. Again, she wore no panties. Cruz inserted his middle finger into her velvet alabaster valley. She was so wet that the juices dripped off of his hand onto his slacks. Summer started to pant and hump Cruz's hand like a nympho in heat. Using his free hand, Cruz freed his erection. Guiding himself into the narrow confines of her womanhood, he stuck the slippery cum soiled fingers of his hand into her mouth. She suckled and licked the juices of her own cunt with great joy.

"How does it taste?" Cruz asked in a low tone.

"See for yourself," she said before ramming her tongue back into his mouth and vigorously grinding her openness onto his shaft.

Snatching her hair, he pulled her head back, forcing her to look up at the high ceiling.

"Oh God!" she shouted as Cruz drove himself deeper.

Cruz began to release his load inside of her. She not only felt the warmth of his hot jism flowing into her vaginal track, she felt the power of his love-muscle beginning to soften. But she was not ready to relinquish the passionate feelings of the moment. Fearing that she might be deprived of the monster erection, she slid down and began rejuvenating his falling stiffness by performing mouth-to-mouth on his external organ. He immediately began to swell. Her pace quickened. Gagging, she took the full length of him. Cruz roughly pushed the top of her head, causing her to fall back.

Standing, he stripped himself completely nude. She just sat there and admired his powerful physique. Pulling her up by her hair, Cruz took her to the balcony. He then spun her around, facing the street below. He lifted her dress and started playing in her love-nest. Instantly the juices ran from her succulent honey dish like sex-scented oil.

"Please Arthur, take me from behind! Here on the balcony!" Summer begged.

Using her own sex juices to oil the head of his penis, Cruz leaned her forward and forced his rod into her rectum.

"Oh God!" she whined in a soft whimper.

Using one hand she reached over her shoulder and clamped her hand on the back of his neck. He in turn began sucking her neck and driving himself deeper.

"Oh, shit! Arthur, you're killing me. Please!" she screamed louder.

"You want me to stop," he asked, breathing the words in her ear.

"No! Please no! I'm orgasming," she whined like a school girl.

Then Summer began shaking uncontrollably. Panting! She could feel the cum running down her legs. At that instance Cruz released his load also. Removing himself from her anus, she calapsed to the floor. Where his seed wasted all over her head and back.

* * *

After the two shared a long hot shower, they slept the better part of the morning away in each others' arms. Cruz was the first to finally rise.

"Morning, lady."

"Good morning to you, sir."

"We need to be gettin' up and at it. I go on at 12:00, then there's a dinner at 3:00, and we fly out of Atlanta at 8:00. It's a two hour drive. So let's get it," he said, slapping her on the butt.

"Ouch!" Summer yelled. "Please don't do that. My ass is sore! I don't think I'll be able to attend any of today's outings, because I can't stand to sit down."

"Are you goin' to be okay?" Cruz asked.

"I think so. You should order us breakfast in bed." Summer excitedly continued. "And have them to bring up some Epsom salt so I can soak my behind."

Cruz started laughing. He really liked her. She was so wholesome and fun to be around.

"That's not funny, Arthur," she said in her childish tone.

When the food arrived, Cruz sat on the edge of the bed and ate. Summer had to lay on her stomach to eat. They ate in silence. She was pouting because Cruz had not allowed her to order any pork bacon.

He then dressed. An all black silk pants set, with black Bally leathers, and a black leather waistcoat.

"You look nice," Summer admitted.

"I know," Cruz agreed.

"Conceited!"

"Confident," Cruz corrected.

"Smart ass."

"Sore ass," Cruz countered.

They both laughed at that as Cruz left to meet the demands of his schedule. Summer relaxed for a bit. Reflecting on last night's activities. She smiled. It had been erotic. Borderline sadistic. He was the ultimate entertainer! Did she love him? That was questionable. Did she need him? Like the air she breathed. Would she do anything for him? Without a doubt or contradiction.

She continued to replay all that they had shared. Touching herself she realized that she had become moist. The thought of masturbation crossed her mind, but she thought better. She merely suckled that which was on her finger and ran herself a hot tub of bubbles and Epsom salt to soak her aching posterior.

As she sat relaxing in the spacious tub, she noticed the book *Black August* sitting on the dresser. Curious! She walked nude to retrieve it. At first she merely skimmed through the pages. She then began to read entire speeches, essays, and letters. Her heart pounded as she took in the information. Her first thoughts were racist. She read on. Passionate! She continued. Sadly, she conceded. It was the truth. And she had to hear it for herself. Checking the time, she knew that his speech had already begun. For that reason, she hurried from the tub and dressed in haste. With *Black August* in hand, she rushed to the hotel's ballroom where the lecture was taking place.

"....as we have witnessed in this bourgeois capitalist society that we call Amerikkka, one man's dream can easily become another man's nightmare. Likewise, a dream unrealized, a dream without proper supervision, the key word being vision, because if this man's dream, or the dream of an organization is not seen or visualized through the eyes of the people, it has indeed become a nightmare!

"The Amerikkkan dream! A dream rooted in a set of complex ideas holding that this land, Amerikkka, is the land of opportunity. Well opportunity for who? And what might that opportunity be? As I see it! As we all have lived it! It is the opportunity for the rich to continue to grow richer, while the poor, the unfortunate and uneducated, the blacks, continue to suffer and die at the hands of our oppressor and open enemy. Blacks have been here in Amerikkka longer than almost any ethinic group, with the exception of the so-called Indians. Yet we have by far accomplished the least....

"....just as you have fought and even died for a physical freedom, which is an incomplete freedom, because we have yet to emerge from the mental bondage placed on us during slavery. Please read the book *Breaking the Chains of Psychological Slavery* by Dr. Naim Akbar. It's no coincidence that we identify everything white as being right, and black as indecent or villainous. Make no mistake about it, *we are what we do and our thoughts reflect our actions.* Mere words mean nothing to Amerikkka, because only equals can come together and talk to reach an agreement. They do not see you and me as equals! So tonight I want you to really consider a complete freedom, and total separation from our oppressors. It's obvious to me, as it should be to you, that we will never be treated as equals nor as human being, here in Amerikkka. No! Not in this Amerikkka....

"Our wisdom lies in our Queens. The Black woman! Brothers we must clean up our Sister; more so mentally than physically. And re-educate her. Respect her! As she is our earth. She is the best and most significant part! The woman is the key to our independence. Why? Because she carries our future! She's the fosterer of understanding! The very link between the family; man and child; and society....The reason we are here today, is to honor these beautiful sisters for their suffering and courage. You see, some woman, or women, took the time to instill that courage and fortitude in them. These women were taught and brought up right, by strong women of character in a strong and balanced household.

"But something has happened. Through the trick-knowledge of our open enemy and oppressor, the devil, our very own women have been used unwittingly to help uproot the black family. Our oppressors have a vicious strong hold on the lifeline of goods and services and are refusing the Black man access. Therefore the Black woman has been elevated to a superior position over her man, causing an imbalance in the home. She has coveted this new role of dominating the household, so now we have a reversed program. She's the man, so she lusts for women, and the man is sleeping around with other men like a common whore for money. Nigga, you a punk! Excuse me, please pardon me. I apologize. But it's true. That ain't the 'Down Low' brothers, that's just plain ole low down.... The sisters do not respect us because we have fallen very low. We lack the essential elements to command her respect, this being knowledge of self, knowledge of God, and the capital to sustain a healthy life style....

"....brothers! Especially my young, strong, and brave little brothers. We can not continue to kill our future leaders by way of drugs, gang violence and abortion. Sisters, what you carry in your womb is very sacred. I know that times are hard, but we need you to help us produce our salvation. The next Malcolm X, T.D. Jakes, Farrahkan, or Bishop Curry is in you! Where would we be if Mary, mother of Jesus, had had an abortion? We'll never realize our greatest potential if it's not allowed to develop....

"Amerikkka, we want what you owe! Reparations are due! We demand justice for all of the Brothers and Sisters being held in prison for crimes committed in reflection to the evil this system breeds. We only want what you yourselves demanded of Great Britian in 1775. Our Independence!"

With that he left the rostrum. Everyone in the ballroom was on their feet clapping. Everyone except Summer Rose. She was not the only white person in attendance, but she was the only one sitting with tears in her eyes. He was....so passionate and beloved! He was so right and needed by his own. With those thoughts she returned to their room.

* * *

Afterwards people began leaving. Cruz stayed back and autographed the books that people in attendance had purchased.

"I enjoyed your speech. And I really understand," a cute and petite, but shapely woman told him. She had a little girl with her.

"Thank you," Cruz responded.

"No," she said holding his stare. Continuing in a most sincere tone she said, "I truly do understand. And I will do better."

"That is a blessing," Cruz returned.

"My name is Mrs. Tracey Carter," she stated with a smile, then extended her hand for Cruz to shake.

"Nice to meet you. My name is Arthur Cruz."

"I know," she smiled.

He felt a little foolish. Cruz then turned his attention to the little girl.

"What's your name?"

"Jai Nadia," the pretty little girl beamed.

"That's a very pretty name, Jai Nadia. What are you going to be when you grow up?" Cruz asked her.

"I'ma be a veterinarian," she answered with much pride.

"That is a wonderful field to undertake. Just remember, open your own, and help to employ your own."

"Okay! Will you sign my book?" Jai Nadia asked.

"Of course! I would be proud to do so...."

He wrote, *To: Jai Nadia my favorite veterinarian. With love, Mr. Arthur Cruz.*

* * *

"Hello," Cruz said as he walked into his room, back at The Winsler.

"Hi," Summer returned in a sad tone.

"What's wrong?"

"Nothing."

"Tears?"

"Of joy."

"What made you so happy?" Cruz asked.

"The truth."

"Truth?" he questioned.

"I heard your speech. I've also read most of your book, *Black August*. Will you sign it for me?"

"No."

"Why?" Summer asked.

"Because I only sign the books of paying readers."

"I'll give you my life," she confessed.

This really took Cruz by surprise. Summer's tone was even and very serious. She seemed to be at the brink of breaking down.

"What's wrong with you?" Cruz asked again.

"I'm white....and we're wrong."

"What do you mean?"

"Before reading this and hearing you speak, I never gave the race issue any thought. I'd never heard of miscegenation before today! I feel so naïve. So stupid!

"When you left the room earlier, I had a talk with myself. During which, I asked myself *'do you really love and need him, Summer?'* I knew then that I undoubtedly needed you in my life. Yet, it wasn't until after I saw the brilliance of your mind that I realized how much the world, your people mainly, needed you more. For that reason I knew that I could not have you. With this I knew that, if I really loved you, I'd have to let you go...Arthur, baby, I love you so much, sweetheart," Summer Rose said before the water gates broke. She sobbed uncontrollably.

"Why?" Cruz asked, feeling himself about to tear up.

"I'm okay. I have had every opportunity that this country can afford a person. I've never lost anything because of my color, until now. My racial identity had been an advantage, until now....I believe in my heart that I may be able to find happiness in a decent white man. Though none, white or black, will ever compare to you. I could not be happy with you, knowing that I'm depriving someone, a sister, of what God intended for her.... I love you," Summer cried.

"Can we be friends?" Cruz asked.

"Always... Promise me, no matter what, you'll never forget me. And, and that we'll be friends at heart...forever."

"I promise," he said. "Now give me that book so I can sign it."

Summer simply smiled and passed him the book. She was sad. Yet she was happy. She had loved and been loved in return.

Chapter 12

In a shopping plaza, several miles outside of Terre Haute, Indiana, a dark-blue Camry sat alone in its parking space, in front of First Union Bank. An armored Brinks First Union truck pulled to the curb, two parking spaces from the Camry; and an old, very dark-skinned, fat women got out of the car. She sat her purse on the roof of the car and began rummaging through its contents. When out of nowhere came two young punks. The taller of the two was the one to speak.

"Gimme that book, bitch!" he yelled loudly.

"Pardon me?" she asked in disbelief.

"He said up the purse, hoe," the shorter man said before punching the lady in the stomach.

The taller man then reached over her to get the purse. At that instance the armored truck driver signaled to his two partners, one riding shotgun and the other in the back compartment with the money, to follow him in aiding the helpless woman. They all jumped out and quickly ran to the car. The driver grabbed the shorter man and slung him to the street. But not before the man pulled a 9mm from his waistband and opened fire.

Pop! Pop! Pop! the little gun screamed, sending its cordless talons to meet the armored truck driver square in the face. The impact sent his lifeless body crashing into the car.

The taller of the two dove on the man closet to him. They hit the ground and struggled for position. The man that had been riding shotgun in the armored truck stood just in front of the old lady and began pulling his service revolver. He never cleared leather!

The old woman put the nose of a short barrel Bulldog .45 to the back of his head and fingered the trigger once.

Boom! the .45 roared. Following the huge slug was a stream of fire, four inches long. The man's hair flamed ablaze as the contents of his head emptied out onto the street.

Removing the wig, Zoe turned and fingered the trigger of the Bulldog twice more.

Boom! Boom! the magnum barked as it regurgitated two crimson lead missiles. They struck the remaining armored truck rider in the chest and stomach.

"Nigga, get ya sorry ass up! We gotta go!" Zoe yelled to Mattula.

By then Karim, the shorter man, had ran and jumped in the driver's seat of the armored truck and the three were off to their mission.

Chapter 13

"Say, baby? This mop-water is fantastic, sweetheart!" Pimpin Boo Baby said after taking a long sip.

"Goddamn, boy! You sho' got a deep throat on you!" Hump exclaimed.

"It's like DP, baby! It's suppose to bubble," Boo Baby capped.

"Pimp! You don't know nothin' 'bout no DP. Ya small time. Ya stumbled cross some poor confused, sex starved girl. Probably just outta the joint. And ya tricked her outta a few dollars," Pop said, taking another sip of his own home brew. "Boy! When you was swimmin' in ya daddy's bag, I was swimmin' in money bags. House fulla white women and animals!"

"That's right, goddamn it! Tell him, Pop! Tell that muthafucka! Tell him 'bout the animals!" Hump yelled, reaching for the jug.

"Well damn you, Hump! You gotta pretty deep throat ya damn self!" Pop said, taking another sip before continuing. "I had a zoo in that muthafucka, boy! Salamanders! Crocodiles, Rhinoceros, and Ostriches! I had big-block gators thick as Brontosaurus hide. You hear me? Elephants and Eels! I'd be in the livin' room with my camel-hair pants set on and holla, 'lizards! Burgundy!' And they'd just crawl to my feet."

"Pop! You outta sight, baby! You sho' outta sight," Boo Baby said, laughing.

"Mainline! Mainline!" the CO yelled out loud.

"Oh! They callin' my name," Hump said, raising himself to leave.

"What they serving?"

"Food! And I'm goin' to get it," Hump said, rubbing his hands together.

"Hold up, Hump. We gon' walk down witcha, 'cause you ain't much boy, but you all we got," Pop said as he got his cane and headed out the cell.

* * *

"Boo, ain't that yo' main man over yonda?" Pop asked.

"Yeah. That's ole Kunta," Boo Baby replied.

"Well what's wrong wit' him. Him and them niggas is up to something."

"Pop, you drunk. Them dudes is mellow."

No sooner than the words left his mouth Kunta sprung into action, hitting the guard with a lighting array of crippling karate kicks and Tyson-like jabs! And right on cue, his men joined the attack. In no time at all, the staff had been subdued and the kitchen doors were locked and secured by Kunta's men.

"He fuckin' them up!" Hump yelled.

"Wow!" Pimp said to himself. "My main man out-the-sky."

* * *

Turning off of the main road, onto the field of white lilies, just outside of the old prison, Karim floored the accelerator, causing the mechanical elephant to roar and strain at its reins as he drove them into battle.

The north and east tower guards were alarmed at the approach of the speeding armored bank truck. "What the hell is he doing?" the north guard questioned.

"You'd betta get on the horn and tell that damned fool he's traveling in a dead zone," the east guard commanded.

"Please! Stop the truck and get back on the main road! I repeat! Get back on the main road. You're on federal property!"

The truck continued on its course. Karim had them twenty-five yards from the main fence. Twenty! Ten! The tower guard continued to warn against further encroachment.

"Get off the horn, East, and let that AR-17 talk to 'em!"

"I copy and concur, North!"

Backa! Backa! Backa! Backa! The two towers fired on the truck. But it was clearly to no avail.

Crash! The truck rammed through the fence and rumbled over the prison rec-yard towards the back of the mess-hall. By now the West tower had began to fire on the armored truck.

Crash! Karim brought down the final fence surrounding the kitchen. Before exiting the rear compartment of the truck, Mattula set precedence by emptying his fifty round drum into the west tower, leaving the helpless guard motionless.

* * *

Upon hearing the gunfire outside, Kunta knew that his savior had arrived. He also knew that he could not take all of the men with him. Seeing the three female guards he came up with an idea.

"Who all want some pussy?" Kunta yelled. "Disrobe these cave dwellers and set 'em out!"

"Hell yeah! Strip 'em and rape 'em!" Hump yelled, beating his fist into his open palm. "We finna see some faces down low, bitches raise them rumps, for the Vicious Hump!"

"Say, baby? That's a little too sadistic for a pimp. Besides, I wants the money. You chumps is content with the honey!" Boo Baby said, distancing himself from the chaos.

It had to be over 120 perverted, sex starved dudes lined up to travel into the sacred valleys of the Europeans' forbidden cunts. Other more morally upstanding, yet still perverted, dudes stood on tables and in corners watching. Some masturbating. The whole scene was sickening!

Kunta and his men used this distraction to make their way out of the back. They opened up the back door to let Zoe and his men in. Pacing off four yards from the rear wall, they began ripping up the floor. Kunta then got on the phone. Dialing the number to the local federal building, he told them of the takeover and gave them his list of demands.

"This is the A.P.L.A. We are now in control of U.S.P. Terre Haute. We are armed and highly efficient! Please, make no mistake about it. We came here to die. And we will slaughter every pig in this building! I want a helicopter on the rec-yard, and a private jet fueled and waiting in Indy. You have four hours! Every minute after those four hours, we will have barbeque at the expense of one of your pigs."

Kunta then called the media and repeated his message. He knew now that he and his men had at least four hours to unload the money from the truck, hit the tunnel, and make it to Chicago; where he had passports and a private jet waiting to fly them to South America. They would then board a commercial flight to Algeria. His homeland. *Liberty! Long live freedom. Long live the Elephant. Triumphant! The Black Guerrilla!*

163

After landing at Miami's International Airport, the three, Cruz, Summer Rose, and Captain Jack all took separate cabs to their respective destinations. Entering the Miami Lakes tenement that he and Breed shared, he saw the latter on the phone shaking his head.

"Look! Lame-ass-nigga! Where the fuck is Cruz? I'm tired of you lying. I know the nigga been getting my calls! Put him on the fuckin' phone!" Ronni spat over the line.

"Listen, sister, I'm sorry you've been missin' him, but I have no control over his schedule. I will give him yo' message though, and thank you for callin'."

"Nig..." Was all she was allowed to get out before the phone clicked in her face. Breed knew that Cruz had been avoiding her. Hell, so did she! The only difference was, Breed knew why and she did not. As he stood to go and fix himself a drink he noticed Cruz standing there.

"What up, Breed?" Cruz asked.

"Man, I'm glad you here. Please, you need to call that girl back or somethin'. She's been callin' here all day on some bullshit."

"So what'd you tell her?"

"That you would holla as soon as you could."

"Aiight. Turn the ringer off. We got a long day tomorrow. I'ma see you in the morning."

It seemed he had just hit the pillow when the alarm clock went off. After a quick workout and a shower, Cruz dressed himself for a full day of activities. Flipping through the stations while waiting for Breed, Cruz couldn't help but to smile when he saw what was on CNN. The unattractive redhead was standing in an open field surrounded by National Guardsmen, local police, and F.B.I. agents. Cruz could see his old home in the background. Terre Haute U.S.P.

"At approximately 5:00 p.m. yesterday, several armed men — an estimated twenty — drove a stolen armored truck through the fence behind me, and successfully tunneled away. Taking with them five men serving life terms. Kunta ibn Ali, Misymbol Allah, Ali Muhammad, Fonzworth Bartholomew Bolinbroke, and G. Hopkins-Bey. They are all believed to be members of the revolutionary group A.P.L.A. The group is responsible for several terrorist acts in the past eight years, and is also leading the current uprising in Algeria. Two prison guards and two armored truck drivers were killed, while a third is barely hanging on to his life. The rebels also severely raped and tortured three female officers. While regaining control of the prison, four inmates were wounded by National Guardsmen. But there is no clue as to the whereabouts of the escapees or the rebels involved. However, this poem, entitled *Unbreakable*, was found on the wall of the escape tunnel."

It will please you to see me beg, cower and cry.
Inflame ashes born burning, ready to die...
Be I become beaten, battered or bruised I shall,
never bend, break or bow. For I am Alpha and Omega,
the Original Black Man Child...
Broken word from distant family friends alike.
Should I continue to bleed, I won't go down
without a fight!
History has shown us murderous atrocities the pale man's
capable. Though wounded and scarred the Drag's on
engendered, Remains Unbreakable!
Liberty. Freedom. Long Live The Black Guerrilla!

"Police are asking for any information that might lead to the capture of these fugitives of justice. Please call 1-800-Hot-Tips. There is a $250,000 reward..."

Cruz cut off the TV and shook his head. He was glad that they all had made it, but the rape of the female staff had really bothered him. Because he knew that once the lines were drawn, and Kunta was placed with the Familiar Post, all hell would break loose.

* * *

After meeting up, Cruz, Breed, Palmer, Wheat, E, and Steve all climbed into their respective rides, en route to what would be one of Cruz's hardest jobs to date. He had faced many demons stemming from his past, but this one by far would be the most ominous. Reaching 103rd and Pee, they pulled in and dismounted.

"Look yall. I really use to fuck wit' dude. So I don't want him hurt. Just watch the perimeter and I'll handle him. Ralo, getta AK and hold the outside. When we go in, E and Diddy, shut it down. I mean get everybody out! Wheat, check the store, then meet me and Breed in the back," Cruz instructed, removing a briefcase from the rear of the Excursion.

Walking into the store, Diddy slipped right behind the counter. Without raising the AK-47 from his side, but making it visible, he emptied the cash register. He then took the black girl's ID and gave her all of the money, brushing her firm breast as he passed it to her.

"Look, shawdy! Take this and be quiet. I'll bring ya ID to you later. Now go home," he commanded her. "Remember, I got yo' address."

The nervous girl took the money, gathered her things, and left shakingly. By now Wheat had swept the store and was going to meet Breed and Cruz in the rear office.

166

"Arturo! Who is your friend?" Poppy asked. He was totally unaware of what was going on.

"Poppy, this is Breed. Breed, Poppy," Cruz introduced them.

At that very moment Wheat entered the office holding an AK-47.

"Oh! What is this, Arturo?" Poppy was clearly shaking at this point.

"Calm down, Poppy. He's with me. And that's only protection. You know, a lotta people aren't too happy to see me. How about you, Poppy? Are you happy to see me?" Cruz asked.

"Arturo? Why wouldn't I be happy to see you?"

"Because time and people change, Poppy. Take me for instance. I've changed, and I'm back to change things. And a lotta people aren't willin' to change. They're, what do us Amerikkkans call it? Yeah, financially secure. Change might threaten that security."

Removing the contract from his inner pocket, he tossed it onto the desk in front of the old man. Poppy looked over the papers quickly, then the old man looked up with even more surprise in his expression.

"What is this, Arturo? I'm not selling the store."

"Oh, yeah! You are selling the store. Today! Right now, Poppy! You've over charged your last customer. And you've sold your last kilo outta the upstairs apartment. I've watched you do business as usual every since I've been home. Yet you told me, 'I don't see our old friends anymore'. Sign the papers!" Cruz said.

"Is this what it's all about? Money! After all I've done for you? You nig..." Poppy stopped mid syllable, realizing that he had slipped.

"Go ahead. Say it.... Poppy, you've never done shit for anybody but yourself. Fuck you! You used everybody that came through that door. Suckin' the blood outta our community to take back to your suburban hideout. Amongst your Jewish friends! But those same friends won't allow you to set up shop in their community. Sign the fuckin' papers!" Cruz spat.

"Fuck you, Cruz! I was good to you! And I won't be pushed around. I'm not signing shit!" Poppy yelled.

At that instance Cruz open-hand slapped the old man across the face. *Whop!* Causing blood and spittle to fly over on Breed. Using one hand to free his pistol, Cruz grabbed the old man and drug him from behind the desk.

"Sign the papers, Wheat! I'ma kill this fuckin' snake," Cruz barked.

"Wait! Please! I'll sign it!" Poppy cried, dropping real tears.

Releasing him, Cruz had to turn his head. This was something he had hated to do. Poppy signed the contract giving Cruz full ownership of the store, the adjoining cleaners (which was being leased by some white folks), and the two apartments which were situated above the store.

"The briefcase," Cruz said, pointing it out to Poppy. "It's yours. Give me my keys and don't ever let me catch you or any of your people in my neighborhood."

The old man took the briefcase containing $175,000, dropped the store keys, and exited the building.

"Wheat, walk him out. Breed, shake this place down extra good. New locks, new alarms, and I want cameras everywhere."

Cruz then began walking towards the front of the store.

"E, stay here with Breed. I'ma send somebody back to help yall," Cruz instructed.

He and Palmer walked out to meet Steve and Wheat at the cars. "Who was the skirt?" he then asked Palmer.

"I don't know. I got her ID, though. I sent her home with all of the money," Palmer replied.

"Okay, find out what kinda sense she got. Make her the manager. I want this place back open and running at 20% profit. The rest goes to payroll and community funds. Tell her to hire someone else to help her. I also want a man here every second that it's open." Cruz continued. "Wheat, I wanna know who's livin' upstairs and what they're payin' for rent. Make it reasonable. And let them crackas know that they need to find somewhere to go. I want 'em out!"

With that said, everybody went about their business.

Chapter 14

They don't live that long/ Before they grown they be dead and gone/ But I'll be waitin' 'til they come back home/ Some niggas died for theirs/ Some lost they lives...I wanna buy me a Benz/ But I'm fifty grand short/ How I'ma get this cheese/ Wit' out a nigga gettin' caught/ Six-two in the jungle now....

The cheap system at Big Mac's blared as girls, both young and old, danced for tips and men sat around drinking and fantasizing.

"You wanna hit this?" Moehead asked DaDa.

"What that is?" DaDa asked as he downed his third X-pill with the last of the Moet.

"Damn, jit! How many of them muthafuckas you gon' take?"

Taking the mixture of weed and cocaine rolled up in the El Poducto, DaDa just looked at him. The death of his cousin Headquartaz had been hard to deal with. Ole Bluey was due out of the hospital today, and they were to bury his cousin tomorrow.

"Where Smash, BoePete and them niggas at? I ain't got all day to be sittin' up in this shit," DaDa said.

"Hey, hoe! Yeah! You! Brang me another *Moe*," Moehead ordered, throwing the young lady a hundred dollar bill. She took it without contest and quickly returned with the champagne.

"You holla'd at Chico?" Moehead asked DaDa.

"Nah. But I see the nigga been textin' me though."

"He say that last money was three stacks short."

"Man, money always a few stacks short fuckin' wit' Chico. My hoe counted that bread twice! Chico either can't count or he fulla shit."

"When you say ya *hoe counted the bread*, who is you talkin' 'bout? Not that hoe, Cola?"

"Yeah! That's who. That's my hoe ain't it?" DaDa shot back.

"Man, that hoe a booster!"

"What the fuck that mean?" DaDa fired back.

"Nigga! It mean the hoe cop her grits and greens by stealing! The hoe a thief! A goddamn kleptomaniac! And we missin' three muthafuckin' grand. You tell me what the fuck it mean, young-smart-ass-nigga," Moehead capped.

"Look, man! I don't wanna hear that sucka shit. We givin', nawl, I'm givin' this nigga $250,000 a wop. And he fucked up 'bout three stacks?"

"Nah, jit. Chico ain't petty, playa. It's ya bitch that's fucked up. Head left you in pocket. Now, if you wanna stay in pocket, you betta get that roguish ass hoe outcha business. Square business! Keep all them bitches outcha business," Moehead told the younger man.

"Yeah, alight. From now on, you count the shit! Since you so damn smart."

Just then Smash and BoePete walked in with Big Shorty. Big Shorty was not originally from around the way, but had come around from Carol City when Dutch and E4 got jammed up. He was a pretty likable dude, so they continued to let him hang around. More so as a favor to Dutch.

"What up, nigga? What they do?" Big Shorty asked as they all sat down.

"Dig, man, I got a line on who killed Head. It was Cruz, man," Smash reported.

"That wasn't no military secret! Yall niggas is procastinatin'. I said from the get start let's pop the nigga's top. Head dead and yall wanna hold all type of UN meetings," BoePete spat angerly.

"Nigga, what you done did beside come to every meeting, complain, and pick yo' money up?" Moehead asked.

"I found out that Cruz ridin' a black Max, and that he fuckin' wit' this real-estate hoe out in Carol City, wit' a silver Act," BoePete returned.

"Then why he still breathin'?" Moehead asked, staring the man down.

BoePete looked to DaDa for an answer. DaDa shook his head.

"I don't know, man. I saw the dude. That wasn't the dude Cruz. So yall make the call. It's whatever wit' me," DaDa stated, still shaking his head.

"Fuck it! I'll call it. Kill the nigga and let the good Lord sort it all out," Smash decided.

Chapter 15

"Bless this house," Cruz said cheerfully as he walked through the door of Tamika's small apartment.

"Fuck you!" Tamika returned scornfully. She wore a frown on her usually happy face.

"You are far too kind." Cruz continued. "Where is my main man?"

"Oh? He's ya main man now, huh? Nigga, please! That boy calls you everyday, and you don't have enough sense in your radical mind to call him back. All that shit you was writin' from jail! Then came ya nasty ass 'round here and raped me, then stole my goddamn car. Why haven't me or Des seen or heard anything from you since the lil' trip to the county fare? Maybe you shoulda stayed wit' Pimp."

"Listen beautiful," Cruz continued softly, pulling her to him. "You know how I feel about my work. But off the no bullshit, things are gonna change. Okay?" He kissed her. "Now where is my son?"

Tamika still pouted in an attempt to suppress her smile. "He's in his room."

Entering the room without knocking, Cruz found his son, Des, listening to Ice Cube's *The Nigga You Love To Hate* and playing video games.

"What's up?" Cruz began.

"Just chillin'," Des responded without looking up from his game.

Still standing, Cruz took a quick survey of his son's room.

"I see you have *Black August*. Do you understand it?"

"Yeah, I've read it a few times. I can't really say I agree with all of it, but it's a good read."

"Maybe one day when you're not too busy with your games we'll sit down and build on it."

Dropping the control, Des spun around to face his father.

"Busy! *When I'm not too busy?* Man, you've been gone my whole life. Then when you get home you're never around. I've seen you maybe eight times in the last ten months. And only then when you...."

Cutting him off Cruz interjected. "Look man, you are one hundred percent right. It's just, man, it's hard to really face you knowin' I've let you down. I never had a pops around to show me shit! So I don't really know how to be one. I do what I do, the money, the books, the clothes, because I love you. Des, all I've ever wanted was for you to grow strong and be a man."

Standing to his feet, young Des spat, "Fuck the money, man! All those nights you was gone, I didn't pray to God for no money. I prayed for you! I need a daddy! You spend all your time playin' daddy to the world, and you forgot about your own family. First Family! What is that when you put your own family last? Grandma don't hear from you, and momma is stupid enough to be sittin' around here waitin' for you to *never show up*. Man, I'm out."

"Look, son, hold on! Shit's gonna get better. I came here tonight to give you and your mother a present, and my word that you'll be seein' a lot more of me. Do you know why?"

"What's up, man?" Des asked.

At that point Tamika entered the room. "What's goin' on in here?"

Des said nothing. He just stood looking at them both. Tamika looked from Cruz to Des and back before asking again. "Well, what's goin' on?"

"Look," Cruz started. "I've been goin' through a lot. It's no excuse, and I truly plan on doin' better. As a matter of fact, here."

"What is this?" Tamika asked.

"It's a blank check signed by me, and a list of homes I've been lookin' at. I felt that you should be the one to pick where we're goin' to be livin'."

At this, not even the angry young Des could suppress his smile.

"Cruz, are you okay?" Tamika asked.

"Yeah! Of course. And that's only part of it. Do you remember that cleaners on 103rd?"

"Yeah, down the street from your mom's old house."

"Well, the paper work is also in there. You and Des are the new owners."

It really pleased him to see the Joy on their happy faces.

"You mean it? When are we moving?" Des asked with much excitement.

"As soon as yo' mother quits her job, picks out the house, and has it decorated and ready to live in. If she starts tomorrow, maybe we'll be in it in a week or so."

Tamika hugged him and passionately kissed him. "I love you," she said.

"I love you even more." Cruz continued. "But I have a few loose ends I need to tie up, and I want you, Des, to come along with me. I'm goin' to D.C. for a few days."

Des just smiled and shook his head yes. Cruz then turned to leave, but before he could exit the front door he was stopped by the sound of his son's voice.

"Dad!" Des shouted.

"What's up, son?"

"I love you, dad."

"And I love you right back." Cruz turned and left.

* * *

The trip to D.C. would be just what the doctor ordered. It would afford Cruz the opportunity to bond with his son, as well as relax a bit. And with the trouble of Kunta's escape on the horizon, Cruz felt it best to put his lawyer on point, clear his schedule for the next week, and arrange for his son, Wheat, and Palmer to meet him at the airport.

As the airplane prepared to land, young Des being seated in the window seat, was amazed at the happenings in Hanes Point. It was his very first trip to the DC - Virginia area.

"Diddy, what is that?" he asked while pointing to a huge statue coming out of the ground.

"Oh, that right there. That's the awakening. I guess it's supposed to be Jesus. I don't know. Let ya father tell it, Jesus was a black man. I'ma take you through there 'fore we leave, aiight?"

"Aiight!" Des answered with a big smile on his face. He really liked ole Diddy. As did most people. He was a very fun-loving dude.

After collecting their baggage, the four men exited the airport to a line of waiting taxicabs.

"Where to?" The cabbie asked.

"Watergate at Landmark, slim, Yogum Parkway," Diddy told the driver.

When the cab stopped the attendant immediately recognized Diddy and opened the gate.

"How are you doing, sir?"

"Fine," Diddy replied, handing the young man a fifty dollar bill. The man smiled and cuffed the bill, knowing that taking tips was strictly prohibited.

As the cab made its way to the rear building, Des' face was plastered to the window; as there were women in g-strings and all different types of one and two piece swimming suits. Upon seeing Diddy they all smiled and waved, "Hey Diddy!"

The men all went inside and everyone showered and got fresh. They dropped Des off in S.E. Washington on Good Hope Road. Diddy's baby's mother and their son lived out Southeast in some very rough apartments. As they all got out and were exiting the elevator on the ninth floor, Diddy was stopped at the call of his name. "Diddy!" Turning to see whom had called him, he came face to chest with a big 260 pound Leviathan. The man had a distinguishing scar running from his eyebrow to the top of his head.

"Bulldog!" Diddy yelled as he embraced the man. After introducing everyone Diddy promised his old friend that he would be in touch with him before he left the city.

Bulldog had been living in those same apartments for the past 30 years.

Stopping at apartment 912, they were met at the door by a radiant sister in a flowered sundress.

"May I help you?" she asked sarcastically.

"Girl, get yo' ass outta the way! Where is Man?"

"He's in his room. This must be Des," the lady said.

"Yeah, this him. I want you and Man to look out for him while we go handle some business," Diddy told his baby's mother while handing her a stack of money.

After the two youths were properly introduced, Diddy made it perfectly clear that they were to stay the fuck off of the Avenue. The Avenue was a very fast paced strip where most of the hustling took place in the city. It was also the very reason why D.C. lead the nation in homicides.

Coming through the lobby doors, the sun glistened off of the shiny burnt-orange 69 Pontiac Firebird.

"Make damn sho' you wipe ya feet off," Diddy said, admiring his customized classic. It had been his dream car growing up. And it was the first car he bought after being released from Lorton in 1984. Now, after serving his last prison sentence, he had spent over $60,000 having it totally restored from the frame up.

"Fuck this old ass car!" Wheat said.

"Nah, fuck you! Young ass nigga," Diddy spat back.

"Go to 51, man."

"Ain't that Jay shit?" Cruz asked.

"Jay who?" Diddy asked.

"Jay! The fat nigga who worked out in mailbags with us. You know, the nigga who say he played with Chuck," Wheat said, laughing.

"Slim? That lying ass nigga! Hell nawl! That nigga probably ain't even from the city."

* * *

After getting two fifths of Remmy Martin V.S.O.P. and a case of green bottles from 51, they headed to Fort Dupont Park for the Jazz Festival.

"Got-damn! This muthafucka packed!" Diddy yelled.

"Yeah! Off-the-no bullshit. Let's go up by the stage," Wheat said.

Looking around for a nice place to settle near the stage they encounter four seductive looking sisters sitting on blankets. Diddy, being the self-proclaimed Mac of the trio, spotted his mark and went into action. The lady was of medium build, light-brown complexion, with hazel eyes. She wore her straight black hair in a ponytail that hung below her shoulders. Diddy could see that she had on yellow panties, matching her yellow mini skirt.

"Hello beautiful. You mind if we join yall?" Diddy macked.

"That all depends," she sassed, still watching the band perform.

"On what?" Diddy asked as he began to seat himself next to her and get comfortable.

"On whether yall sharing what's in them bags. And nigga, how you know my ole man ain't out here, while you gettin' all cozy. You a bold nigga," she returned.

"Sweetness, you ain't seen nothing. I can be down right rude! Ya hear me? Now ya man is the furthest thing from my mind, and to be truthful, I had planned on sharing more than these drinks with ya pretty ass," Diddy capped while moving in closer to her.

"Girl, no he didn't," one of her friends said as they all laughed.

"Oookay!" Continued the first girl. "So what's your name?"

"Diddy."

"Diddy?" She frowned.

"Yeah. That's slick for Daddy. But you can call me either one. What's your name, suga?"

"Meagan, but all my friends call me Juicey."

"I can sho' see why," Diddy continued looking between her legs. "I think lil' man done found himself a new home," he capped,

179

now massaging his slight erection.

By now Wheat had taken a seat between her friends Tonya and Melisa, whom were both a shade darker than Meagan, and wore their hair cut short like Halle Berry. Tonya was the prettier of the two, but they could have easily passed for sisters. Cruz, being the designated driver, removed a book from his things and sat down to read. With all that was going on, a woman was the last thing on his mind. He wished he had brought Des along. As he settled into the smooth sounds of the Jazz pumping off of the stage, he was interrupted by the words *Black August*.

"Huh?"

"*Black August*. The book you're reading," she pointed out.

Cruz looked at the book in his hand and then up into the face of the woman who'd spoken.

"Elga! Elga Wynn?"

"Cruz! Is that you, Arthur Cruz? Boy! I have been looking everywhere for you. I drove all over your neighborhood trying to find your mom's house. What are you doing here?"

"I was tryin' to read until you walked over," Cruz responded.

"So is that how it's gonna be?" Elga asked sadly.

"You said we were friends. Then just left me in prison to bid alone."

"I had problems. But I never stopped thinking about you. I've read your book over and over. Your mind is brilliant! I even came to hear you speak in Atlanta," Elga stated.

"Did you enjoy the lecture?"

"Can I please sit down?.... I'm truly sorry."

From what he could see, she was sincere in her expression. Standing there in her blue-jean skirt and tight fitting Baby Phat T-shirt, her large breast were a very beautiful sight to behold. Her complexion was light. Soft expression. Her eyes were brown. Nice full lips. The micro-braids complemented the roundness of her face. Broad hips. Her thighs were thick and appeared to be soft to the touch. Cruz was open! How could he deny her?

They had been high school friends. Cruz had even dated her cousin Felicia before he'd met Elga. They'd shared hours conversing, laughing, and visiting one another. There always seemed to be an obvious attraction, at least in his mind. Yet, neither of the two ever acted on those feelings.

After Cruz was arrested and convicted, Elga really stepped up and held him down in the beginning. This only intensified what he was feeling. Then one day, just like she'd entered his life, out of nowhere, she was gone.

"Why not?" he answered, allowing her to sit down.

"Thank you. You look good, Mr. *God's Gift,*" Elga said, smiling.

"Thank you. You look very nice yourself."

Her teeth were so even and white. Her nails manicured. Even her small feet were pretty and well kept. Her panties were orange. Imprint, fat.

"So how have you been doing?" she asked.

"Not as good as I could have been doing."

"Under what circumstances?"

"Had I met you before."

"Before what?"

"Before Felicia.... Before all of this...." Cruz answered.

"Are you serious?" she blushed.

"I've always found you attractive. And before you up and left me, you had always been so responsive to my feelings and needs.... Even before my incarceration, I would find myself sittin', thinking about you."

"I don't know what to say." Elga smiled.

"Play a game," he said.

"What kind?"

"An honest game. A game of the mind. *Wish or Question*. You go first," he said.

"Question," she replied.

"Why did you leave me?"

"I was afraid. Afraid that I might start to care too much for you. And, and, I just didn't know what to do."

"Question," he said.

"Why didn't you ever acknowledge what you felt?" Elga asked.

"Because I was too smart to make an intelligent decision. I was stuck between saying something and bettering what we had, and not saying something that we might protect or save what we had. I guess I was afraid just like you."

"Wish," Elga said.

"That we were here alone," Cruz whispered, staring into her beautiful eyes. "Wish," he then said.

"That I had met you first," Elga replied.

With that said, he kissed her. She jumped and tried to retreat, but he advanced on her. Rummaging the innerings of her soft lips with his tongue, they volleyed back and forth before he finally captured her tongue and held it. He sucked it. Tasting the Hennessy and peppermint that she had previously consumed. She reclaimed it and took hold of his. His wish had come true. In that instance they were alone. Until commotion from the next blanket brought them back to this world.

"Bitch! I know you ain't layin' yo' funky ass up unda no blanket with this nigga," the dude yelled.

Recognizing the voice, Meagan's eyes flew open to face her boyfriend, standing before her in rage. Diddy was still laying there with his eyes closed.

"Don't just lay yo' musky-ass there like you ain't heard me, bitch," the dude yelled again before reaching down and snatching the covers off of Meagan and Diddy, exposing the fact that she had been jacking Diddy off.

"Slim? What the fuck? Nigga, is you crazy! Gimme that damn blanket!" Diddy yelled while trying to fix his pants.

"Bitch! I ain't gonna tell you no more to get off ya ass," Meagan's boyfriend yelled.

"And nigga, I ain't gon' tell you no more to set that goddamn blanket down!" Diddy countered.

"You need to mind ya business, slim! This between me and my hoe."

"I got yo' hoe, nigga," Diddy said while coming to a standing position. But before he came fully erect, he was met with a straight-right down the pipe.

Whop! The fist connected. Sending Diddy down on one knee. By now Cruz was up and going over to assist him man. But Wheat stopped him.

"Nah, let the ole nigga work. He got him," Wheat said.

"What?" Cruz questioned.

"Let him work," Wheat said with confidence.

While Diddy was still down on one knee shaking his head, the younger dude rushed him. Diddy stood at the last instance and grabbed him, just holding on while he got his senses together. The younger man struggled to move him, and ever so often he'd reel off a quick combination. Diddy was now standing off, south paw, timing the youth's advances. The younger man threw a jab. Diddy slipped it. Another jab. Same results.

"Man, I'm 'bout to stop this shit," Cruz said.

"Nah, man! Let him work. I'm telling you, he got him," Wheat said.

The dude once again threw that jab out there, but this time he left it out there too long. Diddy got under him and hooked him in the kidney, causing the dude to fold. Then in one swift motion, Diddy came off of his hip in a stabbing motion. Diddy held the man to him and continued to strike in an upward motion.

"Hold up, slim! We better get him. He gon' kill shawdy!" Wheat yelled.

As the two of them pulled Diddy back, the dude collapsed to the ground. Diddy had blood all over him. He was looking wild-eyed and breathing heavily.

"Goddamn, slim?" Wheat exclaimed.

"Come on, man! Let's get the fuck outta here," Cruz snatched Diddy and the trio were off through the crowd.

The helpless man laid there in a pool of his own blood. Meagan kneeled crying beside him. Elga stared off into the direction which Cruz had fled. They had shared a lifetime in only a few minutes. And just as he'd appeared, out of nowhere, he was gone...

Chapter 16

Entering his office for the first time in three days, he saw that Palmer, Wheat, Breed, and Captain Jack were already there waiting for him. As he settled in and began checking his schedule and messages he saw that Ronni had left nearly twenty messages in the last three days, and that there were also eight messages from Elga.

After the awkward scenario in D.C. Cruz had returned to Miami and left that same day with his family – Des, Mother Cruz, and Tamika – to Universal Studios. Everyone had enjoyed the trip, while Cruz was just glad to have escaped the world and its demands for a short period.

"Have you seen the newspaper, slim?" Wheat asked.

"Nah, what's up?" Cruz replied.

"They jive doggin' you, slim. They got you wit' that Kunta shlt. Slim!? They talkin' 'bout niggas is terrorist and some more shit," Diddy said.

"Well, we gotta stop the bleeding before it gets bad. Have Elijah write a statement for the press, denouncing Kunta's actions as none revolutionary. Stating that we support and embrace freedom and its fighters, but the rape and torture of those women

185

was evil; and not the act of a freedom-fighter or a man of God…. I have a speech at Berry University tomorrow where I will personally deal with the issue and any questions concerning it and our supposed association with any so-called terrorist. Then I want it ran in the Familiar Post every week for the next two months, in place of Kunta's column," Cruz instructed before picking up the phone to call Elga.

"Hello…. yeah what's up…. I just got your messages…. Yeah, I was out of town…. of course I enjoyed your company…. Oh yeah?... so old boy died….. That's crazy…. Question…. Of course you'll see me again… I wish that dude woulda made it…. Okay, I'll write it down. What is it?.... Okay, I got it. I'll call before I come through," Cruz said and hung up.

"Damn, slim, who died? Not shawdy from the park in DC, huh, man?!" Diddy asked, worried as hell.

"Now look at this scared ass nigga! Shakin' like that ole ass Firebird. You wasn't scared when you was workin' shawdy," Wheat said, laughing.

"Look, Wheat! This shit ain't no jokin' matter, slim. You play too fuckin' much. Slim? The nigga dead?" Not only was Palmer nervous, but he was sad.

"Slim? What the fuck you thought happened to niggas when you put the knife in 'em? Not once! But we had to pull you off the nigga. Now you scared! If ya freak ass woulda kept ya shit in yo' pants this wouldn't have happened…. You fucked up, slim!" Wheat said, still laughing.

"So it's my fault a nigga sat me on my ass?" Palmer asked.

"Hold up, man! Yall chill. Shit happened, man. It's over wit'. The chick say that Meagan fucked up with you, though. So man, don't even holla at her…. Fuck it man, it is what it is," Cruz interjected.

With that said, everyone set out to accomplish what they may. The statement concerning Kunta was released and Cruz delivered a riotous two hour speech at Berry University to students, supporters, the press, and his critics. There were over 800 people in attendance.

The next two weeks were somewhat uneventful. Tamika found the house and they were indeed a family. Des was happy. Tamika was happy. And Cruz was still Cruz. Living, somewhere between heaven and hell. Existing. Scarred, but still breathing.

<u>One month later</u>.

Kunta, from his Algerian stronghold, released a statement for the first time since his brilliant coup d'etat. The vehicle he used to deliver his statement was his very own newspaper, The Militia. He bashed the United States Government, Cruz and his entire organization for their hypocrisy. He labeled Cruz a *charismatic coward*. He stated that "revolution was action, and not mere words. Arthur Cruz is a reactionary, not a revolutionary, and stands in the way of change with his rhetoric."

Thus the lines had been drawn, and the war of words began. Soldiers from both sides began to choose sides. Some defecting. Others standing strong. Almost everyone was suspicious of the other. There had been many death threats emailed and called in to the offices. It was indeed apocalypse now!

Chapter 17

Ronni sat at her desk shuffling through a mountain of paperwork. It seemed like forever had passed since she'd seen or heard from Cruz. He'd just up and left that night after dinner. Why? She questioned. Hurt. She was sad and hurt. She needed some kind of closure. She had parked and watched the Miami Lakes and North Miami residents. The men would come and go, but Cruz was never with them.

Going through the financial statements of Cruz's foundation, she found a return check signed by Cruz for $180,000. Purpose, a house down payment. He had bought another house, but through another agency. "Wise Satan, dumb devil," she thought to herself. After making a few phone calls Ronni had an address and was on her way out of the door.

Driving along, no music, just painful thoughts assailing her. She questioned herself, "What will I say? What should I say? How will he react?" She wondered should she just turn around. She couldn't! Curiosity would not allow it. Her pride would not let her.

Still driving along, her mind swam in an ocean of emotions. Confusion! This is what love flowered. She wiped a single tear.

Saddened. She wiped another. Anger! The thought of another woman. She banged the steering wheel.

All the while, Ronni never noticed the white Box Chevy following her. It had been in the parking lot of her office when she arrived for work and was now two car links behind her.

"Are you sure that's her?" the driver of the Chevy asked his partner.

"Look, nigga! Don't start wit' that stupid shit! You know damn well that's the bitch! Now the nigga changed sides, so he dyin' for that.... Fuck him!" the man's partner returned.

The two men in the backseat just listened as they continued to load rounds into the AR-15's and Mac-11's.

Crossing County Line Road, Ronni continued driving until she was in Hollywood. After checking the address she knew that she was near her destination. She decided to turn on the radio, taking her eyes off of the road for only a second to find 99-Jams. "Hhhooonnk!" sounded the horn of the oncoming car. Looking up from the radio Ronni found herself in the middle of the intersection, heading for a direct collision with a speeding car.

"Oh, shit!" she yelled.

Snatching the wheel of her car, the silver Acura veered left, just missing the car. Ronni flew through the red light, cursing herself. "Damn! Thank you God," she said out loud. Thinking, "Was that a sign? Should I turn around?" However, her pride wouldn't allow her to. Cruz had to be held accountable for his actions. Damn It! He owed her an explanation.

"You stupid muthafucka! You let the bitch get away!"

"Man, you seen that crazy ass hoe run through that red light and almost killed her muthafuckin' self!"

"I think ya scared ass tried to let her get away."

"Nigga, you can think what you wanna think! I'm out to slump a muthafucka, not get killed. Fuck that!"

"Man, if we don't find that hoe, today, I'ma kill you! Now *fuck that!*.... Sucka ass niggas... make me sick."

* * *

The smooth sounds of The Isley Brothers' *Living For The Love Of You* sounded beautifully throughout the sleek luxury sports coupe. Just as her nerves had began to calm, she spotted the house and was nervous all over again. Inside the gate was a clean '72 Cadillac convertible. It was a shiny royal-blue with a white top and all chrome Daytons. Outside the gate sat the all black Maxima that Cruz had been driving that first day in the park. She had been right! This was where he had been living.

Parking, she knocked on the screen door. Waiting. Her heart pounded! "Oh my God," she thought. Her worst fears had materialized. Approaching her was a short red woman.

"May I help you?" Tamika asked from inside the house.

"Yes, I'm here to see Mr. Cruz," Ronni answered.

"Okay, he here. But who is you?"

"Maybe I should be asking you the same thing."

Tamika laughed. "Excuse me? But you're on my porch, at my house, askin' me about my man. Bitch, I think you done asked enough questions. Now what you maybe should do is find ya dog-ass another lawn to trespass or linger on, because I'm Marmaduke round here," Tamika spat.

"You open this door, *Ms. Duke*, and I'll give you ya bitch," Ronni said calmy.

By now Cruz had walked up. Surprised, he stared at Ronni in disbelief.

190

"What are you doin' here?" Cruz asked.

"What do you think I'm doing here?" Ronni spat back.

"Oh, you know her?" Tamika spun to face Cruz. "Who is this bitch, and why did you give her our address? I can't believe you, nigga! You a disrespectful ass nigga! I hate you!"

Tamika then opened the door and pushed past Ronni, who was merely standing there eyeing Cruz. Tamika was not the only one who hated him at that instance. If only looks could kill. Cruz would have been a dead man.

As Tamika pulled off in her car, Cruz and Ronni began to openly argue. This brought Des out of his room.

"What's up, Dad?" Des asked.

"Nothin', son. Go back to your room. I need to talk to her."

* * *

The Chevy continued to patrol the area in search of the silver Acura. "That hoe gotta be around here somewhere," the driver said.

"You better damn well pray she is. 'Cause yo' life depends on it muthafucka!"

At this point the man in the backseat spoke up for the first time. Pointing, he excitedly yelled, "Fuck that hoe in the Acura! There go Cruz right there!"

"Right where?"

"Right there!" They all looked in the direction in which the dude was pointing.

"Jackpot! Yoke this bitch!"

Making a U-turn they sped ahead and came to a sudden stop. Everybody exited the vehicle except the driver. Guns in hand, they began unloading.

Whoop! Whoop! Whoop!.... Doom! Doom!.... Whoop! Whoop!... Doom! Doom! Doom! Doom! Doom! the weapons exploded.

Satisfied, the men jumped back into the white Chevy and sped off.

* * *

Stopping in mid-sentence, Cruz looked around. Des came running back out of his room. "What was that?" Des asked.

Cruz thought, *Tamika!* He took the Mac-10 from under the couch cushion and ran down the street. His son Des was right behind him. Ronni just stood there for a minute before getting into her car and following them. Spotting the black Max alone at the stop sign, Cruz knew that he was too late. The closer he came to the car, the stronger the smell of gunpowder lingered in the air. He was in tears as he dropped his gun and opened the door. Tamika was plastered to the steering wheel, her right arm laid twitching on the passenger seat. Blood and brain fluids covered the windshield.

By then young Des had caught up to his father. Cruz slammed the door shut and turned to his son.

"Go home, son," he said as tears ran down his face.

"What happen, man? Who is that? Who in Momma car?"

"Go home, son!"

Des tried to dash around his father for the car door, but Cruz caught him and held him.

"Let me go, man!" Des yelled.

"Stop it, son! You don't need to see her like that.... She's gone."

"Let me go, man!" Des broke free. "You make me sick, man! I hate you! If you hada stayed yo' ass in prison, and away from us, my momma would still be here! You killed her, man! You killed my momma...."

"No, son. I'm...."

"Nah, man, fuck you! Stay away from me. I hate you, and I never want to see you again!"

Des then turned and ran. Ronni opened the car door and immediately began to vomit. She sat there and watched as Cruz cried and struggled to regain his composure. Hearing the sirens in the distance, Ronni picked up Cruz's gun and drove away. In tears, she thought, "how could this have happened?"

THREE DAYS LATER

...up early/ Dressed in black/ Don't ask why/ A nigga dressed in a suit and tie/ They killed a nigga that I went to school wit', (Damn!)/ I tell ya life ain't shit to fool wit'... I still hear the screams from his mother/ As my nigga laid dead in the gutta... Ice Cube leaked from Cruz's home system. It was his son's CD. He had not seen or heard anything from Des, personally, since the day Tamika passed forms. He had made several attempts to speak with his son, whom had been living with Ma Cruz, but Des refused to talk. Today would be the day they laid Tamika to rest and an irretrievable piece of both Cruz and Des would be buried with her.

Everybody sat around Cruz's house listening to the music and drinking. They were due at the church in two hours. Cruz would not be speaking. Today he was simply relegated to his misery.... Further discombobulation, security factors and Des' emotions, had divided the family. Cruz would not be riding with the family either, nor would he be seated with them. He had even questioned whether he should go at all.

"Slim really fucked up," Wheat said.

193

"Yeah, I can see it. He feel like it's all his fault. Then his people ain't really fuckin' wit' him. I just hope my guy can pull through this," said Breed.

"He gon' be aiight," Palmer continued. "Trust and believe. The boy a soldier! Just give him some time and space. He'll be aiight."

"Yeah, I just hate to see him like this. Kill me, slim! After we pay our respects, them niggas gon' pay theirs, with they life," Wheat was deadly serious.

"I feel you, man. But we don't have a clue who did this."

"Off the no bullshit, it coulda been the ole Cuban nigga, it coulda been Head them people. Then Kunta.... Damn, him and Zoe and them."

"Diddy, fuck Zoe! And I give a fuck less about Kunta bitch ass. Fuck 'em all! The same shells I'ma use to kill Smash and his lil' set, I gotta hundred more for them funny talkin' muthafuckas."

"I'm witcha, my guy. But let's just wait and see what Cruz wanna do, man."

"Slim? You keep sayin', *but.* The only thang come after *butt* is some shit. Straight bullshit! Look at the nigga! You tell me what the fuck he want! Yeah, I'ma wait. I'ma wait 'til this funeral over. Then I'ma punish every nigga I 'think' had somethin' to do wit' it! Startin' wit' them hoe-ass-niggas in Silver Blue," Wheat finished.

The funeral was packed. There had to be over a thousand people in attendance. Cruz saw people he hadn't seen since elementary school. In fact, a great deal of the funeral attendants he had never seen in his life.

It was a very sad occasion. Young Des broke down twice. As did many family members and close friends. It had taken all of the man in Cruz to keep from falling apart. He had to be strong, because all eyes were truly on him. Some were sympathetic and understanding. Other stares were cold and full of hatred.

By the end of the service Cruz was numb. He had not shed a single tear, though he was dying inside. When it was time for his row to stand and walk to view the body, Cruz went in the opposite direction. Wheat hurried himself to get in front of Cruz, because Breed had been in front of Cruz and had not noticed that he was leaving the church.

Just as Cruz made it to the exit, Wheat reached in front of him and opened the door. Himself going out first with Cruz right on his heels.

Kak! Kak! The two explosions barely above a whisper.

Splat! The liquid hit Cruz, covering his forehead.

"What the fuck?" He looked up to see if it was dripping from the ceiling. Seeing nothing, he wiped his forehead and looked at his hand. "Blood?"

At that instance they sounded again. *Kak! Kak! Kak! Kak!* Wheat was sent flying back into Cruz, knocking him to the floor. As they hit the ground, with Wheat landing on top of him, the church door was riddled with bullets. *Kak! Kak! Kak! Kak! Kak!*

"Get up Wheat!" Cruz yelled. "Get off me, dog! We gotta move!"

But Wheat was dead. It was his blood that had covered Cruz's forehead when the first shots were fired. Cruz heard a car door shut and footsteps approaching as the gunfire grew louder. Reaching in Wheat's waistline he drew the Glock .40 and began firing in the blind. *Tat! Tat! Tat! Tat! Tat! Tat! Tat! Tat! Tat!* the .40 went off.

When Palmer, Breed, and Captain Jack finally made it to the door they opened fire as well. *Doom! Doom! Doom!... Pop! Pop! Pop! Pop!... Doom! Doom!*

One of the gunmen was cut down before he could make it back to the car. The gunfire ceased and people began pouring out of the church, running past Cruz as he kneeled holding Wheat.

"Come on, man!" Breed said. "We gotta get the hell outta here, man!"

"Nah man… I'ma hold Wheat down until the ambulance get here. He gon' make it." Cruz was crying.

"Look, slim! I know it hurts…'cause, 'cause slim was my man, too. But he dead! Now you gotta let him go! Come on man! Let him go," Palmer said, pulling Cruz up. They all jumped into the black Dodge Caravan and sped off.

"Where you wanna go, man?" Breed asked as they drove along.

Cruz just sat there. He said nothing. He thought even less. At that point he was finished.

"Aye, just hit the expressway. He can't go home. Hell, we can't go home. Go to the hotel and let's think this shit through. We gotta get off the street with him lookin' like that," Palmer instructed.

After checking into a cheap motel on Biscayne, the men sat in silence. Each caught up in their own thoughts. Cruz knew that that bullet was meant for him. It was this train of thought that led him to reflect on the dream. *Ronni!* Had she been the cause of it all? In the dream their sexual pleasure had been interrupted. A sign that the relationship was wrong. In the dream his mother was killed. Now, in reality, the mother of his child laid dead. The death of Breed turned out to be Wheat. The images blurred. His thoughts became cloudy. He laid back on the bed and dosed off. His mind had never been so tired.

"Aye, look man. Slim need some clothes. I'm sure he could use some squares, as I'm sure we could all use a drink. Let's go to the store while he's sleep," said Palmer.

"You just gon' leave him here?" Breed asked.

"He'll be aiight until we get back. Nobody knows we here. So just let him rest. He need it."

Chapter 18

"Aye, this the last stop. Pull in right up there. I'm hungry as a slave! 'Sides, once we go in and get to drankin' and shit, you gonna want somethin' on ya stomach," Palmer stated.

The three men exited the van and entered the Haitian restaurant on 54th Street. They all ordered and stood waiting to receive their food.

"Slim, what's up wit' that black ass nigga over their watchin' us?" Palmer asked Breed.

"Diddy, every nigga over there black as a muthafucka. Which one you talkin' 'bout?"

"The nigga wit' the dreads. The one keep lookin' over here."

"Man, I don't know dude. But you know these muthafuckas is funny style. They don't really fuck wit' us," Breed returned.

"Aye, Jack... ain't they said it was a white Chevy that hit ole girl?"

"Yeah," Captain Jack replied.

"Well, I want you to go get in the van. If shawdy get in that Chevy, I want you to follow him. Me and Breed gon' get the food and start walkin' back towards the hotel. We gon' be on front street, so you can pick us up."

The dude left the restaurant, and sure enough, he and two of his friends got into the white Box Chevy. Captain Jack fell in behind them and followed them a very short distance to Palm Gardens Housing Projects. The same place that they had met Kunta's man, Zoe.

"Muthafuckas," Jack said to himself while making a U-turn to go and pick up the others. Making it to Biscayne he turned left and continued down. Palmer and Breed were just ahead of him.

"Aye, the dude Zoe had to be wit' that shit. 'Cause the bamma in the Chevy went right to them damn projects where we met Zoe at," Captain Jack explained.

"That's crazy!" Breed said aloud. He still could not believe that Kunta would do such a thing to Cruz.

"I figured that shit! That's why I told yall from day one that I didn't like or trust 'em." Palmer paused before continuing. "I know I told yall that the restaurant was the last stop, but I'ma need to make one more."

"Where at?" Jack asked.

"Palm Gardens. I'm 'bout to *fuck slim over.*"

"Man, is you crazy? Do you know how many of 'em be out there? Not just hangin', but them dudes be strapped!" Breed said.

"Stop the van, Jack," Palmer commanded.

"What's up?" Breed was confused at Palmer's actions.

"Hand me that joint from under there."

Taking the Mac-11 from the stash-spot, he handed it to Diddy. Still confused as to what was happening, he again questioned, "What's up, my guy?"

"Either I'ma get out and walk to Palm Gardens, or you gon' get out and let me go crush them niggas. 'Cause, slim? You sound like you scared to death."

"Nah Diddy, man. Shit ain't like that! We gotta think, homie."

"Shawdy, we been thinkin' too long. It's time a muthafucka put that muthafuckin' work in. So who getting out, you or me?"

"Nobody Diddy, man. Let's go get 'em," Breed answered.

Captain Jack pulled the Caravan back into traffic. Approaching Palm Gardens, Palmer began to instruct.

"Look Breed, we gon' put you out at the entrance. Get the AK. Me and Jack gon' ride through and see what we can see. I hope Zoe or that young nigga in the Chevy be out there. Either way, I'ma crush as many niggas as I can. You make sure we have a route to get outta this muthafucka."

"Aiight. Gimme one of them pineapples too," Breed said before getting out of the van.

As Breed headed off on foot, Captain Jack drove on.

Palmer left the passenger seat and was now positioned on the second row of seats with the sliding door slightly ajar.

"Look, slim. Look! The young nigga. Keep goin' all the way 'round and come back," Palmer instructed.

Captain Jack did as he was told. But Palmer stopped him. He had an idea. He took the food they had ordered, placed two hand grenades in the bag, and handed them to Jack. Taking the Mac-11, he got out of the van and walked along the side, opposite the group. They were situated about 25 yards from the spot where they had left Breed, near the entrance. So if need be, he was confident that he could make it on foot. Stopping the van in front of the group, Jack let down his window.

"Say, one of you kats got some coc'?" asked Jack.

"Who wanna know?" the driver of the Chevy asked. He appeared to be the leader of the little group.

"I wanna know, that's why I asked you. Now, do you have some coc' or not?"

"No! No coc'. You look like the police."

Jack laughed as he pulled the pins on the hand grenades. Throwing the bag of food near the group, he slowly began to pull away.

"No shawdy, I ain't no police," Jack said as the van drifted forward.

"Oh! You wanna throw shit at muthafuckas?" the youngster yelled.

"I don't want no problems, son," Jack replied.

"But I do!" said Palmer as he began to empty the Mac-11 into the group.

Kak! Kak! Kak! Kak! Kak! Kak! Kak! Kak! Kak! Kak! Kak! Kak! Kak! Kak! Kak! Kak!

The driver of the Chevy was the first to catch it. Since he was the first to speak, Palmer made sure he was the first to die. Two more of the youths were cut down by the invisible swords before they ducked behind the Chevy. Palmer was now at a run, still firing the Mac, because Jack had began to push the Caravan a little faster.

Boom! Boom! The grenades went off, one after the other, sending more of the group to hell. And those who had managed to avoid the deadly offerings of the grenades were forced out into the open, to find Palmer still banging!

Kak! Kak! Kak! Kak! Kak! Kak! Kak! Kak! the Mac-11 spat. It was like shooting fish in a barrel.

Doom! Doom! Doom! Doom! Doom! Came the return fire. The shooter missed Palmer but riddled the van. Palmer fired over his shoulder while running to the opposite side of the van. He heard Breed talking back to the Haitians with the AK-47.

Backa! Backa! Backa! Backa! Backa! Backa! Backa! the AK-47 called.

The van was veering strong to the left, heading right for the empty guard's booth. *Crash!*

Palmer and Breed ran over to the van. Jack was leaning over spitting up blood.

"Damn, slim!" Palmer said.

"Come on, let's get him outta there!"

"Nawl, man…. I think they got the ole boy this time. Can't feel my damn legs. Damn!" Captain Jack coughed a few times before continuing. "Yall go 'head. I'ma… have to stay… But gimme that pineapple Breed, so I can finish the game."

"Nah, slim," Palmer said.

"Go 'head!" Jack yelled. "This ain't nothing. I'm dyin' for something."

Handing him the grenade, Breed said, "I love you, homie."

Jack smiled. "God is the greatest!"

Palmer and Breed threw their last grenade and ran off. They were clear of the entrance before they heard it explode. Still running they anticipated the final explosion, which would guarantee their escape, but seal the fate of a dear friend and soldier.

The Haitians continued firing as they approached the van. After seeing that there was no return fire, they stopped and walked up to the window. The van had been totaled! Looking in they saw Jack leaning on the steering wheel. Jack slowly pulled the pin on the pineapple and opened his eyes.

"Surprised!?!" he said before the deadly apparatus spoke its last words, ending all conversation and all life in that circumference.

At the sound of the double explosion Breed and Palmer began to walk. Throwing the Mac-11 and the AK-47 aside, they sat on the bus stop and watched as the police flew past, en route to the scene that had claimed Captain Jack's life.

Chapter 19

"Damn, slim! You just gon' sleep your life away?"

Cruz looked up. Confused, he began to rub his eyes. The sleep was removed, but the confusion remained.

"Damn, shawdy!" the man continued talking. "What? You actin' like you don't know a nigga, but you lookin' like you done seen a ghost or some shit."

Cruz sat all the way up in the bed. He looked at his shirt and there was blood on it. He then looked up at the man again.

"Man, Diddy said you was dead. Damn, homie! I swear I didn't mean to leave you out there like that.... But you don't even look hurt. Who blood is this?" Cruz asked, referring to the blood that covered his clothes.

"It's my blood, shawdy. But not mine alone. It's the blood of the people. We dyin', slim. We gon' lose a whole nother generation if you don't step ya game up. You gotta make 'em listen," Wheat said.

"Man, stop talkin' crazy," Cruz replied.

"What? I come in the room, after yall done left a nigga, and you talkin' 'bout a nigga dead. Lookin' stupid and shit," Wheat laughed before continuing. "But I'm talkin' crazy, huh? Nigga, do I look dead to you?"

"Nah man, I'm just sayin'. My mind fucked up, homie. Everything goin' wrong! Then Diddy them…. Man, I knew I shoulda stayed wit' you. I knew you wasn't dead."

"Look at this," Wheat said, pulling out a small photo album. Wheat walked over to Cruz and sat down beside him. Opening the album they began looking at the pictures. The photo album was full of old pictures. Pictures of Wheat when he was young. There were pictures of Wheat's mother, his father, his brother, and of course, his daughter. But as they continued to look at pictures, Cruz spotted an older girl in her early twenties that looked just like Wheat.

"Who is that?" Cruz asked.

"Why you play so damn much? Stupid! You know damn well that's my daughter."

"Yo' daughter?" Cruz asked.

"Yeah, my daughter! She took this at her graduation party," Wheat said.

"Graduation party? Nigga, yo' daughter 11 years old!"

"She used to be. Look, I got a lot of pictures. Look at Des."

Flipping through the book he stopped at a picture of Des wearing a two-piece suit, with leather Bally's, and a leather jacket. He looked just like Cruz. He was smiling. Something Cruz had not seen him do in quite a while. But something was wrong with this picture. Des looked to be about 30 years old.

"Where did you get this picture from, Wheat?" Cruz asked.

"Man, I told you I had a lot of 'em."

Wheat continued flipping the pages. It seemed he had over a million and one pictures in this little book. He stopped again. It was a picture of Summer Rose and a little boy. The child was sad. He resembled Cruz. Summer was smiling. Wheat went on flipping, stopping again on a picture of Elga. She was crying.

"Why she crying?" Cruz asked.

"Because of you. Go see her, slim. She really loves you," Wheat stated, staring at the picture. "Look, slim," Wheat said after turning a few more pages. "This is me, Biggie and Pac."

"Nigga, you ain't know no Biggie and Pac!"

"I know. I met 'em today. Slim? You think I'm crazy. These two some funny muthafuckas," Wheat said and laughed.

"Wheat, them dudes is dead, homie."

"I know…. Tamika said she ain't mad atcha, and that she loves you…. And so do I, slim."

Then Wheat just disappeared. At that very instance Cruz jumped up and looked around the room. He was sweating! He looked and the blood was still on his shirt. The room was empty. "Damn, Wheat! Why you had to go?" he asked, looking around the room again. He remembered Elga crying. "Go see her," Wheat had said. Picking up the phone, he called himself a cab.

Chapter 20

....in a land where hearts are cold, (ya ye, ya ye, yall!)/ Livin' in a land where thugs don't live that long/ So, thuggin' day for day with the G's, and we pray/ Help us Lord/ 'Cause I'm, livin' in a land where thugs don't live that long.... Now I done seen it all/ And even lost a coupla dogs/ Everythang from seein' hoes boostin' in the mall/ Niggas who used to ball/ They ain't ballin' now/ Hoes who hated me/ Them bitches callin' now/ Momma told me/ But she never told me when/ She said, with money come sin/ And some fake ass friends....

Click! The thundering sound system went off, silencing Trick's prophetic political assault.

"What the fuck? Cola, if you don't turn my shit back up, I'ma put my foot in yo' ass," DaDa said before lighting his lace-blunt.

"Hmp! It would be nice to have somethin' in my ass. 'Cause you sho' ain't puttin' nothin' else in it. Ya act like ya scared."

"Bitch! I ain't into all that freak-ass fuckin' in the ass shit. Ya ass for shittin'. Girl, ya ass stank," DaDa stated, still smoking his weed and cocaine.

"Nigga, I don't stank! But that shit you smokin' do. Goddamn, DaDa! You got too much coc' in that damn weed! That's why I don't smoke witcha ass."

"Hoe, ain't nobody ask yo' junkie-ass to smoke wit' me."

"Junkie? Nigga, no you didn't!" Cola snapped.

The argument was stopped by the sound of their doorbell. DaDa got up and went to look out the window. Seeing Smash he opened the door.

"What up, nigga?" Smash asked.

"Same ole shit. Get money, get high, and argue witcha hoe."

"Nigga, I ain't gon' be too many more hoes!" Cola yelled from the den.

"Hoe, shut up!" DaDa yelled then turned to Smash. "That white Chevy clean as Bolivian flake. When you cop that?"

"That ain't my shit. I think it's Big Shorty's shit, I got it from Moehead. But while we speakin' on Bolivian flake, what you smokin' on?" Smash asked.

"You know what it is," DaDa said, passing Smash the blunt.

"Dig, lil' one, I'm wit' that *get money shit. Get high and all that.* But I don't do no arguin'. 'Specially wit' no hoe! Grits and greens is on you. The rest on the hoe! Moe told me 'bout the talk yall had. Chico a strickly business type nigga, but he ain't petty, and he don't steal. I ain't tryna tell you 'bout ya business, but you need to straighten ya house."

"I hear ya, man." DaDa took the blunt and pulled it before continuing. "Did that work come in yet?"

"Yeah, that's where Moe and Bluey at now. 'Posed to be 50 of 'em. We'll owe him twenty-two-five, but it's all good. Them Towners, Bo and Roc, need five, and Snake left last night. He got the money for them ten I gave him, plus money for three," he continued to explain.

DaDa heard him but he didn't. He just continued to smoke and think about where his life was headed. *Thugg niggas didn't live that long...*

Chapter 21

Three Days Later

The streets were ablaze! With most of the action centering around Arthur Cruz, his foundation, and the recent deaths of three of his people. It seemed that every day a rumor was uncovered and circulated. And as the days unfolded, Kunta and his Militia grew even more relentless in their attacks; never accepting, nor denying any of the physical harm being perpetrated.

With all of his new found media attention, the interests of the people concerning the foundation soared to new highs. Palmer, Elijah, and Breed did their best to withstand the storm, and direct the whole thing in a positive direction by holding press conferences, rallies, and speaking engagments. People whom had never heard of The First Family Foundation began to pay attention. Black August flew off book store shelves and out of the foundation's offices. All the while, the foundation's star was nowhere to be found. No one had heard anything from Cruz since the funeral. Palmer and Breed had been searching high and low for him after returning to the hotel on Biscayne and finding him gone.

They texted him every hour on the hour, still, Cruz remained a phantom.

* * *

Leaving the Boys and Girls Club on 111th Street, where Elijah had spoken in Cruz's place, Palmer, Breed, Steve, and E decided to ride through Silver Blue Lakes to see if they could catch anyone out there. But before they could turn onto 103rd Street, Breed's phone rang.

"Hello?... Who is this?... Elga?... Where do I know you from?... Yeah, I know Arthur Cruz... He's where?... Okay, okay! What is your address?... Aiight, thank you very much.... Yeah, I'm on the way right now." Breed hung up.

"Who was that?" Diddy asked.

"Some chick named Elga. She say Cruz at her house."

"Elga? You think she one hundred?"

"Talkin' to her, she sounded tired. I believe she's one hundred, because she say he been there for three days."

"Well, one thang we ain't gon' do is play games. Ride through there one time, then we gon' let E and Steve out before we drive up. Yall give us five minutes before yall come in," Diddy instructed.

"You, you thank it's a set up?" Steve asked, somewhat nervous.

Checking the magazine on the Spec-90, Diddy chambered the weapon and looked Steve in the eyes. "It bet' not be."

Pulling into the driveway of the house marked 2285, they parked behind a burnt-orange SUV. Diddy held the Spec-90 under his shirt-front as Breed rung the doorbell. When the door opened, Diddy relaxed. He remembered her as being Meagan's friend from the park in D.C.

As soon as they crossed the threshold they were met by a gut-wrenching stench. Frowning, Diddy turned to face Elga. "Shawdy, what is that smell?"

"Your friend," she said in a sad tone. Her eyes were red and swollen. She had been crying.

"Is he dead?" Diddy asked.

"Not literally. But, he tripping. He been drunk for two days. He won't take no bath or take off those clothes. He talking about the blood of his people is on that nasty shirt. He done threw up all over my house. He was asking for guns, scared to go to sleep. He wouldn't even let me touch him," Elga explained.

"So why you just calling us back?"

"Because he was drunk and tripping. He finally passed out last night. So I got his phone and called back the number."

As Breed and Palmer walked down the hall of the small house, the stench grew richer. Breed had never smelt such an odor come from a living human being. "Damn!" he thought. "She must really love him."

When the door came open Cruz rolled over and immediately began snatching at his waistband. Wide-eyed, perspiration covered his brow. Frustrated! He realized that his weapon was not there. Defeated! He fell back on the bed.

"Don't hurt nothin', shawdy. It's just me and Breed."

Without bothering to sit up, Cruz spoke to them while staring at the ceiling. "So what took yall niggas so long?"

"Man, we been lookin' everywhere for you. Elijah going crazy, your mom is too worried. Even Des called looking for you," said Breed.

At the mention of his son's name Cruz sat up. He was now alert. "Des?"

"Yeah, slim. Shawdy done called a few times. Say tell you sorry. I think he worried about you," Palmer informed him.

Breed had become immune to the smell by then. Yet to see his man, his boss, his best friend, sitting there in a state of near comatose, really hurt the big man. Cruz was almost child-like in his current state of existence. "Dig, I'ma let Steve and E know that everything's mello." Breed turned and walked away.

"So what you gon' do, slim? Lay around and loathe your life away?"

Wheat, Cruz remembered. "So what you gon' do, slim? Sleep your life away?" Wheat had asked him in the dream.

"What did you say?" Diddy asked.

"Oh, nothin' homie. I was just thinkin'," Cruz responded.

"Shawdy, you gotta pull it together! Everybody lookin' for you. The office is so busy I hate to go there. And Kunta, slim? The nigga tearing you a new asshole every chance he get! If you don't come back soon, it may not be anything to come back to."

"Let it fold. Fuck it. I don't care no more, man. People used to tell me 'your mind is so brilliant'. Well this same mind got Tamika killed. My son hates me! I loss Kunta as a friend, and Wheat is dead. I killed Headquartaz! Man, at times I feel I'm losin' my mind." He went silent. He thought. "Diddy man, I'm tired."

Now it was Palmer's time to think. He saw the pain in his friend's eyes. He could also hear it in his words. They had all been friends. So the pain was felt by him as well. He knew then that it would be a grave mistake to inform Cruz of Captain Jack's passing. Yet something had to be said. Not about death, but about life.

"Look, slim! It takes a strong man to do what you do. And it's gonna take an even stronger man to go from this point forward. Now we all make mistakes and decisions that we have to live by. Sure we wish we could take some back, but slim, life don't work like that. You did what you thought was best! You always do. That's why I'll follow you to hell. Because I know in my heart, that you'll bring us back outta there." He looked at his friend, thought and continued. "I remember one time, you probably don't remember, but I was about to quit Unicor, knowin' damn well I needed the money. I was frustrated and tired. You told me about this slogan shit yall used to say at football practice. I still remember it, because it still holds true. You said, *we'll fight until we can't fight no more. When we can't fight no more, we'll lay down, bleed a while, get up and fight some more. One for all, and all for one.*"

Cruz smile. He remembered. Palmer continued.

"If you tired, slim, just lay down and bleed a while. But know and believe you gotta get up and fight some more. You been there for us all. And we're all here *waitin' for when you need us.*" Diddy turned to leave.

"Yo Diddy," Cruz called.

"What's up?"

"I'ma get up."

"I knew you would."

"Leave me a AK and a hand gun," Cruz said.

"Aiight, but what you need is some soap and a rag. Slim? You stank as-e-muthafucka! And that's off the no bullshit."

Cruz smiled. "Off the no bullshit, huh?"

"Yeah, slim. But I'ma leave that. Call me when you need me." Palmer turned and left the room.

Chapter 22

...will I see the penitentiary/ Or will I stay free?... I take a shot of Hennessy just to face the madness/ Nickle-bag fulla cess, weed laced wit' hass/ Phone-call from my nigga, from the, otherside/ Two childhood friends just died/ I couldn't cry!/ A damn shame/ When will we ever change? And what remains from a 12 gauge to the brain?/ Arguments with my boo, it's true/ I spend more time with my niggas than I do with you/ But everywhere it's the same thang. (That's the game)/ I'll be damned if a thang change/ Fuck the fame/ I'll be hustlin' to make a million....

"You hear that shit?" DaDa hit his blunt again before continuing. "This nigga Pac is the greatest! And Moe got some beat in this bitch."

"Fuck Moe! Him and Smash some suckas.... Hatin' ass niggas," Cola spat.

"What is you on?" DaDa tried to pass her the blunt.

"DaDa, I don't want that shit! Smell like crack."

"Don't play that crack shit wit' me, hoe! I bet yo' ass want a pill," DaDa said.

"So now I gotta be ya hoe? Hmp! Anyway, you think I ain't hear Smash doggin' me in my own shit the other day? That shit hurt me, DaDa. Then you ain't even say nothin'. You just let the nigga dog me, when you know who was takin' that money. Long as I was countin' the shit, the nigga could steal and blame me. But soon as I told you to let him count it, shit straight. And you know why it's straight? The hoe-ass nigga ain't got nobody to blame now."

"Slow down, Cola," DaDa said calmy.

"What you mean, *slow down*?"

"I mean watch yo' mouth. You was on point, and I'ma deal wit' that. But all that other shit, slow down."

"See! That's the shit I'm talkin' 'bout. You will defend them soft-ass niggas, but you let the nigga disrespect me in my house! Them niggas don't mean you no good. They some haters and they using yo' dumb-ass. Just like they used Head."

Whoop! DaDa slapped Cola in the mouth with the back of his hand.

"I told you to slow down! I'm sick of arguin' wit' you! Now I told you I heard you, and that I was gonna deal with it."

"Alright, DaDa…. You deal wit' it," Cola said sadly.

DaDa and Cola never saw the black Mark VI pull up next to them at the light. Cola began letting her window down to spit, because DaDa had bussed her lip when he slapped her. As she lifted her head she saw the barrel of the shotgun.

"DaDa!" she screamed.

DaDa looked, but was frozen.

"That ain't him," E yelled and Steve withdrew the shotgun. The Mark VI sped off.

"Damn!" DaDa said to himself. He was shaken to his very core.

Cars behind him began to blow because the light had changed and he was still sitting there. Regaining his composure he finally

215

pulled off. Cola cried. He thought. Serious thoughts. "What am I doing? And where is my life headed?" He really could not answer those questions.

A damn shame. When will we ever change? And what remains from a 12 gauge to the brain?

Part 3hree

Mass Confusion

...friendship which is gained by purchase and not through grandeur and nobility of spirit is bought but not secured, and at a pinch is not to be expended in your service. And men have less scruple in offending one who makes himself loved than one who makes himself feared; for love is held by a chain of obligation which, men being selfish, is broken whenever it serves their purpose; but fear is maintained by a dread of punishment which never fails...

[The Prince]
Niccolo Machiavelli

Chapter 23

You're not alone (no!)/ And no one's gonna hurt your heart again/ And this I know (yes!)/ You can count on me, I'll be there as your friend/ For no one knows the pain that you've endured (no!)/ And no one knows how much it really hurts (no!)....You cried but he played around/ You tried but he let you down/ You gave him everything you had, to treat you all so bad.... Give it a chance/ I'll make it up to you.... Give it a chance/ I'll prove this world was wrong.... Give it a chance/ I'll make it up to you/ And I'ma teach this world a lesson.... And I'll never let you fall....

Cruz was awaken to the sweet melodious sounds of Baby Face and the smell of fried chicken. Raising himself, he saw Elga sitting in a chair next to the bed. She was staring at him. Her hope was that maybe tonight would be different. Better.

"Hello, sleepy head." Elga smiled.

"What's up, lady?" Cruz returned.

"You…. Do you remember that song? You played it for me one night over the phone. I was having problems with my friend and you was there for me. I never forgot that song. I love it! And I never forgot you…"

"I don't remember no shit like that. I hate that stupid ass song."

"What?" She raised her brow.

"You sure it was me?" Cruz asked.

"I can't believe you!" Elga was hurt.

Cruz began laughing. "12th grade. Ted Vincent. You was cryin' like a lil' chump."

"Boy!" She punched him in the arm. "You are such a punk."

Cruz caught the lazy jab before she could bring it back. He pulled her out of the chair onto the bed. She smelt of fresh strawberries. He smelt like a decaying carcass. Together the perfumes and odors made manifest, the true essence of love divine. They laid there. Her head on his chest. Their legs intertwined. She was happy. He was there. Existing. Somewhere between heaven and hell.

"Elga."

"Yes?"

"You must really love me."

"Maybe," she answered. But of course, she knew. *Yes, I do love you,* she smiled inside.

The music continued to play, as did the two. He touched, she panted. He had been right, her thighs were soft to the touch. She rubbed and caressed. He responded. In the worst of circumstances they had come to terms. Affectionate! Terms of endearment.

The TV played without audio. The visual gave the room a romantic glow. A scene that Cupid could not have presented. Such a naturally erotic scene. Glancing at the TV screen, Cruz saw a familiar face. A white face.

"Who is that?" Cruz asked.

"Oh, that's Bishop Michael. He got that big ass church in Aventure."

It was the man from his dream that had tried to help him. He had on the same priest's collar that he had been wearing in the dream.

"Sonofa bitch!" he exclaimed.

"What?"

"Let me borrow that ugly ass orange truck."

"Boy! My truck ain't ugly."

"Can I get it or what?"

"I thought you ain't want it." Elga smiled seductively.

"I'm talkin' 'bout the truck."

"Where you going?"

"I gotta take care of something."

"Can I go?"

"No!"

"Hmp! Go 'head. Nothing better not happen to my truck, or you buying me a 'brand-new one'... And I hope yo' stank behind take a bath before you go."

He laughed to himself. She was cute and kind. *Wish,* he thought. *That the world was a better place and that together, the two of them were in it.*

Tucking the handgun in his waistband, he covered the AK-47 with his coat and left the house.

Eight Hours Later After Breaking Into Bishop Michael's Church

The two men sat quietly for a while. Thinking. The strong smell of Cruz's unclean body lingered. Bishop Michael could see the hurt in his expression. He had indeed lost a lot. Yet even in the dark, Bishop Michael could see that the passion still burned inside of him. He had not come this far to simply give up. Arthur Cruz did not break into Bishop Michael's church just to tell him his story. There was more. And Bishop Michael aimed to help him in anyway that he could.

"That is a painful story, my son."

"Life is painful," Cruz responded.

"Pain is love. It fosters and defines."

"It tears and destroys."

"Only to rebuild. Better and stronger."

"Bishop Michael, what have you suffered? I made these decisions.... I alone...."

"No Cruz. That's where you're wrong. God alone."

"Bishop, they're dead!"

"Well, if life lasts and death passes, things would never change. You know that with change comes sacrifice! Revolution has always been bloody. The unblemished lame. The only begotten son. The innocence of a virgin. All sacrificed to produce and redeem. Life! If you give up now, then the sacrifices were in vain. It would all have been for nothing."

"But it wasn't for nothing!" Cruz screamed.

"Then stand up! Do what God has blessed you to do. Before today, well, tonight rather, I've never thought much of death. Life has always been my lesson. But through you and your story, our meeting has taught me that death is the best teacher of life. Life is, *Something To Die For.*"

"Will you help me?" Cruz asked.

"Emphatically yes!"

"Bishop.... Are you my friend?"

"I would love to believe so. *For all things work together and are fitting into a plan for good to those who love God and are called according to his design and purpose.* Mr. Cruz, what is your purpose?"

"To be about my Father's work. To organize, clarify, and solidify."

"Then we are friends."

Taking the bottle from the table, Cruz took a long draw. He then slid the bottle across the table to Bishop Michael.

"Drink and be merry, Bishop," Cruz continued. "For tomorrow we die."

Taking a drink from the bottle, Bishop Michael wondered, "What am I doing?" Again the warm liquid began to take its effect on him. He calmed. Cruz spoke.

"Bishop, I wanna hold a press conference. Here, in your church, on your TV program. I want you, the great Bishop Michael, to bring me out. Introduce me. Make me acceptable to your people, in your world. I want you to take Black August and deliver it in your words, to your people…. If you're my friend, and you want to help, deliver *a message to the white man,*" Cruz said.

"I'll need some time to arrange it. I have to talk to some people and read the book."

"Time is not a luxury, Bishop. Three days. Three days and the train leaves with or without you."

"I'll be ready."

"Remember Bishop, this is not a war against flesh. These are not common men we're up against. We're at war with principalities and powers in high places. It's a mind-state, Bishop. We're fightin' a sickness! And I've come as far as I can go. And like Moses, I know that I'll never enter into the promise land. So you, Bishop, like Joshua, will have to lead the Israelites into Canaan."

"Cruz, do you know what war is?"

"It's miscalculated perfection."

"Are miscalculations in anyway good for business?"

"Not if one is to be successful," Cruz answered.

"Then know this! Whoever has wronged you does not like the way that things are going. So he, whoever he is, will come to you with a solution to bring about peace. Look into it. Look into them! Love your enemy, for he will expose his deceit."

The two men shook hands and Cruz walked out of the church to begin again. To engage in a new struggle....

* * *

The incident at the red light had really disturbed DaDa. For the past week he had been loathing around the house smoking, drinking, and thinking seriously about his future. And the more he thought on his future, the more he realized how much Cola meant to him. Not only had she been there for him when Head had gotten killed, but she had been right on several occasions whereas his business affairs were concerned. Not to mention she'd saved his life that day at the red light. He owed her. He loved her.

"DaDa, I fixed you some spaghetti."

"I don't want that."

"Why?" Cola asked with an attitude.

"My momma told me don't eat yo' spaghetti."

"Nigga! Yo' momma don't even know me...."

"Slow down. Please, just slow down. I don't want none."

"Well, I'm 'bout to go out to the mall and do some shoppin'."

"That's what yall call it now?"

"What?" Cola asked.

"Stealin'. 'Cause that's all yall hoes do."

"So now I'm ya hoe?"

"You always been my hoe," DaDa shot back.

"You know what, DaDa? I hate yo' ass! You always trippin' on how I score for green, but you ain't givin' me shit. Yeah! I steal from them crackas. So what, nigga? I don't cheat on you, I don't ask you for shit, and I keep you fresh...."

"I know what the fuck you do and don't do. 'Cause I'm the one that let you do it. But that stealin' shit over."

"Well you need to stop sellin' drugs!" Cola spat back.

"I am."

"What?"

Cola was shocked! She had been trying to get DaDa to stop hustling drugs and open a business for himself. Yet her pleas had always fallen on deaf ears. When she had made her demand today, she was only being defiant. She had never expected him to comply.

"You heard me. I'm finished, man.... Smash and 'em on they way over here now. I ain't told 'em yet."

"DaDa, you just made me so happy! I love you, DaDa."

"Yeah, I think I love you too," he said and smiled while taking some money from his pocket. "Here," he said, handing her the money.

"DaDa? What you need, some blunts?" Cola continued. "'Cause I said I was goin' to the mall, not the corna store."

"Girl! That's two hundred dollars."

"I can count, DaDa. And I know you ain't use to breakin' females off, so I'ma just get some nail polish or bathroom supplies. But baby, you gonna have to step ya game up." Cola smiled and kissed DaDa on the lips.

"Yeah, aiight. And you gonna have to get a job."

They both had to laugh at that, because DaDa knew for a fact that Cola would never be on anyone's job.

Chapter 24

...Broke niggas fulla slime/ And they got dirt on they mind/ Catch me slippin' never/ And not once have I ever/ Lost the bank to the bettor/ I'ma muthafuckin fool myself/ But I can't fool myself/ If I'm ever caught slippin'/ They gotta have that there.... Two years ago/ I lost a friend in the line of thuggin'/ He got drunk out clubbin'/ Some niggas followed him home.... Trick pumped from DaDa's system.

"So what up?" Bluey asked as he passed Big Shorty the lace-joint.

Bluey had been out of the hospital for a while now. But the doctors had just recently removed the colostomy bag. With that out of the way he was now able to rejoin the fold, and take his rightful place in the family's business. He had arrived with Moehead, shortly after Big Shorty and Smash.

"You, big homie! You look good," DaDa said smiling.

"I feel good, homie. Now what's the business?" Ole Bluey asked.

DaDa began putting the flames to a freshly rolled El Poducto filled with weed and raw cocaine. He inhaled, held it, and then added his sweet lace scented smoke to the already congested air.

"Man…. I been thinkin'," DaDa began.

"Thankin'? You stopped me from trappin' to tell me that you been thankin'?" Moehead spat as he snatched the joint from DaDa.

"Nah, simple ass nigga! I called yo' greasey ass over here to tell you what I've been thinkin' 'bout," DaDa shot back.

"Well what you want, a drum roll? Big Shorty, give the nigga a drum roll or something…. Spill nigga! I ain't got all day to be fuckin' wit' you," Moehead capped, and on cue, Big Shorty began drumming on the coffee table.

"Now how much one of them cost?" DaDa asked while pointing at Big Shorty.

"Yeah, for real," Smash said, pulling the joint out of Shorty's mouth before he continued. "If you gon' let Moe puppeteer you into foolishness, you can wait yo' big stupid ass outside…. Carol City ass nigga! Go 'head, DaDa."

"Look man…. I, I been thinkin', like I said. And I'm not seein' where all this shit is headed. I mean, Head got killed. Some niggas tried to off me at the red light. Niggas almost kill Ole Bluey…. Man, the crackas snatched up Troy and the lil' nigga Chrizac outta J-Ville…. Man, every nigga I just named had retirement money. I'm talkin' 'bout a least a ticket! What the fuck was they still hustlin' for?" DaDa looked at his partners.

"DaDa," Moe chuckled before continuing. "They was scramblin' for the long cheese, lil' bruh."

"Moe, I know you're an ultra-smart muthafucka and all, but they already had bread. What's the difference in one ticket or two?"

"A whole lotta hoes and a bigger pad to fuck 'em in, ya dig," Big Shorty said, causing Moe and everyone, except DaDa, to laugh.

"Shorty, shut the fuck up!" DaDa inhaled the weed. "The niggas got the only thing they had comin', hell or jail! This shit ain't no career, man, it's a come up. They had done came up! At that point, man, they was just in the way…. Real talk, homie, I ain't tryin' to be in these niggas and crackas way."

"So what you sayin', DaDa?" Smash asked.

"I'm sayin' that I'm finished. Yall can have it! Just give me mines, man. I'm finish."

"Ain't this a bitch! Country-ass-nigga, you finished what? Livin' off real niggas?! How you finished and ain't done shit? Nigga, I'm in these streets for real!" Moehead spat.

"And you gon' die in 'em," DaDa said, removing the nickel-plated .38 from his right pocket. "Just have mine in three days."

"Oh, you uppin' guns on me, nigga?" Moehead asked.

"Moe, you can talk ya ass off. Just get me, me," DaDa returned.

"I ain't givin' yo' country ass nothin'! Nigga, fuck you!"

"Hold up, Moe. Slow down! This the homie. We ain't gon' do no disrespectin' the homies," Smash said.

"Oh, you let the nigga up fi' on me, but I'm outta pocket, huh?" Moehead asked.

"Moe, if you let me finish, I'll handle it." Smash lit a Newport before continuing. "Put the gun up, DaDa. 'Cause that was some disrespectful shit. Moe the homie. We don't disrespect the homies. Now, are you sure this is what you want? You know, to just up and quit. I mean, damn baby, you got it good. You bringin' in at least eight to twelve grand a week without liftin' a finger. You smokin' a half a pound a week. Blowin' off the kilo and poppin' pills like they goin' outta style. Say baby, you wanna give all of that up?" Smash asked.

"Yeah man, I thought about all of that. I'm just tired."

"Tired of what, DaDa? You don't do shit!" Moe screamed.

"I'm tired of the life. I'm tired of pills, coc', and niggas like you!"

"Man, fuck this nigga! I'm up." Moe rose to leave.

"Hold up, Moe. Wait a minute! You just sittin' there Blue, what you got to say?" Smash asked.

"Say man, don't mind me, baby. I'm just here," Ole Bluey capped.

"Nah Blue, man. We jive need you! What's yo' take?" Moe asked.

"Look, jit got a damn good point! Besides, this shit ain't for everybody.... Head was my man, bullshit ain't nothing. This is Head's lil' cousin. I been rollin' wit' Head since middle school. So I'ma respect what DaDa sayin'."

"So what about us? What, we ain't been rollin'? Fuck us, huh?" Moe asked.

"Say Moe, that ain't what I said. We all men in here! We can do whatever we wanna do. Jit don't wanna risk it no more. Why you so sore?" Bluey asked.

"Cause wit' him goes the capital and the resources."

"Moe, you been hustlin' since we was kids. You should be strong as an Ox on steroids. You know the connect! What's the problem?" Ole Bluey asked.

"I'm cool, but everythang ain't everythang. And shit, what about Big Shorty, Smash, and you. What about the niggas we buildin' wit', that ain't got retirement money?" Moehead questioned.

"Look, this what's up. Business gone go on as usual...." Ole Bluey said before DaDa cut him off.

"What? Man I ain't...." DaDa began before Ole Bluey waved him off.

"Slow ya roll, jit. I respect yo' point, but this what it is. Business as usual! We gon' roll-on like speedstick. But Moe, you 100% responsible for DaDa's bread. No question! Me and DaDa won't get our usual take, we'll get five grand for the both of us. Yall betta stack! And make sure yall make them other niggas stack! 'Cause in six months, shit is over! No questions, no extentions. So spread the love. After that you niggas can do whatever," Blue finished and rose to leave.

"Can you live wit' that?" Smash asked, looking from Moehead to DaDa.

"Yeah, I'm cool," DaDa responded.

"Yeah, aiight," Moehead said, heading for the door.

After making it to the car, Moehead just sat there in silence, waiting for Ole Bluey to finish so that they could leave.

The two rode along smoking and listening to the radio. There were very few words exchanged. Bluey was older than Moe, but the two were very close. Not as close as Bluey and Headquartaz had been, but much closer than he and any of the others. Whenever an issue was at hand that required a vote, Bluey had always sided with Moe.

"So what you gonna do tonight, Blue?"

"Shiiid, probably go out near the airport. I got a bad lil' teacher hoe that stay out in Miramar."

"She a animal?" Moehead asked.

"Shiiid, that's what I'm tryin' to see. She fine as a muthafucka, though! Trust and believe."

"What her name is?"

"Meka, Kietha, some shit. Ketha! That's her name. She a vet broad. Use to fuck wit' the nigga Raw Nitty back in the day."

"I don't know her, but how you meet her?"

"She was out at the hospital when I got my shit-bag took off. She was wit' some chump in a wheelchair."

"Her nigga?"

"Nah, she say the dude was a good friend of hers. Fuck him, though. You know I ain't trippin', and he bet' not be, ya dig?"

"You fucked up, nigga. You fucked up for real," Moehead said before taking a long draw of the lace-joint. Blowing the smoke out, he continued. "So what you think about that shit DaDa was talkin'? That young nigga a hoe or what?"

"Moe, I told you what I thought about that back at his crib, when I told everybody else," Ole Bluey calmy replied.

"Yeah, I can dig that. I heard you and all, but how you really feel? We been on these streets forever, dog! Gettin' it! We put the nigga Head in pocket. Bless his soul. Now this young nigga, a country-ass-nigga, gon' get everything we worked for. Shit ain't right, Blue. You 'posed to have that shit! Dig man, I ain't goin' for it. Fuck that!" Moehead spat.

Bluey said nothing. He just rode and continued to smoke. There was a slight grin on his face. Even from behind the dark tints the sun caught his gold-grill and reflected throughout the car. Moehead sensed this as approval, and continued in his selfish tirade.

"....give a country boy nothin'! He lucky I ain't fuck him up. Square business, Bluey. Fuck him! What I got for him, he betta duck."

Bluey just continued to smile and listen. They were about five minutes from the Silver Blue Lakes apartment complex, where Bluey had left his car. As they drew nearer Bluey finally spoke.

"Say, Moe, I ever tell you 'bout that hoe Tara I had?"

"You mean the model broad? That was one ultra-bad muthafucka there! Yeah, whatever happened to her, Bluey?"

230

"Say, Moe, if you let me finish I'ma tell you.... Now dig, you know we was spendin' hella time together. Vegas, Mexico, the Bahamas. I took the broad to the Superbowl, All-Star weekend. I loved shorty. I really did! I had her up in West Florida, quarter of a million dollar spread. Yeah, horses and everything. Brand-new Lexus, you name it!

"You remember I used to up and leave, and nobody knew where I was. Not even Head.... My baby-momma and my college broad, Tosha, would be goin' crazy! Callin' yall and lookin' everywhere for me.... Well, that's where I was, up in West Florida with Tara."

"Okay, so what happened, nigga?" Moe asked.

"Well, everything was roses. 'Cause like I said, I loved her. I was spendin' time, breakin' bread, and we was happy! My baby-momma Keta Black was uptight and all. She felt like a nigga didn't care. You know how hoes be. But I wasn't trippin'. I was there for all three of 'em."

The car stopped, Bluey got out, and walked over to his car. Moe sat there for a minute, thinking. He then blew the horn and let down his window. Blue walked back over and leaned into the car.

"What's up, nigga? What happened to the hoe?" Moe asked.

"Oh, Tara? Yeah, well, I killed her."

"What?" Moe was shocked. "Why you do that?"

"I had to. You see, she was dissatisfied with all that she had. Selfish! I loved her, but she tried to make me choose.... Moe, Head's my man. DaDa is his cousin. Don't make me choose, homie." Bluey turned and walked back to his car. Moe sat there, dumbfounded!

Chapter 25

Walking into his office almost felt strange, it had been a while since Cruz had spent any time in there. Everyone was very enthused to have Cruz back, and greeted him with friendly smiles and loving hugs of appreciation. He felt the love. And he knew in his heart that he needed to be appreciated, for himself, just as much as those people needed him. For that very reason Cruz was back and he was back for business!

"Good to see ya back, slim," Palmer said as they all sat down in Cruz's office.

"It's good to be back, man.... I wanna thank all of yall for holdin' me down, man...."

"Slim? Don't get on all that sensitive ass shit. 'Cause I can't handle no cryin' and shit."

"Whatever, nigga! Ain't nobody done more cryin' than yo' ole sensitive ass," Cruz said before continuing on a more serious note. "We got a lot of catchin' up to do, and not a lot of time to do it. Some people owe us and we owe some people. My aim is to be sure that 'everybody' get what they got comin'.... To begin, I got Bishop Michael to come abroad. With him, we can create a real positive synergy, to counter some of this negativity and to further our progress."

"Slim, you talking 'bout the white boy wit' the TV show?" Palmer asked.

"Yeah. Bishop Michael."

"Yeah! I fucks wit' him. Powerful dude! Wheat got me to watching him."

"Well, we gon' see just how powerful he is, 'cause we 'bout to rock Miami and the entire southern region. I met with him and he agreed to help. We've set a press conference for tomorrow, and from there we'll campaign until they shut us down, or until we get our point across. Whichever comes first." Cruz paused before continuing. "So Elijah, get wit' Bishop Michael's people and work out all of the details. Breed, go over there and see about all the security concerns. We've lost enough good men! From this point on, the opposition takes all of the L's."

"So what about Kunta people and them niggas from the 'partments?" Breed asked.

Cruz paused and looked around the room at his men before he spoke again. He loved the men that surrounded him. His friends. And he hoped to see them all, living and free when the smoke cleared.

"We gon' split-up, fellas. Two different operations of like mind. Physical and spiritual. Mind and body! Myself, Bishop Michael, Breed, F, and Elijah will operate on the surface, in a purely educational and political aspect. Raising the consciousness of the people and galvanizing them into a united front for our betterment.

"Palmer, you will lead Steve and four other chosen men on a military-murder campaign! You all will go underground and enforce every demand that I make above ground. You will not, ever, report to me! From here on, you have to make it happen for you."

Cruz then gave Palmer a briefcase containing $200,000 and an emergency phone number. He informed him that there would be another $200,000 available for him and his vanguard in three months.

Everyone stood and embraced. Maybe for the last time. Each in their own thoughts as they cleared the room. The plan was to live and every man was willing to die for it.

* * *

Bishop Michael's Church was filled to its capacity. His church, which would become the headquarters of CLARI (Christian Liberation Against Racism and Injustice), was an old college that sat nicely on five acres of land.

Today there were people everywhere! The library, auditorium, and the main sanctuary were standing room only. Supporters as well as reporters and mass protesters covered the large campus. Love and hate lingered. Confusion was strong! Black fists and cameras flashed. For every black, brown, red, or yellow face in attendance, there was a white face to meet its stare. Wondering! They all were there for answers.

According to the beautiful colored brochure, there was to be only three speakers. One of Bishop Michael's junior ministers had nervously introduced Bishop Michael, then the Bishop himself had taken the next 90 minutes to explain, as best he could, what the day was all about. He used the Bible, with the guidance of Black August, to express the future of his works as a man of God; and friend of Arthur Cruz.

Ronni had heard most of the Bishop's speech as she drove to the large church. A lot had happened between her and Cruz. Confusion and pain! Yet, First Family was still an army! Her army! And she was going to continue in the support of its leader. The two of them had talked for hours the day before the press conference.

Cruz had explained his relationship with Arthur X, and why he had discontinued the relationship that she and him had held. It was sad, yet the end results were beautiful. The loyalty that he represented towards his teacher and friend somehow sparked a consciousness in her. They, Ronni and Arthur X, had also talked and written one another in an attempt to become better friends, and hopefully regain what so many years apart had slowly degenerated.

Unable to find a parking space at or near the church, Ronni parked at Adventure Mall and caught a cab back to the church. This had taken quite some time, and caused her to miss a lot of Cruz's keynote speech. She arrived and found a seat reserved for her not too far from the rostrum.

"…. this intense darkness is ignorance! It is ignorance that causes us to *cast evil suggestions in firm resolutions*, meaning to twist the truth until it fits the purpose of the liar that whispers it into the ears of an ignorant listener! It is ignorance that facilitates our need to gossip, lie, back-bite, and envy one another! Envy is worst than slaughter. Because it's like a cancer. It destroys from the inside! Most often it's hidden, so it goes unchecked. This sets a sinister mind state, and places evil in the hearts of, otherwise, good men and women….

"There is a loose-association in the minds of the family, and it manifests itself through the ignorance of our actions. Mothers lie to the child in respects to the father, the father lies to the mother in regards to their future together, and the child lies to them both. As should be expected! *For if the child forever ingests the words of the parent, and the parent be a liar, how could the child ever be of the truth?* It was ignorance that killed Tamika! Not Arthur Cruz! It was a dumb-devil that gunned down my brother and close friend, Wheat. But it's a very wise Satan pulling the strings!

"According to the theorist and psychiatrist Frantz Fanon, *the Black man has two dimensions. One with his fellows, the other with the white man. A Negro behaves differently with a white man and with another Negro.* That this self-division is a direct result of colonialist subjugation is beyond question…. This self-division, or split-mind, is in fact a most serious mental process such as thoughts and feelings.

"Such thinking, as is witnessed in the Black man and woman, and poor whites, causes or incorporates delusion of persecution, anger, anxiety, argumentativeness, extreme jealousy, lack of motivation, poor social skills, deteriorating personal hygiene, and loose associations. People, something is wrong with us! Look around at the filth, and smell the funk of our loathsome situation. A wise Satan has effectively disrupted our sense of connection! He has divided our way of thinking, and divided us as a people. He came to steal, kill, and we have been destroyed as a people….

"As you all know, there has been a split in the ranks of our foundation, The First Family. There has been some words exchanged, and losses on both sides. Are these losses a result of decisions being handed down from the leadership? Undoubtedly no! He was a father and a teacher to me. Over three years ago I gave him my word that I would *allow no one to commit a nuisance on or near my past.* Well, I've come to a fork in the road, and I need advice, man…."

Cruz paused. He thought. He removed a handkerchief from his pocket and wiped the stream of tears from his face. He took his time refolding the handkerchief. The room was absolutely silent. Composing himself, he looked up at the crowd and continued.

"I know what it is that you would want." Cruz smiled. "You would want me to *seek refuge in the Lord of men, The King of men, The God of men, from the evil of the whisperings of the devil, who whispers into the hearts of men.* Well, Kunta I've sought refuge! And I've been walking my post just like you taught me, man…. I know that you have not done this to me! And I know that a wise Satan would like for me, and others on both sides, to believe otherwise. I know that a sinister mind seeks to exploit our situation to the detriment of our personal safety, and to the detriment of our people!

"You people! Our people! You love me, but you hate me! You were born so beautiful, yet we act so ugly. You say that you want the truth, but you reject it at every turn! You want to be taught, yet you cannot stand to be seen or associated with the teacher; for fear of what Rome and/or coward Negro professionals might think. So you come by night like Nicodemus did with Jesus….

"Please! Please people. Consider what I and the good Bishop have said today. Research and see for yourselves that what we speak is indeed the truth. Then I ask only that you give me, or any organization that is fighting to give this world a better reality, some of your time. Invest in yourselves by investing in your people!

"With this, I leave you with love and in peace."

The crowd thundered with applause! Everyone was on their feet. Blacks and Whites alike held their closed fists in the air! Some women, and even men, cried at what they had just witnessed. And this was merely the beginning. Cruz and the Bishop went on to rock North Amerikkka with a murderous series of speeches and TV interviews.

* * *

Palmer had finally decided that he would not be going back to DC. After what had happened in the park with Meagan's boyfriend, and the loss of his good friend Wheat, he reasoned not to return. BadLand, Miami would be his home.

Leaving the train station, where he'd just picked up his recently shipped Firebird classic, he was en route to pick up Steve, whom had stayed out all night. The engine of the burnt-orange machine rumbled as he pulled up in front of the duplex and blew the horn. A little boy came out. A little girl came out. Then two more little boys came out with another little girl in tow.

"Goddamn! This young nigga done found him a Breeder's Cup finalist," Palmer said to himself.

The curtain moved in the living room. It was another boy. He was a lot older than the others. Letting the curtain fall back in place the young man disappeared. The curtain moved again. Palmer had expected to see another child, but to his surprise it was Steve. Palmer blew the horn again and yelled out the window. "Ralo! Boy, brang yo' stupid ass on!" Steve held up one finger and disappeared. Two minutes later he came out of the door with his pants hanging low, no shirt on, eating a sandwich. Behind him trailed one additional child, followed by all the others. Standing in the doorway was indeed the cause of it all. "Lord! Have mercy!" Palmer exclaimed. The lady had to be about 5'10" in height, about 180 pounds, and she was black as coal. She had almond shaped eyes and wore her hair combed straight back, it hung far below her shoulders.

"What it do, ole school?"

"Let me fucka, man," Palmer said seriously.

"Who?" Steve asked.

"You, nigga!"

"What?"

"The broad, fool! Standing in the doorway," Palmer spat.

Steve looked and saw Tikeisha standing in the doorway waving bye to him. "Oh, hell nawl! That's my Amazon-dot-com right there."

"Oh, everybody else fuckin' her, but I can't fucka?" Palmer stated.

"Now why would yo' ole-ass say some dumb shit like that? You don't even know the girl."

"Hell boy, I ain't got to know her. I can see! It got to be twenty of them lil' muthafuckas runnin' 'round, and ain't none of 'em look alike. So they gotta have different fathers."

"Man, them ain't her kids! She babysits. You a stupid ole nigga," Steve spat.

"And you a vicious bamma. You got on some plaid slacks and a Hawaiian shirt. I don't know how you managed to pull shawdy back there. 'Cause that's a woman, slim."

"Nigga this fly!"

"Shawdy, that's country."

"Where we goin'?" Steve asked as they rode along 79th Street heading east.

"To the *Take One*. We gotta meet these four dudes we gonna be workin' wit'."

* * *

Wake-up everybody/ No more sleepin' in bed/ No more backwards thinkin'/ Time for thinkin' ahead/ The world has changed so very much/ From what it used to be/ So much jealousy and hatred/ War and poverty.... The world won't get no better/ If we just/ Let it be (No, No, No, No, No!).... Harald Melvin and The Blue Notes sounded throughout the small dimly lit strip club.

"Man, what kinda shit you got me in?" Steve asked. "Look at these ole ass hoes. And what the fuck is they playin'?"

"That's some playa music, shawdy. This a playa spot! Me and Wheat used to always come in here and shoot pool."

"Hey Diddy!" an attractive older woman in a pink catsuit yelled over the music.

"Hey suga," Palmer returned.

"You lookin' good," the woman said.

"I know," Palmer winked and handed the lady a fifty dollar bill.

"You a ole ass trick," Steve laughed.

"Shawdy, I'ma muthafuckin' playa! Everywhere I go the hoes yellin' *hey Diddy*. 'Cause it's real slick for, Daddy," Palmer capped.

Walking to the rear of the club, Palmer spotted his man. It had been a long time since he had seen him. The two had met in prison. When Fast Long looked and saw Palmer, he stood up to greet him.

"Say Diddy, what's happenin', slick?" Long said as the two hugged.

"Shiiid, Long, I'm just makin' it. How 'bout ya'self?"

"Still two-steppin'! You lookin' good."

"I know," Palmer returned and winked at Steve. "Long, this is Ralo, Ralo this is Long."

"Fast Long," Long extended his hand as he continued. "Pimp and kill! Love guns and whores, and always will. In that order! How ya doin', lil' bruh?"

"I'm good. Happy to meet you," Steve replied.

The three men sat down at the table with the man that had already been seated with Fast Long.

"Diddy, this my man, Chuck, the one I was tellin' you 'bout. Chuck, this here Diddy," Fast Long introduced.

"Good to meet you, slim. I hear you an ex-marine and a real good dude."

"Yeah, I did about twelve years in the service. Green Beret. Served in Desert Storm and the early part of the Iraq war. I'ma soldier, my nigga," Chuck said all in one breath.

"That's big, slim. But what make you wanna risk it all fuckin' wit' this?" Diddy asked.

"The big homie, Boo. Me, him, and Fast Long are super-tight. So if Boo Baby and Fast Long fuck witchu, then it's whatever. You told Long that you got some problems, I'm here to clear them shits out."

"This shit is serious, slim," Diddy reiterated.

"I'ma soldier, dog! Line 'em up and I'ma cut 'em down," Chuck stated with confidence.

"I thought it was 'posed to be four of yall."

"Yeah, it was. But they found my man OJ dead in the trunk of his Benz. And the fourth man, well, he right there," Chuck said, pointing behind Palmer.

Palmer turned around to see a very dark-skin brother slumped down in his chair. He sat alone at his table staring straight ahead.

"What's wrong with that nigga? Is he high or something?"

"Nah man, he chillin'. OJ was his man. But even still, he don't talk much. He good. Straight soldier."

"Where you know him from?" Palmer questioned.

"From the cradle, that's my lil' brutha, Lenard. We call him Ninja."

"Aiight, well, we ridin' tonight. First dark! Yall meet me at this address and we're rollin'." Palmer handed them the address and $75,000 before him and Steve got up and left.

Later That Night

"Okay fellas, this what it is. Long, you and Ninja gon' hit 60th. The niggas got a spot over there. It's some apartments sit right there on 60th and 14th. Hit 'em quick and get outta there," Palmer said.

"Anybody in particular you want stretched?" Fast Long asked while toying with his twin .357's.

"All of 'em!" Plamer continued. "Now Chuck, you, me, and Steve gon' hit they primary spot, Silver Blue. We gon' make it hot for 'em. Cut off they money, ya dig?"

The five men got into two different cars, headed in two different directions; yet their mind frame and absolute objectives were the same.

Coming through the entrance of the Silver Blue Lakes Apartment Complex, Palmer stopped the black Mark VI and let Steve out.

"You go down four gangways befo' you come out. Just run along the back. We'll be in the front," Palmer instructed.

He then waited a while before he started the car towards their destination. They had just made it to the sixth gangway and bussed a U-turn when Steve's Mac-10 went off.

Tat! Tat! Tat! Tat! Tat! the Mac sounded.

Two men were cut down by the deadly projectiles as they tried to flee, BoePete was one of them. Palmer cut off the head-lights and sped towards the hurd of running men. Leveling the AK-47 after he brought the Mark VI to a screeching hault, he began firing.

Wacka! Wacka! Wacka! Wacka! the AK-47 called. Three more men fell to their deaths.

Without saying a word Chuck sprung from the passenger side of the car like a cannonball being fired from a cannon. He was quickly closing the distance between him and the tall hefty man he was pursuing. Once within reaching distance, Chuck lunged forward, landing with his left forearm in the small of the man's back, slamming him into the wall. For his lack of height, Chuck jumped and in one smooth motion swung downward. There was a very grotesque scream as the twelve inch blade burrowed its way through the base of the man's neck and into the concrete wall. Turning, Chuck headed back to the car, leaving Big Shorty's lifeless body hanging as if it were part of the building's original structure.

AT THE SAME TIME ON 60TH AND 14TH

Ninja was ducked down in the backseat of the old Dodge with a 12 gauge automatic. Fast Long brought the vehicle to a stop in front of the building where Smash and Moehead's workers stood.

"Say there, *round!* You got some blows?" Fast Long asked.

"Yeah, what you need?" the young dude asked as he approached the car.

When he reached through the open window to get the money, Fast Long fired one of the .357's through the car door into the man's stomach. *Boom!* At the same instance Ninja began unloading the 12 gauge. *Boom! Boom! Boom! Boom!* Three more men fell as Fast Long leveled both 357's and joined Ninja in the assault. There was no return fire. Just desperate men fleeing for their lives!

These attacks were repeated for the next three weeks. Sometimes twice a day. Palmer led his men on a campaign that brought F.B.I. and national news coverage to the issues that Cruz demanded money and support to change. Drugs were killing the inner-city youth and incarceration was not the answer.

Palmer raided the Palm Gardens stronghold held by Zoe and his men and came away with a quarter of a million dollars in drugs and cash. The body count was up to 47 people dead and steadily rising as the months passed.

Palmer may have been lying about the tours in Lebanon, but he was fast proving himself as a very worthy general in the streets of BadLand, Miami.

Chapter 26

There had been continued business on the streets of BadLand, Miami, but it was far from usual. Homicide and the special drug/murder task force were working overtime. The F.B.I. and A.T.F. had also joined in an attempt to quiet down the media and get things back to normal. There had been no arrests, but plenty of shakedowns and added police pressure was placed on the underworld figures of Miami. Payoffs were simply not enough. Everyone was made to suffer under the Foundation's campaign – the bribers and those being bribed. The whole situation was an embarrassment to the city as well as to state and national government officials. The overseas druglords felt the bite just as well as the flat-foot corner hustlers.

"Dig man, this shit is gettin' crazy!" Smash said, looking at the flat screen TV in his home-office. He just shook his head as he watched officers, from what appeared to be over ten different agencies, take two men and an old woman into custody. The entire facility of the large Hialeah warehouse had been surrounded by Hialeah police and different alphabetical agencies. According to the reporter, they had seized over 2,500 kilos of uncut cocaine, at a street value of over $62,500,000.

"I can't believe this shit! At least a mil' of that was supposed to be mine, my nigga," Moehead cried while trying to pass Smash the lace-joint.

"Nah, man.... I'm too depressed to smoke."

"Well, if you that fucked up 'bout it, why the fuck ain't you doin' somethin' 'bout it?"

"Moe? What you want me to do? Open sesame or some shit?"

"Yeah, if that's anotha way to murda a muthafucka.... Nigga, just do what we do! This ain't nuclear physics we doin', homie." Moe paused and hit the lace-joint before he pointed to the contents on the table. "And these ain't no nuclear reactors we dealin' wit'.... These guns and drugs! We dope dealers, and we kill niggas! So why the fuck you act like you scared to kill Blue, that big-foot country boy, and Cruz bitch ass?"

"What the fuck you wanna kill Blue for?" Smash questioned.

"'Cause he wit' them niggas. Fuck Blue! Look man... Is you forgettin' what we here for?"

"Nawl, nigga! I'm just sayin'."

"Sayin' what? Dig, Smash! I'm out here, man. And I'm serious 'bout this shit. Niggas is in the way, homie."

"Aiight, look.... I'ma deal wit' Cruz. And at the same time, I'ma get him to deal wit' DaDa. You just handle Blue."

"How the fuck you gonna get Cruz to do DaDa?" Moe asked.

"You just deal wit' Blue, nigga. Let me handle the nuclear reactors."

* * *

The next day Smash was up and on a mission. Everything had to be handled just right. For that reason he was doing it himself. It was one thing to drive up, empty a few clips, and drive away. Hell, his daughter could do that. But it was altogether another ball game to have your enemy to kill your enemy and go to jail for his stupidity. Yes, Smash was dealing with high explosives.

Pulling the white Box Chevy up in front of DaDa's house, he saw that Cola's car was inside the fence and that Headquartaz's Surburban was parked out front. He then blew the horn before getting out. Just as he was closing the fence, DaDa came out of the house wearing some cut-off Dickies and bedroom slippers.

"What up, kinfolks?" DaDa said, giving Smash dap.

"Ain't shit, lil' ole nigga. What you on a diet? You skinny as a muthafucka, nigga! I can see all ya ribs and shit."

"Man, I been skinny. But you see that six pack, nigga," DaDa capped, rubbing his stomach.

"Yeah, well, you look sick, nigga. What, the hoe won't cook?"

"Slow down, man…. I just been chillin'. You know I don't be smokin' shit no more. So, I don't really be eatin' all that bullshit no more."

"Oh, yeah?! Well do ya thang, lil' ole nigga. The more of you niggas that detox, the more weed and coc' for me. Shiid, nigga, you stop gettin' money, you don't get high…. Fuck it, stop breathln', I need the air."

"You trippin', nigga. Anyway, what you doin' in Big Shorty Chevy? I thought Moe put it up since he got kill?"

"Yeah, he did. But his car fuckin' up on him, so he got mine. And now I done got stuck goin' to pick up some work from Boca. It 'posed to be 'bout ten kilos, and that Chevy won't hold ten in the spot. So I'ma need the 'Burban for the day."

"Yeah, aiight. I ain't doin' nothin'. Let me go get the keys."

After the two exchanged car keys they gave each other dap and Smash was off to complete his mission.

DaDa went back inside to play Madden and listen to Tupac. But was he really listening when Tupac said, "watch for phonies! Keep your enemies close. Nigga, watch your homies...."

* * *

Cruz sat at his desk amid all the junk mail, books, and papers that he needed to look over. He had been so busy with his speaking engagments that he had not been able to come to his office as often as he needed to. For this reason he'd spent the last two days playing catch-up.

There on his desk, with the junk and paper work, sat a half empty Red Bull energy drink and a pack of No Doze. Cruz had stayed up at his office until 1:30 a.m., only to return at 8:45 a.m. to try to complete his work-load. Because in another week he and Bishop Michael were going on the road again for three weeks.

Last night had been the first night that he'd slept in his own bed, in his own home. The home that he had once shared with his family, Tamika and Des. Him and Breed had even uncovered the Cadillac and drove it to work this morning. The last time he had driven the car it was just him and Tamika. The two had just dropped the top and took off up the panhandle to Daytona for a week.

"Mr. Cruz.... Mr. Cruz!" his receptionist called out.

"Yeah, what's up Sherry?" he finally answered.

"Arthur, are you alright?" Sherry asked.

"Yeah. Just a little tired."

"Okay. Well, Ms. Wynn is here to see you," Sherry said and smiled.

"Okay, send her in."

Cruz had been spending a lot of time with Elga lately. Whenever he was in town he stayed with her at her house. Everyone was happy to see him finally opening up to someone, because he had been an absolute mess every since the death of Tamika and Wheat. Elga was like a clean breath of fresh air to everyone in his camp. Even Breed liked her. And Big Breed did not like anyone! So this even allowed her to travel with them on some occasions.

"Hello, sweetie!" Elga beamed as she entered the office and kissed Cruz on the lips. "How are you?"

"I'm cool," Cruz answered dryly.

Elga turned to put down her purse before taking a seat and saw that Sherry was still standing in the doorway of Cruz's office. She looked at Cruz and then back to Sherry, who smiled at her before she closed the door and returned to her desk.

"What is up with her?"

"Who?" Cruz asked.

"The red chick with all the teeth. Why she smilin' all at me? Yall got somethin' goin'? 'Cause she don't know me to be all showin' me her grill."

"Elga…. Think about what you just asked me. Then think about where you are. That is my receptionist. It's her job to be sociable with people that come to 'my' office."

"Okay, you right. You always right. That's why I love you." Elga smiled at Cruz before continuing. "Why you ain't come home last night?"

"I did go home last night," Cruz returned without looking up from the papers he was reading.

Elga narrowed her eyes and stomped her heels on the marble floor before she spoke through clinched teeth. "You know what I'm talking about, Arthur Cruz. I waited for you."

"I told you not to wait up for me. I was here until about 2:00 and I did not want to bother you. So Breed and I went to my house," Cruz said, rubbing his eyes. He then looked off in the distance, towards the door of his office.

"You thinking about her?" Elga asked in a sad whisper.

"Who, Sherry?" Cruz raised an eyebrow.

"No…. Tamika."

"Elga…. Are you crazy? How many times do we have to go through this? How many times do I have to go through this with you?" Cruz stood and walked over to the window. There was anger in his voice, and pain in his expression.

Elga walked over behind him and hugged his waistline. With her face buried in his back she held him.

"I'm sorry, sweetness…. I'm sorry…. I just love you. I can't help it. I'm just insecure when it comes to you…. Are you mad at me?"

It was all baby-talk. Yet it was sincere, and Cruz knew it, because he knew her. She had been through a lot with men. They had really ruined the best part of her. The part that allowed her to love and trust. The part of her that was most essential to having a positive relationship. They had taken from her that which allowed her to be a woman. Yet she was not alone. He saw this in most women. Even Sherry.

"Nah, I'm not mad atcha. I am kinda busy though. Why don't you go and get somethin' nice for me to look at you in tonight." He smiled that smile that she loved to see. He then kissed her lightly before continuing. "I'll stop by the Familiar Spot and get us somethin' to eat and drink, okay. I'll be in before 10:00, I promise."

"Okay…." She looked him in the eyes, still holding on to him, not wanting to ever let him go. She tip-toed and kissed him. "I'm sorry for being so insecure. I'ma do better, okay?"

"Okay," he said before Sherry knocked on the door. "Come in."

"I'm sorry to disturb you, Mr. Cruz, but a Mr. J. Jackson is out here and he says that it is an emergency."

"Okay. Send him in. And show Ms. Wynn out please."

This was indeed a surprise. What in the hell was Smash doing at his place of business? After all, they had no business. He had not seen or heard from Smash since that day, long ago, at Big Mac's. Cruz was now seated behind his desk, thinking, when Smash finally walked in. He was smiling. A beautiful smile. It reminded Cruz of their childhood. Man had times changed! Yet they remained so much the same. Smash was stylishly dressed as always. The gap between his top six gold-teeth was still in place. Cruz watched. Smash continued to travel deeper into his space. Nearer. He stopped and extended his hand.

"What it do, big homie?" Smash asked, still smiling.

"Same ole two-step…. What brings you here?" Cruz stood and accepted his old friend's hand.

"Shiid, ain't a whole lot…. Just been thinkin' is all. Decided it was 'bout time we really sat down and rapped-a-taste."

"Dig, Smash, it's been years man. I mean, I tried to rap wit' you when I touched down. And man, I was down for nine and a half years and you never got at me. No letter. No visits. Man, not one dime! Ole Bluey was the only nigga to holla."

"Say, man. I can't speak for the fellas. I'm here on behalf of Smash. Period! Shit wasn't all gravy when you fell, jack. A nigga jive struggled wit' Busta gone. And Poppy wasn't fuckin' wit' no niggas. But I stayed down and fought to give you more than a dime when you got home, nigga…. From first street, all the way to Palm Beach. To Duval, up to Sumptor and back. You lookin' at the nigga that's stampin' the work. But you don't want that! So what a nigga 'posed to do? Huh? Tell me, man."

"You was supposed to be there, man. Fuck Moe, Head, and Shorty! You and Bluey was supposed to hold me down! We was friends."

"We still is friends! Dig, Cruz, this shit gotta stop. We both losin'. We've both lost too much. Especially you.... Man, I'm so sorry 'bout Mika.... Shit done went too far." Smash dropped his head and began sobbing. Cruz was speechless.

Regaining control of himself, Smash removed a small hand towel and wiped his face. Looking up at Cruz, he began to speak again. "Look, man.... Like I said, shit really done got outta hand. I'm here to jive make it right, if I can.... I told you that if I wasn't wit' you that I'd leave. Well, I'm gone, homie. But before I leave, I gotta get something off of my heart." Smash stood and walked over to the window and gazed out before continuing. "I had nothin' to do wit' this shit, man. I had no knowledge of it until after the fact. I just, well, I.... I ain't say nothin' because it wasn't gonna bring her back."

"What the fuck is you talkin' 'bout, nigga?" Cruz spat.

"DaDa, man. Big Shorty.... Tamika."

"Hold up, Smash. You losin' me. Who is DaDa and what do him and Big Shorty got to do wit' Tamika?" Cruz was now standing.

"DaDa is Head's lil' cousin from Tennessee. Somebody told him that you was the one that hit Head. Me and Blue told the young nigga to let it be. Besides, we knew that you ain't have shit to do wit' hittin' Head."

"And?!" Cruz snapped.

"And, the nigga wouldn't listen.... Nobody wouldn't ride wit' him so he paid Shorty to go."

"How do you know it was them for sure?"

"I was there when they left. But at the time, I didn't know where they was goin'.... Then I saw the news. I heard the report about the white Chevy.... Cruz, man, they left in DaDa's white Chevy."

Cruz could not believe what he was hearing. Flashbacks of that fatal day flashed through his mind. Tears began to stream down his face. He had murder on his mind and blood in his eyes. Smash could see it.

"I'm sorry, man. I really am...." Smash said as he reached into his coat pocket and removed an envelope. He placed it on Cruz's desk, patted his old friend on the shoulder and headed for the door. Smash opened the door, stopped and looked back at Cruz with tears in his eyes. "I'm, I'm sorry Cruz," he said and walked off.

"So am I," Cruz said to himself as he stood there. Opening the envelope he found a check for $50,000 made out to the foundation and there was also an address. The name above the address said, DaDa.

Chapter 27

Fast Long, Steve, Chuck, and Ninja all sat quietly, readying themselves as Palmer drove them closer to their destination. Palmer slowed the white cable truck as they turned off of 54th Street into Palm Gardens.

"What is today?" Chuck asked as they cleared the entrance.

"Sunday. What, you Muslim or something?" Palmer returned.

"Muslim? What are you talkin' about?" Chuck was puzzled.

"Yeah! A Muslim. Worship on Friday. 'Cause any good Christian gon' remember the Lord's day. How ya forget somethin' like that, Chuck? Less you Islamic. Moor, Nation, Talibane, it's all the same."

Chuck looked around the truck for support. Was Palmer serious? Steve caught Chuck's expression as he looked about and bussed out laughing.

"You can't always reason wit' Diddy, big homie. He stay on one," Steve said, still laughing.

"What that 'posed to mean?" Palmer asked.

"I'm just sayin', Diddy, man. You pick the craziest times to say the most 'off-the-wall' ass shit." Steve laughed some more before continuing. "We in a stolen van, with AK's and hand grenades, goin' to kill some niggas, and you talkin' 'bout *it's the Lord's Day*. You fucked up, big homie."

"That is kinda crazy, ain't it man," Palmer said with a chuckle.

"Looks like we ain't the only cable men on the block," Fast Long said, pointing to the white cable van that sat near the building they were going to.

"Yeah, I saw that," Chuck commented while scanning the area. "It's a lot of work going on 'round here on the good Lord's day."

"What you mean?" Palmer asked.

"It was a phone truck posted near the entrance."

Palmer parked the van and they waited. Meanwhile it was business as usual for the people of Palm Gardens. The hookers and the hustlers were moving back and forth. From car to gangway they were making moves. Palmer and his men had been posted for an hour and a half before their man decided to show his face. Accompanied by three huge men, Zoe made his way out of the building towards a brown station wagon.

"There we go!" Steve yelled, making his way to the door.

"Hold up, jit," Chuck said, raising his hand.

"Hold up? You gon' let 'im get away," Steve returned, AK-47 in hand.

"Trust me, jit…. Hold up for a few seconds."

"Man! This nigga scared! Who runnin' this shit, Diddy, you or him? 'Cause we been waitin' too long to let Zoe get away," Steve argued.

Chuck did not reply. He just continued to scan the area.

"Yeah, slim. Off the-no-bullshit. What is we waitin' on?" Palmer finally questioned.

"Look, I've been doin' this shit for a long time. And something ain't right," Chuck said.

"Shiid, Diddy! You been to Lebanon," Steve countered.

"Yeah, six tours, 32 confirmed kills," Palmer boasted.

"I thought it was three tours, 27 kills," Fast Long interjected.

"Six tours, three tours, it's all the same. I stopped countin' after 20 kills. It coulda been 100."

"Well this ain't Lebanon, fellas. Look!" Chuck said, pointing to the other cable van.

Just as Zoe and his men closed the doors of the station wagon and started the engine, the cable van began to move.

"1, 2, 3, 4, 5, 6, 7, and 8," Chuck pointed to the entrance. And sure enough, a big brown U.P.S. truck came in followed by a blue Tahoe and a white Surburban. The U.P.S. truck stopped just past the building, while the two SUV's sped in the direction of Zoe's vehicle.

"1, 2, 3, 4, 5, 6, 7, and 8," Chuck counted again and pointed to the entrance. The phone truck had closed it off by parking across the mouth of the entrance. The back of the U.P.S. truck flew up to reveal two men standing behind M-60's on tripods.

"1, 2, 3, 4, 5, 6, 7, and 8," Chuck pointed overhead.

"What?" Palmer asked. He was dumbfounded.

"Listen," Chuck said in an even tone.

Just then they began to hear a helicopter coming over the building. Three men stepped out of the cable truck with M-16's shouldered. The two SUV's came to a sudden halt right behind Zoe's station wagon. Six men emerged from both vehicles, donned in all black with ski masks and M-16's. At the same time men also began pouring out of the U.P.S. truck.

"God-damn! You see this shit?" Steve was shocked.

At that instance one of the men fired into the driver side door of the station wagon. *Tat! Tat! Tat!* Killing the driver and causing the occupant on the driver's rear side to jump out running. *Tat! Tat! Tat!* He was cut down before he cleared the door.

Boom! One of the men that exited the cable truck fired a large gun into the rear passenger side window. The canister shattered the window and the entire car was filled with smoke.

The three men from the Suburban continued to advance on the station wagon. The door of the window in which the canister had entered flew open. *Tat! Tat! Tat! Tat! Tat! Tat!* The dead man fell out onto the concrete. Snatching open the front passenger side door, two of the men drug Zoe's unconscious body to the Suburban.

The phone truck led the way into traffic. Followed by the Tahoe, the Suburban, and the cable truck. The U.P.S. truck was the last to leave. The rear door still up, showcasing its awesome firepower, daring anyone to pursue them. Just as suddenly as the helicopter had appeared, it was gone. The kidnapping took place in less than a minute and a half.

"Slim? Did you see that shit?" Palmer asked.

"Yeah. I don't know who this kat Zoe is, or what he's on, but he done pissed off the wrong muthafuckas," Chuck commented in his usual even tone.

"Off-the-no bullshit!"

"Come on. Let's break befo' boe-nine get here. 'Cause it's three dead dudes out here, on The Good Lord's Day."

Chapter 28

After dinner and a few drinks, Cruz laid in Elga's king-sized bed in only his silk Miami Heat boxers, smoking a kool. It had been a very long time since he had smoked one. But tonight he needed it. He laid there playing back the day Tamika had died, as well as the conversation that he'd had with Smash concerning her murder. Placing the cigarette butt into the ashtray, he downed the last of his XO just as Elga came into the room. She had on a leather bra with the nipple coverings removed. The panties were also leather, and crotch less. The sandy-brown hairs on her vagina were lightly shaved. As she stood wide-legged in the doorway, Cruz could see the lips of her pink pussy slightly gapped. He felt himself growing erect.

Elga walked over to the foot of the large bed and began crawling onto it like a starving feline approaching its helpless prey. She advanced further. Stopping between his legs she leaned forward and kissed him deeply. His erection grew larger. Feeling it on her inner thigh she reached down and squeezed it. Cruz cringed.

"I told your ass I was a great kisser," she said, looking him in the eyes. Still holding his manhood in her hand, she began kissing him again. She massaged his love-muscle as she ran her long tongue in and around his mouth.

Cruz took both of his hands and squeezed her breast, one in each hand. Applying more pressure, Cruz kissed her harder. He then slid her bra up, freed her big soft breasts. Continuing upwards, Cruz placed his hands on the top of her head and forced her down towards his shaft.

"Is this what you want?" she asked, looking him in the eyes, his dick still in her hand.

"No. It's what I need," Cruz capped.

She kissed it. Then ran her long wet tongue from below his testicles, up the bottom of his shaft, and over and around the head.

"Promise you won't leave me...You can't leave me." Elga was all baby talk.

"Promise me that you won't give me a reason to leave you." Cruz was all real talk. This was his element, Cruz-control.

"I promise!" was the last words she spoke before waging an all-out assault on his tower of power. Head work, she bobbed. Taking the full length of him, she worked the body. Never gagging once. That was out of the ordinary. The service was extraordinary. She was phenomenal in her ability to fellate.

Lifting herself she straddled Cruz, then reached behind herself and inserted Cruz's dick. Elga leaned forward and began to maneuver her hips in a slow circular motion. The secretion's of her vagina streamed down his pipe and onto the sheets like an open faucet.

Taking one of her large ripe breast into his mouth, Cruz nibbled and sucked at it. She increased her pace. Faster! More frantic! Until they both climaxed and collapsed in each others' arms. Only to repeat the act several more times that night.

Up early, Cruz dressed and headed for the door.

"Arthur!" Elga yelled.

Cruz turned to find her standing in the hallway completely nude. She had tears in her eyes. "You promised me that you wouldn't leave me."

"What?" Cruz asked.

Her entire demeanor was antipathetic. He was confused.

"You're leaving," she whined.

"Only for the moment..." Cruz then turned and walked out of the door.

* * *

It was very cold in the room where Zoe sat handcuffed to a chair. His head was killing him. The Haitian drug-boss had no idea where he was, or what time of day it was. The last thing that he remembered was closing the door of the station wagon; and all hell had broken loose. He was worried, but not scared. Because had they been killers he would've been dead already. In his mind, they were faking! They did not realize that by committing such an act against a man of his sovereignty, that they were dead already.

Then, all of a sudden, a tremendous pain exploded in his chest, sending him crashing to the floor. The chair that he was cuffed to shattered under the pressure of the impact.

"Stand that black son-of-a-bitch up."

There were footsteps, and Zoe felt himself being lifted to a standing position. His entire head was hooded and the handcuffs remained. Again there was an explosion. This time it was in his stomach. The pain caused Zoe to fold-over and fall to his knees. There were more footsteps. It seemed to be at least three or four men in the room.

Zoe's worst nightmares were realized when the hood was snatched from his head. He cringed! Not only from the violent spectacle of lights, but more so from the potential violence of the small pale man that stood before him.

"Ma, Ma, McIntosh. Boss, what I do?" Zoe asked.

McIntosh did not bother to answer. He simply back-handed Zoe across the face. *Whooop!* Sending Zoe down on his side.

"Uncuff the son-of-a-bitch!" McIntosh commanded.

"Sir, are you..." one of the suited men began to ask.

"You fucking heard me! Get those got-damned cuffs off and get the fuck out of here!"

The men did as they were instructed. Quickly they left McIntosh alone in the cooler of the small store. This was one of the many Arab stores that served as fronts to launder drug proceeds and operate foodstamps schemes. The CIA had many such fronts, and used them to fund Black Operations. This allowed them to operate outside and above the law. For they did not have to bow or report to Congress, and conform to their budgets and/or limitations.

McIntosh was a seasoned animal. He mainly operated under the alias Ya'acov Nimrodi, but was known as Al Shaitan, The Devil. McIntosh joined the F.B.I. in '72, but was later initiated into the C.I.A. in '77. He'd served to organize the Shiite Militant Muslims In 1979. As the Administrative Executive of the Ayatollah Khomeini, McIntosh had helped to overthrow the Shah of Iran. This was his very first assignment as a C.I.A. operative, and it helped to corrupt and alter the 1980 presidential election.

Zoe, after the cuffs had been removed and his eyes and mind had adjusted to the circumstances of his situation, attempted to raise himself.

"Remain on your fucking knees, you black sack of shit," McIntosh barked.

Zoe remained as told. McIntosh removed a folder from the table and threw it in Zoe's face. Papers spew everywhere.

"Collect 'em!"

Zoe began picking them up. He looked nothing like the murderous general that commanded the streets. If Zoe's Pound could see him now, bowing before this cracka, he would no longer have a Pound.

"Do you know what that is?" McIntosh asked.

Looking over a few of the papers Zoe saw his name. He saw Kunta's name. He saw locations that included Palm Gardens, The Matchbox, Scott Projects, The Pork and Beans, and places in New York and Algeria. There were homicide and gun transactions. Bank records, as well as personal criminal records. Aviation reports. There was a complete narrative of his history involving organized crime, not to exclude all of his current and ex associates. And he'd been the narrator of most of the reports.

"Yes, it's Kunta's original criminal complaint and my statements against him and others," Zoe responded.

"I saved your black ugly ass from prison. Where you'd most likely have become some strong man's nigger-bitch.... Now how do you show your gratitude to Mr. McIntosh? The man who gave you power and crowned you over all other niggers. You let some ex nigger-flat-foot hustler, turn revolutionary, come home and take my streets! What do you have to say for yourself?"

"Boss, I...."

"Shut the fuck up!.... and listen. You listen good! The ghettos and projects, world-wide, were designed for nigger destruction, not improvement. I allow you to operate towards those ends, and those ends alone. You, for your part, get to enjoy some luxuries and help your little nigger friend, Kunta, feel like he's accomplishing something. Very well." McIntosh mockingly applauded while smiling before he continued. "You see this scimitar? It was given, well, I took it from the Shah of Iran.... I'm going to take this same scimitar, and I'm going to drive to Lake Land and cut that mammy bitch of yours to pieces! Then I'll come back through Hollywood and kill your wife and every one of those little coons that the two of you have produced.... Do you understand me, boy?"

"I understand, boss."

"Good.... Now you get your black ass on a plane to Algeria. And you tell that black son-of-a-bitch, Kunta, that it was I, Ya'acov Nimrodi, that allowed him to escape. That I'm his boss, and that the two of you had better deal with the monster he created, Cruz.... Now leave me...."

"B, b, boss...."

"Get the fuck out!" McIntosh yelled.

And Zoe was off to do the biddings of his true boss-man.

Chapter 29

As the small G2 came in for its landing, Zoe took in all of the beauty of Algeria. It had been almost twenty years since he had last been in such a place.

Exiting the plane with two of his own men, Zoe was greeted by a score of heavily armed men in fatigues marked A.P.L.A. After formal salutations had been exchanged Zoe and his two men were escorted to a line of black Hummers. As the vehicles bumped along the rickety dirt roads en route to Kunta's Algerian layer, they saw a group of mandrills wrestling and eating mango on the edge of the jungle. Then, just beyond the river, there stood a battery of old mangonels lining the entrance to the huge palace.

Before Zoe and his men had time to exit their Hummer a dozen beautiful women, also dressed in A.P.L.A. fatigues and head dresses, descended on them. The leader of the group, the darkest and most attractive, approached Zoe with the intentions of searching him. She reached towards Zoe and he caught her arm and turned it. But before he could fully apply the arm-lock, the woman stumped the toe of his designer shoe, causing him to release her. "Bit-" Zoe started to yell before being silenced by an open slap to the face, *Whoop!* Zoe's men went for their guns, but were immediately stopped at the sound and sight of thirty-one automatic guns swinging in their direction.

"We are not in Amerikkka, Mr. Zoe! Such language and aggression towards women will not be tolerated…. Now! Conform, or get back into the vehicle and be on your way," the lead woman instructed.

Zoe eyed the woman with pure hatred! How dare anyone, especially a black-bitch, get indignant with him. Chastisement! This woman needed to be chastised; and a good sodomizing would serve essentially in her punishment. Looking from her to all of the guns pointed at him and his men, Zoe spat a hunk of spit on her combat boots. He then raised his arms above his head to be searched. Never once did he take his eyes off of the very attractive leader. And neither did she divert her stare from his.

After finally entering the palace the woman led Zoe to the rear of the house, where they passed two more armed women. Taking a stairway, Zoe was led further down a long dark hallway. The woman knocked three times on the wall panel before the opposite wall panel slid open, giving them access to a small cargo-elevator. In the dark, they rode in silence. There were no buttons or light indicators to tell whether they were traveling up or down. Again, they walked along a dark corridor. This time they stopped in front of a heavy steel door. The woman knocked three times. Zoe heard the sound of locks being turned. The door opened. Opposite them stood another woman. Only she wore a pants suit. Zoe was given entrance to the large study. The two women disappeared into the dark hallway.

Sitting in the far corner of the room, in black military garb, was Kunta. He was reading Richard Evans' *The Third Reich In Power.*

Upon seeing Zoe, his oldest and dearest friend, he closed the book and stood to greet him.

"Zoe! How are you? It is so good to see you!" Kunta smiled brightly.

"What is with that bitch you have in charge?" Zoe barked.

"Bitch? What is wrong with you, Zoe? What happened?"

"That woman has no respect! She pointed guns at me.... She demanded that 'I' allow her soldiers to probe me and my men. She...."

"She was only doing her job. She meant you no disrespect, nor any harm."

"Her job?! Her job does not include me. Or have you become so great that you even distrust me? The one who...."

"Zoe.... Please. We both know that the Judas is always on the inside," Kunta said calmly.

"Judas? Did you just...."

"I did not mean it that way. We 'all' simply have to be very careful. We have protocol that we must follow."

"Protocol, huh? Have you not received my messages?"

"How are you, Zoe?"

"How am I?" Zoe repeated.

"Yes, your health. You look a little heavy around the gut," Kunta said jokingly.

"My health?" Zoe closed his eyes and shook his head before continuing. "Would you like for me to go back outside and come back in so as we can start this all over again?"

"What do you mean by that, Zoe?"

"I mean, what the fuck has my health got to do with anything? I did not fly all the way across the earth to be humiliated by some bitch, then have you play mind games with me! I sent you several messages. You have not responded! So I came myself! Now what and thee fuck are you going to do about Arthur Cruz?"

"Zoe, has the man not lost enough? After all, was not this the plan? To clean our people up? To bring about a change."

"Whose plan? And whose people? I have no such plan! Those foolish Amerikkkan negros are not my people! Therefore they are not my problem.... My agreement was for my people," Zoe snapped.

"Zoe! You are wrong! And I did not build this organization to turn a blind-eye to any injustice. I did not sacrifice; my father was not sacrificed to the ends of which you speak...."

"Your organization? Your sacrifice? McIntosh was right about you. You really are fucked up. You've read too many of your own speeches," Zoe chuckled as the words left his mouth.

"McIntosh?" Kunta questioned.

"Yes.... Ya'acov Nimrodi. Al Shaitan!" Zoe said.

"What has he to do with this, or us, at all?"

"He has everything to do with us! Do you really think that your rhetoric brought you this?" Zoe laughed aloud as he pointed around the room. "Please, do not answer that. You will only sicken me further. You are not in power because you read some books. You are in power because of my sacrifices! Because of me and my political ties."

"What are you talking foolish about? I built the A.P.L.A. I...."

"I, I, your ass! You had an i-dea! You had a dream. One that got you sent to prison to die! I made the proper moves to avoid falling with you. I took your movement and made it a reality. Do you think that I, or anyone could operate like I do without help? Do you think that you could have escaped from a max prison like Terre Haute without help? Do not fool yourself! You could not get an extra orange out of the mess hall without the authorities' knowledge of it."

"You mean to tell me...." Kunta started to speak.

"Yes! I mean to tell you that you are only a pop-u-lar pawn. I mean to tell you that McIntosh and thee Amerikkkans are the key to your success."

"I can not believe you, Zoe!"

"And I do not understand you! Everyone needs strong political ties to survive. Did you not learn anything from your father's mistakes?"

"Don't you mention my father! You, you...."

"Fuck you! Your father was a fuckin' fool...."

"I'll kill you!" Kunta screamed.

"And Algeria will be a cloud of smoke before the week's end... Go ahead, great general.... Yes, just like I thought..."

Kunta was devastated at what he was hearing. He was mentally and spiritually broken. "Zoe, what have you done to me?" Kunta asked.

"I have assured you victory! You told me in the beginning that *losing was not an option*. Well, I sacrificed some pawns and bishops to protect you, the King. I went outside of the box and got you a win! Now you must sacrifice. You must kill one black Amerikkkan negro for the betterment of 17 million Algerians."

"Zoe, you broke the rules."

"No! I broke the cycle. There are no rules! Winning is what McIntosh has taught me. Victory is what 'I' guarantee."

"You can't guarantee nothing! God alone decides."

"I am God! Have you not heard that we all were...."

"You are nothing! And you will burn in hell...."

"Fool, God never made a hell, nor a heaven for man. We are creators, and we make our own. You, Kunta, have a chance to create heaven for the 17 million."

Kunta sat thinking. He had never been so confused in his entire life. Looking up at Zoe, with anger and deep sorrow in his voice, he began to speak.

"I will do this…. I will continue this evil you have brought for me. But I 'alone' must do it. And after it is done, I want nothing to do with 'you' or your keeper, McIntosh."

"As you wish, your greatness," Zoe smiled mockingly.

"Please, leave me…. I will arrange your trip back."

With that said, Kunta pressed a button on the wall and began walking away. The two women reappeared in the doorway to escort Zoe out.

Chapter 30

Cruz sat on the passenger side of the dark-blue Honda Accord screwing the silencer into the barrel of the small 9mm. Big Breed sat at the wheel. They had been sitting and watching DaDa's house every since dawn. There had been no movement, with the exception of the paperboy and some woman coming out to retrieve the paper he had thrown on the porch. She was young. Her skin was paper bag brown. She had long brownish hair with full lips, Chinese eyes, and though she was tall and slender, she was quite curvaceous.

"Cruz, you don't think we should let Diddy 'em handle this?"

"Big Breed, we already done been through that. Now you can haul ass, it's all on you. But me, this nigga killed my people, and I'ma personally see to it that he get his due justice."

"It's yo' call. I was just...."

"Sayin'! Yeah aiight, but you said enough! Fuck all that talkin' shit."

The two continued to sit in silence. Breed toyed with the Mac-11 that he was armed with and Cruz continued to check his phone every three minutes on the minute.

"Damn! This girl is blowin' my shit up!"

"Who that?" Breed asked.

"Elga."

"You sho' know how to pick 'em."

"You got that right. Either they crazy or they goin' crazy."

"Say no muthafuckin' more…. Look right there!" Breed pointed to the house. Cola was dressed and heading towards the white Chevy.

"Come on…. Follow her. She might be goin' to pick up the nigga."

Cruz's theory proved to be false. Cola led them to a house where she picked up an older version of herself, her mother or an aunt maybe. The two went to an expensive little restaurant on County Line Road, and then to Ebony Drugs on 17th and 60th. Cola then dropped her older version off and returned home.

"So what we gon' do, homie?" Breed asked.

"We gon' wait."

Two hours later Cola emerged again wearing a different outfit. Breed and Cruz followed her again, but this time they ended up at Westland Mall, where Cola embraced two other women at the mall entrance before going in. It was another two and a half hours before they came back out, loaded with shopping bags. They all embraced again before Cola returned home.

"Hey man, I'm tired of sittin' out here and playing security for this broad," Breed said.

"So stop waitin', then."

"What?"

"The next time this bitch come outta that house, and the nigga still ain't wit' her, we gon' snatch the bitch," Cruz stated.

It took another two hours, but Cola did emerge, again wearing a different outfit, and again she was alone. Pulling the white Chevy out of the yard she headed east. Like most *square* women, she was not paying attention to what was going on around her. She never saw Breed and Cruz get out of the car behind her as she walked towards the salon entrance.

"Excuse me! Beautiful," Cruz shouted as he made his way over to her. "May I please speak wit' you for a moment?"

Cola turned to see Cruz approaching her. "Cute," she thought. But quickly turned to go inside the salon. As she grabbed the door, Breed grabbed her arm, his gun was in his other hand.

"Bitch! You heard my man callin' you. Get yo' ass over here."

Cola was shocked to see the huge man and the gun he held.

"Homie, that's no way to talk to a woman. Is it, suga?" Cruz said as he put his arm around her waist and began walking her back to the Chevy. "Just get in and it'll all be over soon…. Okay?"

Cola was too scared to speak. She merely nodded her head in agreement. Breed drove the Chevy while Cola and Cruz rode in the backseat.

"You gon' be alright, babygirl, but you gotta help me…. Will you help me?" Cruz asked while removing the 9mm from his waistband.

Cola nodded her head up and down, indicating yes.

"Okay, good. I have some questions. And you're gonna have to talk. Can you talk?"

Cola nodded again. Cruz raised an eyebrow and shifted in his seat.

"Oh, I'm, I'm sorry…. I mean, yes. I, I can talk," she stuttered.

"Very good…. See homie, I told you we might not have to kill her."

"Whatever, man," Breed responded, playing the bad guy opposite Cruz's good guy role.

"No! Please, please. Don't kill me. I, I'll tell you…."

"Shhhh," Cruz said, placing his index-finger over her beautiful full lips. "You'll be fine. As long as you tell me the truth. Can you do that?"

"Yyyeess," Cola whined.

"Aiight.... Now, who the fuck is DaDa and where the fuck is he?"

* * *

Bluey laid in the queen-sized hotel bed looking up at the mirrored ceiling. This gave him a perfect overhead view of the whole scene. And in his own words, "he really dug it!"

Deion laid between his legs giving him some of the best head he had ever had in his life. She moaned as she served him; because Miay was on her knees with Deion's ass spread as far open as she could hold it, licking her from pearl-tongue to rectum. The trio had been going at it for hours. They had started out with a pill a piece, but once the cocaine was brought out, all of the freak came out with it.

This was tradition for Ole Bluey. And Deion, though she was not his main girl, she was the closest thing to it, and she always made sure that Bluey was happy.

As he laid there, his phone began ringing. His first mind told him not to answer it. But with all that had been going on, he went against his better judgement and decided to answer it.

"Yeah.... What up?.... Yeah, this Blue! Who the fuck you lookin' for.... Moe, slowdown, homie.... Okay, I can dig that. But.... Seventeen! The shit is only doin' seventeen?.... Aiight, I'ma call Chico.... Why not? It's his right.... Yeah, I'm at the 'tel with Falion."

"Nigga, what?" Deion yelled, still holding Bluey's dick in her hand.

"Oh, girl, no he didn't," Miay commented, taking a break from pleasing Deion.

"What?" Bluey asked, looking at the two of them. He had not realized what he had said.

"Nigga, you called me Falion! I can't believe you, Blue. You fuckin' my lil' sister?" Deion asked.

"Bitch! Hell nawl!" Bluey lied.

"Nigga, I can't tell! I'm 'round here settin' my friends out for you, and tryin' to keep yo' no-good-ass happy…. And this what you go do?" she said, now in tears.

"Hold on, Moe, my nigga." Bluey then continued with Deion. "Look here, pussy-ass-hoe! I told you I ain't fuckin' ya sista…. Punk bitch! You ain't had no business I-spying my convo' noway, hoe!"

"But Blu-"

"Nah, bitch! Shut the fuck up…. You and ya punk-ass friend go in the bathroom somewhere…. Find you some business."

"Okay, but…." Deion tried to speak.

"Hoe, I said get!"

"Come on, girl," Miay said, walking her friend to the bathroom.

"Okay, man, look. You know I don't know a whole lot about that shit…. What? You wanna re-rock 100 birds?…. Man, you trippin'…. Aiight, I'm on my way…. Yeah, nigga, I'm comin' now…. Yeah, I'ma be by myself."

Bluey hung up his phone and called DaDa. There was no way Moehead was going to have him stuck over his house for two days re-rocking cocaine. DaDa was good at that shit and would cut the time in half.

"Say, lil' one, what's up?…. Dig, I need you!…. This nigga Moe got some fucked up work and wanna re-rock it…. Yeah, I know you don't fuck 'round no more, but I need you! Just this once…. Cola got the car?…. Aiight, look, I gotta drop these two chicks off. So just jump a cab, I'll pay for it, 'cause I'ma already be there…. Yeah…. See you in 'bout two hours…. One."

Bluey hung up the phone and started getting dressed. He then walked into the bathroom to urinate. Deion and Miay were sitting there naked, talking about the issue with Falion and Bluey.

"Yall hoes get dressed. Get ya shit. I gotta go," Bluey told them.

Deion stared at him. At that moment she hated him. "You gon' get yours nigga," she said as they walked out of the bathroom.

"Whatever, hoe."

But Bluey had no idea how right she truly was….

* * *

"Please, I don't wanna die…. I have some money. And, and, you can do anything you want to me, but please…. Not DaDa, please," Cola whined. She looked Cruz right in the eyes as tears ran down her face.

"I wish that it was that simple, lil' momma. But unfortunately it's not. I'm not here for the money. I've come for his life."

The girl began to shake uncontrollably. She held herself and doubled-over next to Cruz. He was sadden by this whole affair. For he truly had compassion for the brave, young, beautiful girl. Yet, it was what it was, MURDER.

"Are you willin' to die for this nigga?" Cruz asked.

"I don't want to."

"Well if I don't find him you will die…. DaDa owes me, and I aim to collect."

"I'll pay you. I swear…."

"He owes me his life…. Your DaDa is a fuckin' croward! He killed my wife. Now I'ma kill him, or you, and still kill him! The choice is yours."

"DaDa would never do that...."

"Why wouldn't he? He did it in his car! This is his car isn't it?"

"No! No this Moehead car.... They, him and Smash, needed DaDa's truck, so Smash dropped off the car and took the truck...."

"Smash?" Cruz questioned.

"Yeah, Smash. He dropped it off yesterday morning."

"Yesterday morning?" Cruz thought to himself. Smash had just came to his office yesterday, right before noon, with the information concerning Tamika's murder. *What in the fuck was going on?* he wondered, then remembered Bishop Michael's words, their conversation, "Are miscalculations in anyway good for business?' 'Not if one is to be successful.' 'Then know this. Whoever has wronged you does not like the way that things are going. So he, whoever he is, will come to you with a solution to bring about peace. Look into it. Look into them! Love your enemy. For he will expose his deceit." Cruz could not believe it. Smash had really been studying his Art of War. And he had almost fell victim to his tactics.

"Are you bein' honest with me?" Of course, Cruz already knew that she was.

"Yes! I swear! DaDa ain't left the house...." she stopped mid-sentence, but it was too late. She had already disclosed DaDa's whereabouts.

"Breed, send somebody back to that house. Keep an eye on DaDa.... Now listen, baby, what's your name?"

"Cola," she said, sniffling.

"Okay, Cola, look, if you tellin' me the truth, nothin' will happen to you or DaDa.... But for some reason, somebody wants somethin' real bad to happen to DaDa. Do you have any idea who?"

"Well, him and Moe was arguing the other day when DaDa told them he was finish with the hustling."

"Why were they arguing?"

"I don't know really. But Moe was real mad. DaDa pulled a gun on him about some money he owed."

"DaDa owed Moe?"

"No, Moe and Smash owe DaDa."

"Okay, look, Smash is the one who sent me. Now if you wanna help DaDa you gonna have to help me. Will you help me?"

"Yes...."

"Good! This is what we're gonna do...."

Chapter 31

As Ole Bluey walked along the side of Moehead's house, a strange feeling came down over him. The vibe was all wrong. "Vibe," he thought to himself. Maybe it was those damned X-pills he had taken. That along with the argument he and Deion had had was indeed enough to rock any sane man's ethers. He could still see the hatred in her eyes as she said, "you gon' get yours nigga." Deion was a real cool chick, Blue thought as he closed the privacy fence and walked up the back stairs. He promised himself that he would make it up to her as soon as he concluded his business with Moehead.

"What up, my nigga?" Moehead said, opening the door.

"Heeey."

"What's wrong, nigga? You lookin' crazy as a muthafucka."

"Man, I'm off that."

"Off what?" Moehead questioned.

"Off that! What you smokin'?"

"Nigga, you know what it is."

"Let me hit that…. I'm feelin' crazy."

Moehead passed Ole Bluey the joint as the two walked through the kitchen into the living room. Moehead had a very conspicuous pad. It reeked of fast living and blood investments. Ole Bluey hated to be there. Looking over at the breakfast bar, Bluey saw the Vision Ware pot that held the piss-color liquid that was supposed to be crack cocaine. Bluey smiled to himself and took another long draw off the lace-joint.

"Say there, Moe. What's the muthafuckin' hold-up?"

"Blue, every since that nigga Cruz came home it's been a lot of high-stakes and bad-breaks for a nigga."

"I can dig it, man…. I really can."

"What happened wit' the teacher hoe you met at the hospital that you was tellin' me 'bout the other day. Tell me 'bout that, Blue."

"Say, man. One word. Expensive!"

"What you do? A stack?"

"Nawl, nigga! I ain't gave the bitch nay dime. You-hear-me? It's what the bitch gave me! Say, man? It's hard to dig how a dame can have an Oxford head on her shoulders, with Bentley potentials, yet they'll devour whole crews of dudes like some starved bitch carnivore or whatever…. I'm talkin', on the strength! Free of charge. And not even have greens to score grits when it's all said and done. Say man, I really can't dig that." Blucy shook his head in sorrow, still smoking the joint.

"Shit Blue! Look at you! You mobbed-up…. Brand new ride. And you're a real bitch connoisseur to begin wit'…. Shit, anybody can see why they hoe-up for you."

"Oh, shit, Moe! I wasn't talkin' 'bout me. I was talkin' about them other niggas! Off-da-no-bullshit, a hoe betta know that all my visits is conjugal and 100% tax free."

"Nigga! You fulla shit...." Moehead laughed. "Gimme my muthafuckin' weed!"

"Nah, nah, for real. Off-the-no-bullshit.... You remember the nigga, Dream?"

"Big dumb-ass-nigga, got the hoe wit' the one dumb-ass goldtooth in the front?"

"Big Dot!"

"Yeah, what about her?"

"Not her! The nigga, Dream."

"Fat-ass-nigga, use to work for you?"

"Yeah, yeah! Well, you remember Hog, his homeboy?"

"Black ass skinny nigga? The one you pistol-whipped in the projects that day?"

"Nawl, nigga! That's the nigga that used to fuck wit' the hoe Sheba."

"Hog?"

"Bone, stupid-ass-nigga!"

"So what Hog got to do wit' this?"

"Hog is who I'm speakin' on."

"So why you pistol-whip Bone? Kill me, my nigga! That was some funny shit!"

"Moe?"

"What up?"

"Is you really that fucked up, man?"

"Okay man, okay...." Moe was in tears thinking about that day when Bone came over to Sheba's house trying to hide from Bluey. He had been owing Bluey for over a month. Yet had no idea that Bluey had been fucking Sheba. So when he walked in the house, he didn't just catch Sheba sucking the blood out of Bluey, but he got pistol-whipped, stripped, and ran out of the projects.

"So you remember Hog?"

"Used to work for you right?"

"Who said that?"

"You did!"

"No I didn't! I said Dream used to work for me."

"Aiight."

"Anyway, the nigga Hog was gettin' his money. See, he was gettin' work from a nigga, that was gettin' work from a nigga, that was gettin' work from the nigga I was givin' it to."

"So how you meet Hog?"

"I didn't. He had this hoe, Keisha. Dog! Pussy was on one thousand! You-hear-me?"

"So what about the nigga Hog?"

"Fuck Hog! It was Keisha. She introduced me to Smelly Mel."

"Keisha introduced you to Mel?"

"Yeah, yeah! So the nigga gettin' a unit right...." Bluey hit the lace-joint again before continuing. "Well, he hit me one day. Say he needed one. So I told him to come through. I was at the crib in Homestead with Keta-Black and the kids. But by the time slim got there, Keta-Black was gone. So it was just me and Monisha there."

"So what happened, Blue?"

"If you let me I'ma tell you.... Simple ass nigga.... Anyway, he had a hoe wit' him. Bad-red-bitch! She was 'bout yo' height, slim, nice ass! China-doll eyes and big lips. Cold cum-drinka.... He was callin' the hoe San or some shit.... So dig! I'm breakin' the unit for the nigga. We was in the kitchen. He facin' me and I was facin' the living room. All the while I'm 'bout to cook one for Mel so he knows it's straight. Slim? The hoe keep eyein' a nigga. So I'm peepin' her and shit. Remember, I told you that Monisha was there wit' me. She was 'bout one at that time."

"Okay, what happened?" Moehead asked excitedly. He loved to hear Ole Bluey's hoe-tales.

"Moe?"

"Yeah?"

"Will you shut the fuck up... Or do you wanna tell the story?"

"Aiight, Blue, my nigga, go 'head."

"Dig, I told you the nigga Mel was facin' me. So he couldn't see the hoe, and she knew it. Monisha was playin' on the floor. The hoe stood wide-legged and bends over. My nigga? Skirt, no panties! Pussy spread like the Red Sea! I automatically rocked-up. You-hear-me? She looked back over her shoulder at me and smiled. I really could not believe it."

"So what you do?"

"Shit, I put the coc' in the microwave. Let it cook, and tried like hell to drop it. It would not fall.... So I was fucked up at that point. But the nigga Mel stepped up. He said that he had a spot that he could shift it down and gram it out in blow, *if I gave him a play on it.*"

"So what you do?"

"I gave the nigga a play. Him and the hoe left."

"So did you fuck the hoe later on?"

"Nawl, man! I don't just go 'round fuckin' everybody hoe."

"So what's the point?"

"The point is, soon as they left Keta-Black and Marquis walked through the door. And like I said, I was fucked up at that point, because I had nine more of them muthafuckas in the room, and I didn't feel like goin' through it with Chico."

"So what you do?"

"I was sittin' there, face in my hands, sick as a dopefiend in police custody. You hear me, man? So Keta-Black walked over to me. 'Nigga what's wrong wit' you?' I just looked at the hoe. So she said, 'Hmph, you can't talk when it comes to Black, but you can't stay from rappin' wit' them punk bitches.... Nigga you somethin' else…. That bakin soda in the bag'. So I say, 'Bakin Soda?'And she say, 'yeah nigga! You sent me way 'cross town to get that Pure Bakin Soda. Like you too advanced for Armor Hammer. Fake ass cook'.'"

"So what you tellin' me this for, Blue?"

"You is a stupid muthafucka…. Look, man, I sent the hoe to the store to get some bakin soda. Hint! I was out! Fuckin' 'round wit' that hoe, San, or whatever her name was, I forgot and put the coc' in the microwave wit' no bakin soda. It wasn't nothin' wrong wit' the coc', it was me. I gave that slick-ass-nigga Mel a good unit for dirt cheap."

"And?"

"And? Stupid-ass-nigga, you wastin' my time. I'm lookin' at the pot, and it looks just like that shit that I forgot to put the bakin soda in…."

Bluey got up and walked over to the breakfast bar where the pot sat. He picked it up and knew right away that he had been right.

"You might be right, Blue. I was rushin'," Moehead said.

"Where is yo' soda, man?"

"Under the cabinet."

Bluey bent down to get the bakin soda. And when he lifted up and turned around, he was staring down the barrel of Moehead's Glock .40.

"I hate an ultra-smart nigga!" Moehead said as he pulled the trigger. *Boom! Boom!* the gun sounded. "Now, tell me what's missin' now…. Hoe-ass."

Ole Bluey died with his eyes open. Deion had been right, and he would never get the chance to make it up to her. At least not in this life time.

Chapter 32

"Hey Smash," Cola spoke into the cell phone.

"Who the fuck is this?"

"This Cola, boy."

"Oh, what up? Where is DaDa?"

"I don't know…. He just up and left this morning. He been actin' real funny, man…."

"Hold up, hold up. Cola, what do you want? You know that we don't do this *you call cryin' and I tell on the homie shit.*"

"Smash, ain't nobody asked you nothin' 'bout no DaDa. Boy, please! You the one brought him up, anyway…. scared ass."

"Scared? Cola, what the fuck is you on?"

"Yeah, scared! DaDa first and now you…. Look Smash, man, I'ma be one hundred wit' you. I ain't wit' this square shit. I met DaDa in the streets 'cause I wanted a street nigga. Man, I'm still in the streets. How 'bout you?"

"For life," Smash shot back.

"So you not scared?"

"Of what?"

"Me."

"Hell nawl! Smash ain't never been scared of a muthafuckin' thang. Shit! What you tryin' to do?"

"I'm tryin' to guarantee my future in these streets, baby…. You a smart dude. I need a 'man'. Smash baby, I need yo' help…. 'cause, 'cause I'm leavin' DaDa. I can't take this shit."

"Heeey, I hate to hear that. But I can dig it, and I'm always willin' to help a friend in need. Say, where you at?"

"About eight minutes from your house," Cola answered.

"Well, why don't you fall through so we can really rap-a-taste. Hell, I could really use-a-taste right now, anyway."

"What?"

"The door will be open…. Oh, and leave ya shoes on the porch, 'cause that there is *mank* on the living room floor…." Smash hung up the phone.

Playa, Playa, he thought to himself. Standing, he viewed himself in the full-length mirror. He was a very slim, red dude. Yet he had started to develop a gut. Rubbing it, he turned side-ways. *Damn! I gotta start workin' out…. No bullshit! Once Cruz bitch ass kill DaDa and I hip the fuzz to it, my cash count gon' be longa than a broke hoe's dreams! Please believe it! And I'ma need my strength and stamina to count and carry all my millions…. and to ball all the bitches!* With those thoughts Smash prepared himself for his coming guest.

* * *

Cola parked the Chevy and sat there for a moment to calm herself. After applying some lip gloss and taking a last look in the car mirror, she grabbed her purse and headed up the walkway. Cola opened the door, remembering to remove her shoes, she entered the large house. It was absolutely beautiful! Mink floor. Ivory and gold was tastefully splashed throughout the entire room. High ceiling with a sky-view. "Damn-it, man!" she thought to herself. "The nigga got some class."

"Smash! You here?" Cola yelled.

"Yeah! I'm in the back. Come on in here!"

Cola walked down the long hallway to find Smash laying on the biggest bed she had ever seen in her life. He was smoking a joint and watching *JD's Revenge* on a huge flat-screen.

"Don't just stand there, baby boo. Come on and take a seat. Lay back or something.... You want a drank, a pill, or a blow? It's whatever in Smash Daddy's Dream Palace."

"Nah, I'm aiight. But your house is very nice."

"Yeah, I know," he said while standing.

The light from the flat-screen reflected his 16 gold-teeth as he spoke, and brought the many diamonds that he wore to life. A rainbow flashed in the dark.

He stood toe-to-toe with Cola and looked into her beautiful eyes. She returned his stare. He kissed her lightly on the lips. She continued to stare. Placing his arms around her waist, he kissed her deeper. She responded by putting her arms around his neck. Smash then took the liberty to explore the secret confines of her body. He lifted her skirt and ran his finger beneath her G-string and found her sex-cavity moist. She jumped! He continued. Pushing her to the bed, she landed on the cool silk sheets with him on top of her. She could feel his erection rubbing against her clitoris. She hated herself, because she liked it.

Smash reached between her legs and played in the juices that her vagina had produced. Then, in one swift gesture, he tore away her panties.

"Wait! Smash, please...."

He silenced her by placing his cunt soiled fingers in her mouth. She accepted it.

"We ain't gonna do a whole lotta rappin' and playin', suga…. Daddy Smash gon' getcha right."

Moving down her body, he kissed her clitoris. Lifting her legs slightly, he positioned himself to enact a full-range assault on her sweet quivering pink quiver.

"Oooh, God!" Cola moaned. *I hate myself*, she thought.

"Don't call, Him. Suga, this ain't God's pussy. This here Smash pussy! Say my muthafuckin' name!"

Lifting her right leg, she placed her foot on his shoulder. He dined, she moaned. Cola then drew her leg back slightly from his shoulder, and pushed it forward with great force, sending Smash flying from the bed to the floor.

"Bitch, is you crazy?!" Smash jumped up. "Hoe! I'ma beat yo' funky…."

His tirade was cut short by the butt of a 9mm against his skull. The blow sent him crashing to the floor.

"Say, man? What the hell is…."

"Shut the fuck up, nigga!" Cruz demanded.

"Oh, Cruz. Man I'm glad to see you…. Shit, I thought maybe some funky hearted niggas was out to cross me, you know." Smash chuckled a bit to mask his fear.

"You a real piece of shit, Smash…. Man, and I almost went for it."

"Say, man, why the sour look? Cruz, what's wrong? If it's a problem, I can help you fix it."

"You the problem, nigga! You a fuckin' disease! You, Moe, and every nigga like you!"

"Cruz, this is me, Smash! What are you talkin' 'bout, man?" Tears were now running down Smash's face.

287

"You know what the fuck I'm talkin' about! DaDa didn't kill Tamika! That Chevy belongs to Moe! You niggas killed Tamika…. Now I'ma kill you." Cruz aimed the gun.

"Wait a minute, man! Please, just wait a minute. I'ma playa, Cruz! You know that. I ain't no killa. Lord knows I ain't! It was Bluey and Moe, homie. I swear to God! I tried to stop 'em, but they threatin' to croak my daughter and my ole-girl…. Look man, I got money. You can have it all! I'll leave right now. Please man, I don't wanna die! Cruz, don't killa nigga like this."

By now Cola had fixed herself and gathered her purse. She was standing right behind Cruz.

"I ain't gon' kill you, Smash."

"Thank you, my nigga…. Thank you! Thank God."

Cruz handed the gun to Cola and stood back. She raised an eyebrow and looked from Cruz to the gun. Cruz said nothing.

"Hold on, man! Nawl! Cruz, no man…. Don't let no bitch kill me," Smash yelled and lunged for the gun.

Pop! Pop! Pop! Cola squeezed off three shot as she pedaled backwards to avoid Smash's attack. Each shot hitting its mark. Smash laid dead in his Dream Palace.

"Here, drop the gun in here. Remember, it's got your fingerprints on it. So I'ma hold on to it, to help us both forget that 'you' killed a man today…. You understand?" Cruz asked.

Cola shook her head yes. She understood completely.

"Breed," Cruz called.

"Yeah homie?"

"Find all of that money the nigga was talkin' about. Then burn this crib to the ground."

"Aiight."

"Take the truck out there and meet me back at her crib."

Putting his coat around Cola, Cruz held her as they walked to the Chevy.

* * *

"Hey! Hey, man! Can you turn that radio down please?" DaDa yelled from the rear of the cab.

"Mun, you no like i-land music?" the cab driver responded.

"Not like that. Damn-it-man! I'm from Ten-A-Key, playboy. Rap and old school slow grooves," DaDa capped.

"Yankees."

"Yankee? I said Tennesse, not New York. I'm country! And bruh, what the hell is you smokin' up there?"

"Earth, you want some?"

"Nah, man. But you need to let ya window down.... God-damn! You know it's against the law to be gettin' loaded and drivin' folks 'round."

The cabbie said nothing in return. He just continued to drive. Him nor DaDa noticed the dark-blue Mark VI following them. Nearing Moehead's house DaDa instructed the cab driver to stop.

"Right here, man."

"$17, mun."

"Let me run in and get it."

"No, no, no! No run, pay! Now...."

"This nigga Blue done got me again. I ain't gon' never get my money back from his tight ass," DaDa said, handing the man a twenty.

He turned and began walking up the side of Moehead's house. Ole Bluey's Lexus was out front. Nearing the privacy fence he heard two shots go off inside the house.

"What the fuck?" he said, coming to a crouching position. He stood there, not moving for several moments, hoping to hear something that might help him to know what was going on inside of the house. He heard nothing. DaDa removed the nickel-plated .38 from his pocket and proceded to the rear of the house. He opened the privacy fence and what he saw caused his knees to buckle. Moe was dragging Bluey's body out of the back door.

"Blue!" DaDa shouted.

Moehead dropped Bluey's body and looked in the direction of the scream.

"Bitch nigga!" Moehead said, reaching for his .40 cal.

DaDa raised the .38 and fired. *Tat! Tat! Tat!* Moehead retreated, stumbling over the dead body he fell. All three of DaDa's shots landed in the kitchen door. Now crawling, Moe returned fire over his shoulder. *Boom! Boom! Boom! Boom!* DaDa laid below the steps at Bluey's head. Blood was running down the steps. The kitchen door swung closed. Hearing the lock turn, DaDa stood and fired three more times. *Tat! Tat! Tat!* There was no return fire. DaDa cleared the gun's cylinder of the spent shells and reloaded. He then kicked the door open and found Moehead face down in a pool of blood. He was struggling to move. DaDa stood over him and fired twice more. *Tat! Tat!* The shots put Moehead to rest.

DaDa quickly filled a bag with the money from Moe's safe and sped away in Bluey's Lexus.

* * *

"Yeah, this Cruz.... They had a shoot out?.... So where DaDa at now?.... Okay.... So Ole Bluey and Moehead dead?.... Okay, okay.... Well, look, clean everythin' up. Move Bluey's body, but torch Moe and his house.... Aiight.... One." Cruz hung up the phone.

"What happened, my guy?" Breed asked.

"Is DaDa alright?" Cola chimed in.

"DaDa's aiight, but Blue and Moe dead. He say Moe killed Blue and DaDa killed Moe. Then he left with a bag in Blue's car."

"Damn! What they trippin' on?" Breed asked.

"I don't know, but they sho' savin' us a lotta bullets."

"Say no muthafuckin' more! Jit just pulled up in a cold ass Lexus."

Cola shifted in her seat. She did not know what to think, or what to expect from DaDa when he walked through the door. Did they still know one another? How could DaDa have killed a man? How could she have killed one also?

"Hey, Cola! You need to...." DaDa stopped mid-sentence at the sight of Arthur Cruz sitting in his living room. "Man, what the fuck you...." he said, reaching for his pocket.

"Come on, young blood," Breed said as he grabbed DaDa's arm. "Let me get this lil' bittie gun off ya befo' ya get yo'self hurt."

DaDa turned in surprise, but did not resist. He hadn't seen the big man standing behind the door when he walked in.

"You on a roll today ain't you, DaDa?" Cruz asked.

"Man, what are you talkin' about? And why you and yo' goon layin' in my spot like this, man?"

"I just came to check on my niece...."

"Yo' niece? Cola! This yo' uncle?"

Cola said nothing. She just shook her head yes.

"You can understand an uncle's concern for his niece, can't ya? What, with you jumpin' outta cabs and shootin' niggas and all."

"Hey man, I was just...."

"What's in the bag, DaDa? Money?" Cruz questioned mockingly.

"Yeah."

"My money?" Cruz asked.

"Nah, my money!" DaDa snapped.

"How much is it?"

"A lot."

Cruz smiled. He liked the little dude. "You get it from Moe and Blue?"

"Just Moe.... He owed me."

"So I've heard.... Do you wanna keep it?"

"Hell yeah!"

"Then why did you leave a crime scene, that a taxie driver dropped you off at, wit' two dead bodies, six .38 shells wit' your finger prints on 'em and a ram-shacked house wit' an empty safe wit' your finger prints on it also.... Then, in your brilliance, you brought the murder weapon home wit' you.... Nah jit, you don't want that money, your life, or my niece. You wanna go to prison for life."

DaDa said nothing. Cruz was right and he was wrong. He had seriously fucked up! This was all too much. DaDa was in over his head.

"Cheer up, jit. Uncle Cruz got you," Cruz said as he kicked a large sack over to DaDa.

"What is this?" DaDa asked.

"It's *'a lot'* of money. It belongs to my niece. She loves you and seems to trust you. Even with her life. So take care of it for her. Take care of her, DaDa. She loves you and I love her. We don't want that fucked up, do we?" Cruz asked.

"Nah. Not at all."

"So you feel me?"

"For sho'," DaDa answered.

Cruz stood up to leave. Cola walked over and hugged him. She then kissed him on the cheek. Cruz, in turn, extended his hand to DaDa, who accepted it with a smile.

"Here's my card. Come by the office or call. I'll put you with my accountant, Ms. Sims. She'll put all of that *lotta money* to work for you," Cruz said jokingly. "I'm here if you two need anything, okay."

"Thank you, man," DaDa said.

"Yeah. Thank you for everything, Uncle Arthur."

"No, thank you, baby girl."

Cruz and Big Breed exited the house.

Chapter 33

It had been business as usual at the office for Cruz and his staff. His speaking tour with Bishop Michael had been a success. Now with greater awareness in communities near and afar, as well as in white minds, the winds of change began to blow with greater strength and consistency. First Family branch chapters and other organizations of similar aim were being born everywhere.

BLACK BY GOD's DEMAND had been completed and was listed as a New York Times best seller. Cruz, Elijah, and Bishop Michael were preparing to do a regional tour in celebration of the book's success. But for now, relaxing was the order of the day.

"So what it is, my guy?" Breed asked as they sat in Cruz's office.

"Not a whole lot. Probably head over to Elga's as soon as this meeting with Palmer 'em is over," Cruz responded.

"You and ole girl been hangin' pretty tough there lately.... You ain't been bit is you, playboy?"

"Bit? Whatcha mean?" Cruz asked.

"By that love-bug, homie.... Look atcha! We don't hang. You ain't been workin' out or nothing! You gettin' a gut and everythang."

Cruz looked down at his stomach, it was protruding his belt-line a bit. He had to smile as he thought, *the woman can cook!* And though they did not make love with great frequence, the frenzied times in which they had made love were fantastic. But even more than the cooking and love making, he enjoyed her. In laughing, the conversation; just her smell. She was normal, and that... Cruz loved the most.

"Okay, you two ultra-soft-ass whitecollar, corporate niggas, look alive! It's some field niggas in this muthafucka, boy..." Palmer said with much joy.

"Hell yeah! Straight outlaws, fresh out the trenches.... Niggas, what's happenin'?" Steve chimed in.

Breed stood and the three men embraced. It had been a very long time since any of them had seen each other.

"I been readin' 'boutcha, boy. You doin' ya thing! Me and the youngin' got that new book. It's a good one," Palmer said.

"Yeah, I don't even read and I read it," Steve stated.

"Thank you, thank you.... Shit! I been readin' 'bout yall too." Cruz smiled.

"No bullshit, slim! I told you I was *'like-that'*.... See, it take a *hell-of-a* man to survive eight tours in Lebanon. I had 43 confirmed kills! Braveheart, slim! The natives of Lebanon named me Diddy. Al Diddy! They use to shout it befo' they all broke out runnin'. Didda Do-nitz! Ruthless Italian general that made Napoleon look like a school-boy.... You-hear-me?"

Laughter erupted in the small office. Palmer was on another one. Looking about the room, he was as animated as ever when he spoke.

"What the fuck is so funny?" Palmer asked.

"Palmer.... Hold up, man! Last time, in the van, you said you had 32 confirmed kills on six tours," Steve said.

"Yeah! And you said that Ms. Witheral named you Diddy in prison, 'cause she ain't want nobody to know that she called you Daddy," said Breed.

"Well, Jesus H. Christ! Holy son of Mary…. What the hell is goin' on?" Palmer shook his head before continuing. "What, you niggas take notes when I'm talkin'? If ya hadda paid half as much attention to ya parents and teachers growin' up, I never woulda met you niggas in the joint…. Here I is, from Lebanon to Miami, done put on one of the greatest performances by a nigga, for you niggas, and you question me? Now I know first-hand why Jesus wept…."

"Why did Jesus weep, Diddy?" Steve asked.

"He wept 'cause of you niggas! I see how Muhammad, Elijah, Drew Ali, and Neo felt…. I don't much like talkin' 'bout Lebanon, but boy, they had to cut the trigga guard offa my AK-47."

"For what?" Breed asked.

"Cause I'd come in out the bush, finger swoll' this bigga 'round from bussin' my gun! Workin' that joint! They cut the guard off 'cause I couldn't get my finger through it…. Out just killin'! Al Diddy, the Killa…. The hoe Witheral read all that in my P.S.I. 'Cause it's in there…. She changed the meaning to Daddy."

"Nigga! You fulla shit," Breed yelled.

"Aiight, aiight…. Enough about Diddy. Let's get down to business. I'm callin' yo' team in. The campaign was well served, we got some things done and it's outlived its course…." Cruz said.

"Damn, slim! We still…." Palmer began.

"Nah, man, that's it. We got our point across. The people, as well as our opposition knows we are out there. They've felt our strength. Now we must allow the system an opportunity to step up. We have to give the law and the underworld an out. Art of War, *an enemy with no way out will fight without restrain to the death!*

Causing much unnecessary death. Diddy man, we lost too much already," Cruz stated.

"Aiight slim, it's your call."

"Good! Now look, I've been thinkin' this over. I never mentioned it before, but I gotta letter from Kunta...."

"Kunta? Man fuck that nigga...."

"Hold on, Diddy, hear me out. It's been a lotta bad words and bad blood between us. We've all lost. The season for war is over. We are all BLACK BY GOD's DEMAND. Now we gotta get 'back by' that same demand. You read the book! We have to apply it. So I got Elijah gettin' things together. We gon' rent the old Miami Arena. It'll be the start of our new tour celebrating the book."

"You makin' a mistake, homie," Palmer said.

"Who will it cost, Diddy?"

"Us all! We fuck wit' you, slim.... This is a set-up!"

"I doubt it.... But hey, if life lasts and death passes, shit'll never change. You said Jesus wept for the niggas, well, he also died. Because you all, my niggas, are *Something To Die For*...."

"It's your call, man," Diddy said.

"Well, I've made it...."

Steve and Palmer got up to leave.

"Oh! Say there, Diddy, man. I was sittin' here thinkin' and shit, 'bout what you said earlier and all. And, well, I know Muhammad, Drew Ali, and of course, Jesus. But who is Neo?" Breed asked.

Palmer chuckled. "Ain't you a smart muthafucka.... Hip him Steve."

"Man, Neo the nigga off Matrix. 'Like-that'! We watched Reloaded last night.... Come on Diddy, I'm smarter than this nigga." And the two continued out of the door.

* * *

....heart laced with venom/ Smokin' sherm, drinkin' malt liquor/ Father forgive us…. Me and my girlfriend hustlin'/ Fell in love with the struggle/ Hands on the steering wheel, Blushin'/ While she bail-out bustin'… Fuck 'em all, watch 'em fall screamin'/ Automatic gunfire, exorcising all demons…. Mafioso on the side/ My congregation high, ready to die/ We bail-out to take the jail back, niggas united!…. all I need in this life of sin/ Is me and my girlfriend/ Down to ride to the bloody end/ Just me and my girlfriend… Tupac had the perfect words for a perfect moment as DaDa and Cola raced through traffic in Ole Bluey's Lexus sport. They were on their way to hear Uncle Cruz speak at the Miami Arena.

"DaDa, baby, I like that song."

"Yeah, I'm feelin' it too. But hey, no disrespect Cola, but yo, don't call me that baby shit."

"Why?"

"'Cause it ain't proper. Cruz gave me a 'bad-ass' book by this hoe…. Damn! I gotta stop sayin' that shit. By this psychiatrist outta Washington, D.C. Dr. Frances Cress-Welsing. Like that! She broke down that whole baby shit, and the origin of the word muthafucka."

"Oh yeah, well what she say?"

"She said that there are like five catagories of human existence. Man, woman, boy, girl, and baby. She says that our reference to the white man as not just 'man', but as 'The Man', strongly suggests that he's the only man…. And of course, we would not allow ourselves to be called women, or girls, and have faught to not be called boys; so all that remains is baby. So we began, as bein' hip, callin' one another 'baby'. Even you just said 'DaDa baby'. Not man, but baby. And to a degree you're right. Because we as black men have become dependant on the black woman, and the white man—The Man— for our income, housing, our overall survival. A baby depends on others for shit like that! So we, the babies, call him 'The Man', and we call yall black women momma. Well, if I'm fuckin' you, and I am, and you my lil' momma, then I'ma muthafucka. And I ain't no muthafucka! So don't call me baby no more."

"Teach then, nigga!" Cola said laughing.

"What?" DaDa exclaimed.

"I'm just playin', ba-, I mean, man. My man! I'm so proud of my intelligent new man."

"Yeah, whatever Cola."

"No! I'm serious. Did you learn all that from one book?"

"Yeah, but Cruz give me all kinda books. I just been readin'."

"That's good, DaDa…. I love you."

"I love you too."

* * *

The two arrived at the Miami Arena and found that it was almost impossible to find parking. The place was packed! The arena had not even seen attendance like this when the Miami Heat was using the building. After finally getting parked, DaDa and Cola made their way into the building along with the other 40,000 spectators.

Getting seated, late of course, they saw Elijah do his best Arthur Cruz impression. Elijah was entertaining, but he was no Cruz! Bishop Michael was a little better than Elijah, but they had missed him. He was the first to speak. Cruz was scheduled next, and last would be someone from Kunta's organization.

Just as Elijah finished his speech by wishing "Peace and Love" to everyone within the sound of his voice, the lights went out.

There was a gasp by the audience before a silent calm fell over the entire auditorium. Quiet! You could hear an ant pissing on cotton.

Bring 'im out/ Bring 'im out/ It's kinda hard to speak wit' the barr-ell in ya mouth…. Bring 'im out/ Bring 'im out/ Bring 'im out…

T.I.'s hit single blared from the Arena's sound system as spotlights began lighting the middle aisle. The rest of the Arena remained in darkness. The audience stared wide-eyed as men in Storm Trooper outfits filled the lighted area. The men moved swiftly! Quickly filling the walkway. Then, just as the last two were taking there place, an explosion went off, *Boom!* Sparks fell on stages. *Boom!* A secound explosion went off. And up the middle of the Storm Troopers came Arthur Cruz in an all white three piece suit. Once firmly behind the rostrum, the Troopers fanned-out around the stage, and the lights came back on. The crowd went crazy! Everyone was on their feet yelling along with the sound system. "Bring 'im out/ Bring 'im out/ Bring 'im out!" Cruz raised his arms and the music went quiet, along with the cheers from the audience.

"Cola, yo' uncle is 'like that'! He may be the baddest dude I ever seen," DaDa said.

"He aiight," Cola said and smiled at DaDa. "But you the baddest."

They both had to laugh at that. Yet DaDa promised himself that he would one day be just as good, if not better. Through Cruz, DaDa had finally found his purpose.

"Who is the greatest?" Cruz asked.

"God's the Greatest!" the crowd roared back.

"Who-is-the-greatest?"

"God's the Greatest!!!"

"Surely Allah is Akbar," Cruz said.

Doom! Came another explosion.

Cruz leaned over the rostrum, the crowd applauded! Then silence. Cruz lifted up slighty. The front of his suit was red. The audience gasp! Cruz clasped to the floor. At that point it was mass-pandemonium!

"Damn, slim!" Palmer cried. "I told you, slim! Why?"

His questions would go unanswered. But not his aim at finding and dealing with his friend's killer. Nor would Cruz's dream end there. In mission and spirit, Arthur Cruz would live on…. For he'd given them all sOmEThInG 2 DiE 4.

Epilogue

Unspoken Thoughts (Cruz's Last Ride)

I don't shed tears, I shed blood for the masses/
See, I've fed and made moves for them bastards
I can't cry, Blood in My Eye, extreme measures/
The existence of pleasures are non-existent, life's treasures
Have been taken, so Momma please, pray for your Boy/
Drama these days are complicating all I stand for
You got Boys taking boys, extorting boys/ Exporting
Funds off of importing boy
In the pen, the pen has, made your Boy a man/
And if life lasts and death passes, shit'll never change
Therefore look man, in hell love is treated as a contraband/
But if need be, look, I'ma ride for you man
'Cause I got love for you man, but man it's getting hard/
Questions that man can't answer, so I'm pleading to the Lord
Often bleeding from the heart,
orphaned at three by the Ole Boy/
My third offense, plea offered, too steep for the Boy
It's time to ride, blew trial, sentenced to a lifetime/
We made Amerikkkas' Most, viewed here at prime time
I told you we'd be great, yo (!) Diddy, Breed, we did it/
1-0-3 and Pee is the realist thing Miami's ever witnessed
Life's fluids in my eye, see through it never die/
You said you'd never leave, together you and I
Baby Girl I know you tried, still the Lord had the last say/
I went to visit your gravesite on your birthday
On a Saturday, it was a sad day, yet I promise/
Few tears, more cheers, until my demise appears

Be it Heaven or Hell, just give me a sign and I'm there/
I got your name tattored on me just to show that I care
Scribed to coincide with the last letter you wrote/
And I struggled to relive, as often I quote – you
For you'll never know what you mean to me/ For words
Can not describe what you mean to me
For when the world was mean to me, and life was cold/
You'd always intervene and bring warmth to my soul
Shattered dreams, I've seen 'em unfold,
please tell Tyson I love him/
See, I never got a chance to tell him that I love him
And if you're listen homie, you were more than a brother/
You were all I've really ever had,
and there will never be another
Tell me, who can I trust Tee, when there's no one to turn to/
No place to run to, and guns are few
Real friends are far less,
and I can't even trust those that I'm Kin to/
we've all fallen victim to the evils that men do
Evil men, hypocrites (!), turned me in to these people (!)
We've died, For "Something 2 Live 4" the sequal...

PLEX PRESENTS
LOVE & THUGGIN

BY BO BROWN

BADLAND PUBLICATIONS
PO Box 11623
Riviera Beach, FL 33419-1623
www.badlandpub.com

Shipping address

Name:

_____

Address:

_____

City: _____ State: _____ Zip: _____

Title	Author	Price
STREET RAISED: The Begin...	Mike Harper	15.95
BOO BABY: The Secret Of...	PLEX	15.95
SERVED: With No Regard!	PLEX	15.95
STREET RAISED: The Raw Deal	PLEX	15.95
BUCKIN' DA' DICE Vol. 1	BOOK GANG	15.95
NO TURNING...	Big Nation	13.95
ONE LOVE	PLEX	13.95
SUGAR	Mike Harper	15.95
LOVE & THUGGIN	Bo Brown	15.95
CRUMBS TO BRICKS	Capo Cat	15.95
EROTIC DESIRES	BOOK GANG	13.95
PROMISCUOUS	PLEX & C. Williams	10.95
GET IT HOW YOU LIVE	Big Gemo	13.95

3.75 (S&H) for 1-5 Books _____

For quantities over 5 add $ .75 per book _____

If you enjoyed this book by PLEX, please see the list of titles that are also available.

BOO BABY: The Secret of Sweet Donnie Mac
LOVE & THUGGIN [Co-written with Bo Brown]
ONE LOVE
SERVED: With No Regard!
STREET RAISED: The Raw Deal
BUCKIN DA DICE Vol. 1 [Edited and contributed a short story]
EROTIC DESIRES [Edited and contributed three short stories]
PROMISCUOUS [Co-written with Calvin Williams]

Coming Soon!!! [The Third Quarter of 2014]

IF YOU KNEW MY STRUGGLE... [Co-written with Treasure Hills]
YOUNG-N-THUGGIN [Co-written with Troy 'Disco' Jones]
GET IT HOW YOU LIVE Vol. 2 [Co-written with Big Gemo]
LOVE & THUGGIN Part 2 [Co-written with Big Bino]
ONE LOVE Part 2 [Co-written with Big Gemo]

Log on to www.badlandpub.com for updates on releases.

Ain't Nobody Pen'in Like Us, Man!!!

www.ingramcontent.com/pod-product-compliance
Lightning Source LLC
Chambersburg PA
CBHW070224260626
47160CB00002B/674